R.V. BOWMAN

JABBERWOCK'S CURSE

BOOK 1
LOOKING GLASS CHRONICLES

Northern
Estates
Faelands
Pearl
Mountains
Kingdom
of
Wonderland
Red Palace
Gilded
Mountains

Contents

Chapter 1

"IT'S NOT YOUR FAULT."

Chess found himself licking his paw and stopped. The longer he was in this cat form, the more he operated on animal instinct. It was unsettling, and he wondered how quickly his humanness would fade if they didn't break the curse.

Zander's rumbling voice interrupted his thoughts' downward spiral.

"How can you say that? I killed that man." Zander's giant head dropped onto his forelegs, and steam rose from his nostrils, disappearing into the shadows of the cave ceiling.

The Jabberwock's reptilian face showed little emotion, but Chess could hear the self-loathing in his friend's voice. He felt a pang of sympathy, but impatience pushed it away. He stood, his nails clicking on the stone floor, and swished his plumed black tail. A slant of the early morning light caught the white tip.

"Well, the other option is that we'd both be dead, so I can't find it in myself to wish for a different outcome. Can you honestly say that you do?"

Zander turned his head away from Chess. "Perhaps." His voice was so low that Chess wasn't sure he had understood him.

"You're saying you want to die?" Chess paced in front of the Jabberwock, his back rigid. "Well, that's just perfect, Zander. Go ahead. Give up. Because of course, nothing matters but your tender little feelings. I certainly don't matter. Your Kingdom doesn't matter. Let it fall into the hands of that witch. It's much more important to marinate in your noble guilt." Chess shook his head. "I must give the Red Queen her due. She recognized just how to break you. I suppose I'm the fool because I assumed you were stronger than this."

The Jabberwock lifted his head, blinking at the cat at his feet. "What would you have me do, Chess? I can't go anywhere without someone trying to hunt me down because they assume I killed their beloved prince. If I do, I end up having to defend myself, and you saw how that turned out last night." He snorted. "I can't tell anyone what's happened because they can't understand me, and my birthday is less than a week away. Don't you think I realize I'm dragging you down with me? Don't you understand I can't bear the idea of my people at the mercy of that woman? But time is running out. I don't see a way out of this."

"Then do something about it. Don't just lie here and give up. Citrine would—"

The Jabberwock reared up and let out a roar. "NO!" The gout of fire passed over Chess's head, singing the tufts of fur on his ears.

"But, Zan, she could help us."

The Jabberwock's horned eyebrows lowered, and steam rose from his nostrils. Flames flickered behind his friend's teeth, and Chess backed up a step.

"She can't break the curse, Chess. Isn't that what you've been telling me all this time—that it has to be someone from the Mirror World? I won't have her endangered just because she has the Creature Gift."

Chess licked one paw and washed his ear. He didn't know why, but he found the action soothing. "Okay, okay. We won't go to Citrine." He peered up at his friend. "But you're underestimating her." He shrugged a furry shoulder. "It doesn't matter though, because I've found someone in the Mirror World who *can* help us, and she's even the daughter of a gentleman."

The prince drew back his head. "Isn't the Looking Glass portal guarded?"

Chess allowed a grin to stretch across his face. "It is, but the Rabbit Hole isn't."

"But how did you— It's impossible..."

Chess winked. "It helps if you aren't entirely human. I knew my tainted blood would come in handy one of these days."

Zander frowned. "I don't know, Chess. You can't drag some unsuspecting person here. They won't be able to understand us, and seeing me might frighten them to death."

"Oh, ye of little faith." Chess stood and swished his tail under the Jabberwock's snout. "I've been watching one girl in particular, and I'm almost positive she has the Creature Gift. Of course, you can't identify it in the Mirror World, but..."

Zander rolled his eyes. "What a surprise—it's a girl. I suppose she's pretty, too?"

Chess smirked. "Of course, but that's a delightful bonus." His expression turned serious. "As you said, your birthday is next week. We no longer have a choice. We must get someone to help us."

For a moment, Zander looked hopeful. Then his head drooped, and he turned away. "Even if she has the Creature Gift, why would she come here? It's not fair to drag some poor innocent girl to another world and expect her to break a curse in a matter of days. Especially not when she has to avoid the Red Queen's clutches." He sighed, his olive-bronze scales glinting in a patch of sunlight on the cave floor. "No, I can't involve anyone else. It's bad enough I dragged you into this mess. I won't ruin another person's life."

Chess hissed in irritation. "It's not only your life here, Zander. It's mine too, and I'm willing to take the risk. I'm not going to just stand by and let Lyssandra take everything from me, and you shouldn't either."

The Jabberwock drew himself up and stared down the length of his snout. "I am still your prince, and I am saying I don't want to involve anyone else. That isn't a suggestion."

Chess sniffed. "You lost the right to command me when I got cursed along with you. I'm sorry, Zander, but I refuse to let the Red Queen win without even trying."

He turned and bounded towards the back of the cave.

The prince stood to his feet and arched his neck. A low growl rumbled from his chest. "Don't disobey me, Chess. I mean it."

Chess paused in the shadowy arch of one of the tunnels that twisted into the heart of the mountain. His voice floated back, mocking.

"Or you'll what, Zander? You've already proven you don't have the stomach to kill your enemies, never mind someone who stuck out his neck and got cursed for his troubles."

With those last words, Chess trotted into the tunnel. He wasn't giving up his life as a human because Zander was too noble for his own good. He snorted out a laugh. Nobody could accuse him of having that problem.

Chapter 2

ALICE SNEEZED AND BUMPED her head on the underside of her sister's bed.

"They aren't under here," she said, as she rubbed the sore spot.

She sat back on her heels.

"I don't think anyone's cleaned under here in ages," she said.

Rommy laughed and her face popped up over the edge of the bed, her enormous hazel eyes sparkling. "Mother has all the maids hopping with the wedding coming up. They don't have time to clean all the nooks and crannies. Let's just hope she doesn't find out, though, or they'll be looking for work."

A line appeared between her eyebrows. "I need to find those shoes," she said. "I can hardly walk to my groom with my hem dragging in the dust."

Alice pushed to her feet and sat on the blue coverlet next to Rommy, who reached out and pulled a cobweb from Alice's black curls.

Alice grinned at her sister. "Finn wouldn't care if you rolled in the dirt."

Rommy flopped over onto her back with a dreamy sigh. "And I wouldn't care if he wore a loincloth."

There was a beat of silence before both girls dissolved into giggles.

The door opened.

"I found them," Mother announced. She stopped and stared at them. "Andromeda Cavendish! What in the world are you doing lolling around on the bed? The seamstress is going to be here in less than a quarter hour!"

She bustled into the room. "Honestly, you two act like you're still schoolgirls."

Rommy sat up, an unrepentant smile on her face. "Alice just graduated a few weeks ago. You can't expect the schoolroom to have completely rubbed off."

Mother shook her head, and her narrowed gaze moved to Alice. "And what have you been doing? Your hair is a mess, and you're covered in dust. You need to get cleaned up. Mrs. Chambreaux will want to do your final measurements, too. We just don't have time to squeeze in another fitting before the wedding."

Alice exchanged a guilty look with Rommy. She didn't want to get the maids in trouble. She got up and batted at her dark-blue skirts with little success.

"I'll just change into my bridesmaid dress now, and I can put on a fresh dress for tea later."

Mother shook her head. "That won't work. Hadley Beechworth hinted he might call this afternoon. You can't greet him looking like a chimney sweep, especially now that his parents have given him their approval to court you."

Alice felt the color drain from her face. The last person she wanted courting her was the Beechworth heir. He'd always been terribly polite, and all the girls thought him handsome, but there was something about him that made her skin crawl.

Rommy wrinkled her nose. "What does Alice want with that gongoozler?"

"Andromeda! What is wrong with you? The Beechworths are an excellent family, and he's one of the most sought-after bachelors in the area." She sniffed. "Even if Alice doesn't return his regard—and I see no reason she wouldn't—his parents' blessing and his interest will be seen as a stamp of approval for her." Mother gave Alice an apologetic smile before turning back to Rommy. "Your father may have adopted Alice, but with her background, the Beechworths' acceptance is important for her future."

Alice tried to ignore the prick of hurt at the reminder of her past. She had worked hard to flatten her Cockney accent and learn to look, move, and speak like a lady. It hadn't been easy, and sometimes she felt suffocated by the strictures of polite society. She knew their stepmother meant well, but since Papa James had married her five years ago, when Alice was 12, the woman always seemed to be the one to bring up Alice's previous life in London's slums. When it had been just the three of them, neither Papa James nor Rommy ever mentioned her life on the street.

Alice swallowed down her resentment and forced a smile. She had no desire for Hadley Beechworth to court her, and she didn't give a tuppence about his parents. The last thing she wanted to do was embarrass her family, though. They had done too much for her, so she would put on her polite mask for their sake.

Rommy slung an arm around Alice's shoulders. "Alice is too good for the likes of Hadley Beechworth. That puffed-up popinjay weaseled out of doing his part in the Great War. He should be glad nobody's painted him yellow."

Mother glared at Rommy. "He's not the only gentleman's son who stayed in England. His family needed him here."

Rommy snorted. "They needed him about as much as I need a second nose."

"That's enough!" Mother pulled out her watch pin and looked at it, pursing her lips. "Mrs. Chambreaux will be here in just a few moments. I suggest you both make yourselves presentable before she gets here." Without giving Rommy a chance to reply, Mother turned and whisked out the door.

"She's so old-fashioned." Rommy picked up a brush and pushed Alice into the white tufted stool in front of her dressing table. She ran the brush through Alice's curls before she picked up the hair comb Papa James had had designed, one for each of them, and slid it into Alice's hair. "You'd think we still had knights and peasants, the way she goes on."

Alice's violet eyes met her sister's hazel ones in the mirror. "She's not completely wrong, you know, and she means well. I've heard more than one person refer to me as *the Cavendish charity case*."

Rommy set the brush down with a thump, her cheeks flushing. "What do they know? Since the war, things are changing. Out in the country, everyone is still so narrow-minded, but in London, rich and poor rub elbows. Do you think an aristocrat cared who was next to him in a trench somewhere in Europe?"

Alice found her eyes prickling with tears. She glanced down, trying to hide the emotions that crowded to the surface. The war had been a difficult time. When Finn had enlisted, Rommy had gone to London to do her part. Papa James had tried to prevent her, but once her sister made up her mind, there was no stopping her. Besides, Alice knew their father was secretly proud of his daughter's grit and courage. Alice was still in school, so there was no question of her going, too. She didn't like to remember the constant fear that had gripped her for both Rommy and Finn or the awful hollow feeling of being left behind to wait.

Fortunately, both Rommy and Finn had come home. They had loved each other forever, and only the war had kept them from marrying earlier. Alice was happy for them, but she once again felt like she was being left behind. And that made her feel horribly selfish. Alice blinked back the tears and drew in a shaky breath.

Rommy set down the brush. "Come now, what's wrong? Don't tell me Mother got to you." She sucked in a breath. "It's not Hadley, is it? You don't... care for him, do you?"

Alice grimaced. "Hardly. Besides, I'm not ready to marry anyone." She wrinkled her nose. "Especially not any of those boring idiots Mother keeps parading in front of me. It's just sometimes I wish..." She clamped her lips shut. She couldn't say what she really wanted—to attend veterinary school. Papa James might not take her seriously, but he'd indulge her. Mother, on the other hand, would have a fit—and, Alice had to admit, for good reason. It would ruin her chances of making a suitable match—and that would reflect on her family.

Even if Mother would allow it, being accepted into a veterinarian program at university would be difficult. From what Alice had read, they only accepted a certain number of students each year, and as a woman, she wouldn't be high on their list. Lost in her thoughts, Rommy's hand on her shoulder startled her.

"You wish what?" Rommy said.

Alice forced a smile onto her face. "I wish nothing had to change," she said. "I'm so happy for you and Finn, but I'll miss this."

Rommy threw her arms around Alice and squeezed tight. "As will I!" she said, her voice catching.

Alice pulled back, a shaky laugh escaping. "Listen to us, getting maudlin. It's not like I can't come and visit you and Finn in London." She smiled and wiped at her eyes. "Maybe I'll come for a prolonged visit, and Hadley will forget all about me."

Rommy gripped her hands more tightly, and tears brimmed. Alice's stomach dipped, but before she could ask what was wrong, Rommy spoke in a rush.

"Alice, dear heart, we've just gotten word. I don't want you to think I was hiding anything from you." Rommy bit her lip, and her gaze dropped to their clasped hands. Alice waited, her breath trapped in her chest. After a beat of silence, Rommy continued.

"Finn and I, we won't be in London because"—she inhaled—"we're moving to America when we come back from our wedding trip."

A hole opened inside of Alice, and there was a ringing in her ears. Rommy's mouth was still moving, but the words seemed to come from far away. She shook her head.

"But, why?" She pulled her hands away from her sister.

The tears in Rommy's eyes spilled over. "Alice, I've been waiting until we knew for sure the position came through," she said. "Finn wants a fresh start."

"Fresh start?" Alice's mind felt wrapped in cotton, making her thoughts sluggish and stupid, so all she could do was repeat Rommy's words.

Rommy sniffed back her tears. "London is—well, darling, everywhere you look there are signs of the Great War. Poor Finn, he can't get away from it there, and there are no jobs around here for him unless he takes over as estate manager." She shrugged her shoulders. "It's important to him that he makes his own way, without Papa's help."

"But... America? It's so far." Alice swallowed hard. She didn't want to be selfish, but the sense of claustrophobia was threatening to choke her. Rommy and Finn, London, they had been her escape hatch. Even if the university wouldn't accept her as a proper student, she had hoped to at least attend some classes, maybe help Tom with the animals once she learned more. Without London, Alice saw the future. The line of foppish young men Mother would force on her, the constant pressure to make a good match, the reminder of her duty to make her family proud.

Rommy dug out a handkerchief and dabbed at her eyes. "Alice, we want you to come with us. I know it means leaving Papa and Mother and your friends, but you could go to university there."

Alice's mouth dropped open, and Rommy bumped Alice's shoulder with her own. "Did you think I didn't know?"

Excitement bubbled in Alice's chest as the possibilities opened up in her mind. She could not just attend a few classes, but maybe get a degree. Her mouth curved into a smile as she thought about how different things were in America. They said class wasn't even a consideration over there. Nobody would care where she came from. She couldn't help bouncing a little, but she tried to tamp it down, to not let her hopes grow too big.

"Really? You want me to come with you? What does Finn think about that? Surely he doesn't want a tagalong when you're newlyweds."

"Don't be silly! Finn loves you like a little sister." Rommy's eyes sparkled. "Plus, he wants to keep his new wife happy, doesn't he? So what do you say?"

Alice had a moment of doubt. Could she leave Papa James and the only home she'd ever known? But her dream was in reach. She clasped her hands, her eyes shining, and nodded. "Yes, oh yes!"

The girls threw their arms around each other just as the door opened. Mother poked her head in and then shook it in exasperation. "Alice, Mr. Beechworth is here to see you. Carter put him in the parlor."

Chapter 3

ALICE'S STOMACH SANK, AND she cast around for an excuse not to receive him. "But Mother, I need the last fitting done on my dress. You said yourself that the next few weeks will be busy. Surely, Mr. Beechworth would understand that the wedding is taking so much of our time."

Mother's mouth thinned. "Carter has already shown him in. We can't send him home now."

Alice gave Rommy a pleading look, and her sister stood to her feet. "It's just Hadley, Mother. Tell him Carter forgot that Mrs. Chambreaux was coming."

"I'll tell him no such thing. Goodness, you wouldn't think it a hardship to visit with a handsome young man." She stepped into the room and gave Alice's skirts several pats. "Well, I suppose it's too late to change now." She put a hand on Alice's cold cheek. "Smile, dear—with that beautiful face, maybe he won't notice your dusty skirts. Come along now." She looked back at Rommy. "Mrs. Chambreaux is in the morning room. Run along so she can get you fitted."

Alice's feet dragged as she followed her mother towards the parlor, and her mind whirled with what she could say to get rid of her caller as quickly as possible without upsetting anyone. She dreaded the next hour, but she hugged Rommy's invitation close. She could survive an hour or so.

Mother swept into the room to greet their guest, but Alice paused in the parlor's doorway. Hadley rose from the high-backed jade sofa, his back ramrod straight. A ray of sunshine peeked through the open draperies and gilded his blond hair to gold. He was a handsome man. She knew many girls would envy her.

Mother turned to her, and Alice inhaled before she stepped into the room to greet her guest.

Hadley's face brightened, and he bowed over her hand. Alice forced her lips into a smile. "Mr. Beechworth, how pleasant to see you this afternoon."

"The pleasure is all mine, Miss Cavendish."

Mother sat in one of the chairs that flanked the fireplace, and Hadley moved to make room for Alice next to him on the sofa. The other chair called to her, but she knew Mother would find it rude if she sat there and would no doubt lecture her later.

Instead, she perched on the far end of the couch and folded her hands in her lap. Mother asked about Hadley's mother and his sisters, while Alice kept a smile on her lips and nodded periodically. Mother kept shooting glances her way, but Alice ignored her.

When Hadley and Mother stood, Alice blinked. Her mind had wandered, but her shoulders relaxed. Oh, good, he was leaving. Although it was odd that Mother hadn't even offered him tea. Alice stood, too, a true smile on her face, ready to offer her goodbyes.

Mother didn't offer a farewell, though. "Alice, why don't you take Mr. Beechworth out for a walk? The roses are blooming right now, and the scent is heavenly. He has something he'd like to talk to you about."

Alice's shoulders tightened again, and her hands gripped the sides of her skirt. There was only one reason her mother would leave her alone with a young man. Her mind cast about for an excuse, any excuse to avoid what promised to be an uncomfortable and embarrassing encounter.

"Mother, surely Mr. Beechworth would like some tea. Cook makes the best lemon tarts, and I know I smelled them baking earlier."

"Nonsense, dear. There will be enough time for that later. We hope." Ignoring Alice's wide eyes, Mother swept out of the parlor, leaving Alice alone with her unwanted suitor. She gritted her teeth, but forced another smile. There was no way she was taking Hadley to their gardens. It was much too romantic.

Instead, she ignored his outstretched arm and strode towards the front door. Hadley frowned at her but followed in her wake. Once they stepped out in the sunshine, he grasped her arm.

She looked at him and then his hand. He took the opportunity to thread her arm through his elbow. "Aren't your gardens out back?" he asked.

"Oh, I'm sure you aren't interested in some silly old roses." Alice dragged him towards the stables. See if he wanted to propose in there. She was sure he wouldn't get down on one knee and dirty his clothes.

When they got in sight of the building, Hadley wrinkled his nose. "Certainly, there's nothing to look at in here, Miss Cavendish." He tried to turn back towards the rose garden, but Alice was determined.

"Oh, but Papa got a marvelous new jumper. I just know you'll want to meet him."

"I'm sure he's lovely, but I really must—"

"Yes, you must. I'm so glad you agree."

Alice towed him through the doorway into the dim interior of the stables and made a beeline towards the second stall. She only prayed that the horse was in here and not out in the pasture. She let out a puff of air when his sleek bay head emerged from the stall. The horse whickered out a greeting.

She walked over and patted his nose, and the horse blew a warm breath over her hand and nosed at her skirts. Her lips curved into a genuine smile.

"I'm sorry, boy. I didn't think to bring you a treat this time."

Hadley snorted. "Treats just spoil good horseflesh." He tilted his head and took in the tall gelding in front of him. "He is a good-looking animal, though."

"Pirate isn't just good-looking. He's very talented and has a lovely temperament, too."

One dark-blond eyebrow rose. "Pirate? Did he come with that ridiculous name?"

Alice opened her eyes wide. "Oh, no. That's just Papa James's little joke about his previous life on the high seas."

"I see." It was obvious he didn't, but Hadley didn't have a sense of humor. His mouth pressed into a thin line, and Alice bit back a laugh at his struggle to hide his irritation.

By this time, the other horses had heard them, and they were all peering over their stall doors. Alice moved to the next occupant, evading Hadley's outstretched hand as she did. She patted the nose that pushed into her chest, and she chattered on about Biscuit until Hadley's foot tapped on the stable floor. After another minute, she moved on to the next horse. She hoped by the time she got to the end of the row, he would give up his pursuit and go home.

She was only halfway down the row before Hadley's patience snapped. He stood next to her and pinched the bridge of his nose. While his tone was still polite, his voice was strained.

"Thank you for showing me your father's horse, and every other horse in your stables, but we should go to the gardens now. After all, that's where your mother is expecting us to be. I wouldn't want her to think I am untrustworthy."

Alice waved a hand. "Nonsense! Mother is used to me and my odd little ways, I can assure you, Mr. Beechworth. Besides, I couldn't possibly leave until I've said hello to everyone. They'd be so disappointed if I neglected any of them. I need to check on Daisy, too. She's due to whelp any day now." She looked up underneath her lashes, gratified as a muscle in Hadley's jaw ticced.

She thought his politeness might give way then, but he gave a tight smile and gestured her onward. "By all means, then. Let us hope *nobody* will be disappointed today."

Alice smiled brightly and drifted from one stall to the next. She lingered with each horse, but eventually she came to the very last stall. Hadley still hadn't given up, and her hopes of avoiding a confrontation dwindled. She gave him credit for his tenacity. Too bad his show of character had to come now.

She turned her attention to the last horse, a black mare with a white star on her forehead. "This is Star, for obvious reasons. She's a beauty, but she knows it, don't you, girl?" The horse tossed her head and whinnied as if in agreement. Alice let out a peal of laughter, and even Hadley smiled.

He reached out and fingered one of Alice's curls. "Spirited and beautiful. It's a combination I greatly admire." His voice turned husky, his gaze heavy with meaning.

Alice ignored him. "She's got a canter as smooth as butter, but she's not above bucking off a heavy-handed rider."

Hadley sniffed. "I would never allow any filly to throw me out of the saddle, not if she was the horse I had selected."

Alice held back a snort. She had hoped the atmosphere of horses, manure, and dust would deter him. She supposed she should just let him speak, but her skin prickled and she rubbed at her arms. All she wanted to do was get away from him.

"Not all horses want to be selected." She regretted the words almost as soon as they left her mouth. A tense silence hung between them. A low-pitched whine broke through it.

Alice ducked under Hadley's arm and ran down the aisle.

Hadley hurried after her. "Miss Cavendish?"

Alice ignored him and skidded to a halt in front of the far stall. Inside, Daisy, one of several of the estate dogs, was lying on her side. Five tiny bundles squirmed in the straw next to her, but one wasn't moving. Daisy licked at it and nudged it with her nose. She looked up at Alice's approach, a low whine in her throat, her big brown eyes sad.

Alice forgot about Hadley. She dropped to her knees next to the mother and gently lifted the pup. Warmth radiated from the small body. Hope flickered low, but she'd seen other pups come back. Tom would know what to do, but he wasn't here right now. There was no time to find him, either. With her thumb, she cleared the little nose and mouth of any lingering debris. She looked around for a cloth. When she didn't find one, she jumped to her feet only to run into Hadley, who was standing in the doorway. His mouth twisted as if he'd bitten something sour.

"I just need a cloth. I might be able to save him." She tried to push past him, but he didn't move. There was no time for his foolishness. Using both hands, she shoved at his chest. Surprised, he stumbled back a step, and she brushed by him. Her fingers had just closed over the rag Tom used to wipe down the tack when Hadley jerked her around.

"This is no place for a lady, mucking about in the filth for some flea-infested dog. I insist you stop this at once."

Alice tried to pull away, but his fingers dug into her arm. "He's going to die if I don't help him."

"Then let him. This is what you have servants for."

Alice growled and jerked her arm away. She tried to dart around him, but he blocked her.

"Blast it!" Alice stomped on Hadley's foot, hard. He swore as Alice pushed past him. She knelt again and picked up the pup. Alarmed by the little body's drop in temperature, she took the cloth and rubbed him all over. Was that movement?

She didn't even hear Hadley. Without warning, pain seared through her shoulder as he yanked her to her feet. In the process, he swatted the pup from her hands. It made a dull *thunk* against the side of the stall. Daisy exploded in a fury of barking and snarls. Hadley kicked at the dog as he pushed Alice out of the stall. Daisy whimpered in pain, and he slammed the door shut.

A red haze dropped over Alice's eyes, and her hand balled into a fist. Before she quite knew what she was doing, she had drawn back her arm and punched Hadley Beechworth in the nose.

Chapter 4

"MY NOSE!" HADLEY YELLED and covered his face with both hands. Pain streaked over Alice's knuckles and she shook out her hand. Her breath came in pants as she tried to regain her composure.

She realized she should apologize, claim being distraught to excuse her behavior, but the red haze wasn't completely gone—and she wasn't sorry. Besides, she was leaving in a few weeks. She didn't have to be afraid of the Beechworths.

"I think you need to leave." She offered him the cloth in her hand, but he grimaced and fished out his own handkerchief to stem the stream of blood coming from his nostrils.

His blue eyes never left hers as he mopped up his face. He smeared blood on his cheek, but it didn't seem prudent to tell him that. The truth was, he looked a little crazed. A lock of golden hair hung down over one eye, and his polite mask had cracked to reveal an ugly expression.

"I still haven't spoken to you, Alice. I can call you Alice, can't I?" He laughed, the sound harsh.

A cold chill settled over Alice's skin. She stepped backwards, her heel kicking up dust motes in the dim light. "Whatever you have to say, I don't want to hear it." Despite her hammering heart, she lifted her chin. "You need to leave."

The smile that twisted across his face made ice skate up her spine. "Not until I say what I've come to say."

Alice squared her shoulders. "I said—" He moved so quickly, Alice found herself shoved against the wall, her head connecting painfully against the wood. His hands gripped her upper arms. She'd have bruises there tomorrow.

"And I said, you will hear me out." He spoke through clenched teeth, his eyes dilated and wild.

Alice stilled. She had the sense of standing at the very edge of a cliff. The wrong move would send her plummeting. She would listen to him. She could put off answering and get back to the house. Once Papa James found out what happened, she'd never have to see Hadley again.

When she spoke, it was in the soothing voice she used to coax the feral cats. "All right then, I'm listening."

Hadley inhaled, his nose flaring. He closed his eyes for a moment. When he opened them, his expression had calmed. "I'm sorry. That was most ungentlemanly, but you forced me to lose my temper. You must stop doing that." He let go of her arms and straightened his coat.

"I had hoped to do this in a more romantic setting, get down on one knee and all that." He looked around at the barn and grimaced. "But you would insist on coming in here."

When she said nothing, he continued. "The thing is, despite Mother's protests about your unsuitable beginnings, I would like to marry you, Alice."

"How... very unexpected."

He smiled and drew himself up straighter. "You are most likely overcome by the compliment I am paying you."

Before Alice could respond, he continued. "A lot of men would have been put off by your less than savory start in life. I mean, you might have the Cavendish name, but everyone knows you weren't born with it."

She goggled at him. This was his idea of proposing to her? She resisted the urge to roll her eyes. The sooner he was done talking, the sooner this would be over.

He leaned in and gave her a conspiratorial grin. "You know, Father agreed with me about your beauty, but he wanted me to take you as my mistress." Hadley chuckled and shook his head. "Of course, that was out of the question, and we both knew it. Lord Cavendish can be so unpredictable, and it's widely known how he spoils not just Andromeda, but you too."

He finally stopped to take a breath. Alice stared up at him, afraid if she opened her mouth, she'd tell him what she really thought of him and his proposal. After a moment of silence, Hadley frowned.

"Well, didn't you hear what I said? I want to marry you. You'd be a Beechworth."

She narrowed her eyes. "Oh, I heard you, all right," she said. Hot words rose in her throat, but she bit them back. She wouldn't embarrass her family, even if Hadley

Beechworth was an idiot. "I'm sure I should be beyond flattered, but as you said, it's all so overwhelming." She put a hand to her throat and looked up at him from under her lashes.

He reached out and traced a finger down her cheek. "You are so beautiful, and you have that spirit I so admire." He shifted closer and Alice shrank away from him, but with the stable wall at her back and his big frame blocking her in, there wasn't anywhere to go.

"Mr. Beechworth—"

He waved a hand. "You must call me Hadley if we are to be engaged."

Alice gave a tight smile. "Hadley, I'm sure you understand I need a little time."

Hadley's eyelids drooped, and his hand strayed to her curls again. He wound one around his finger. "What's there to think about? We were made for each other. Imagine how stunning our children would be."

Bile rose in Alice's throat at the thought, and she swallowed it down. "I really must insist we go back inside. Mother will be wondering what's become of us."

Hadley's smile faltered and his eyes narrowed. "I don't know why you're stalling. You'll say yes eventually. There's no need for all this maidenly modesty."

Alice straightened her shoulders and lifted her chin. She channeled Mother's no-nonsense tone. "I would really like to go in now. I am not ready to give you an answer yet." She tried to move past him, but his arm shot out, blocking her.

He leaned in close, his tone conversational. "You know, Alice, it would be a real shame if Father had to call in your family's debt."

Alice's eyes widened.

"Oh, didn't your father tell you about the loan he took out against his ship for all those property taxes? Nasty thing, those taxes. They've hit a lot of the old families." He knocked on the wall behind her. "These old estates cost a pretty penny to maintain, and Lord Cavendish has always liked to dance on the edge of risk. Father's warned him before, but the man doesn't take advice very well."

Alice's mind reeled. "I don't believe you."

"Believe me or not, it's true." Hadley shrugged. "Of course, if we were to marry, I'm sure Father would be happy to forgive the loan. After all, we'd be family."

Alice stared up at him, not able to speak around the burning lump in her throat. Hadley's smile held more than a hint of triumph as he brought his face close to hers. She turned her head at the last minute, and his sloppy kiss landed just shy of her mouth. He growled and slid a hand into her hair, anchoring her head as his lips found their target. His other arm snaked around her waist, pulling her body flush against his. She tried to kick him, but her skirts were tangled around her legs and both her hands were trapped against his chest.

Suddenly, something dark flew through the air. Alice was left reeling in the empty space next to where Hadley had just been.

Chapter 5

CHESS'S TAIL LASHED, AND his fur bristled. He crouched in the shadows of the barn. He'd been waiting for the man—the girl had called him *Hadley*—to leave so he could bring her to the portal.

But the idiot wasn't taking no for an answer. Heat welled up in his chest, and he growled low in his throat. He hated bullies.

Then the bloke shoved his stupid mouth on the girl's, and Chess rolled his eyes. Some men had no finesse. He shook his head. Clearly, the girl needed his help. Why did he have to always fix people's problems? He stood and shook himself. If he wanted to free Zander in time, he was going to have to intervene.

He hopped down from the ledge and sprinted across a wooden beam. He launched himself through the air, his target the blond head.

His weight knocked the other man sideways, and he dug his claws into skin. A howl erupted out of the man and he grabbed at Chess, trying to pull him off. Chess dug in deeper. The girl fighting Hadley off flashed in his brain. More than anything, he wanted to teach this fellow a lesson.

Chess slashed at the man's face and sank his back claws into a padded shoulder. Hadley screamed, his hands flailing. He got an arm underneath Chess and tore the cat off. More skin ripped, and Chess hissed in satisfaction. Hadley tried to fling him away, but Chess wrapped his large body around the man's arm and sank his teeth into a hand.

The man swore and shrieked, "Don't just stand there, you stupid cow! Help me!"

Chess heard footsteps running out of the barn. His lost focus cost him. Hadley rammed his arm against the wall, and Chess felt the breath whoosh out of him as his spine thumped against a stall door. Inside, a horse whinnied and pranced in the straw. Chess grimly hung on, and his weight pulled at Hadley's body.

"Get off!" Hadley banged Chess against the wall again, and this time Chess's skull made contact. His ears rang. He shook his head to clear his vision.

Hadley pushed against Chess's chin, wrenching his neck at an awkward angle. Chess glimpsed the man's face. Blood dripped from his cheek, and a vicious satisfaction surprised Chess.

Cold water drenched his body. He gasped and dropped to the ground. Water dripped in his eyes, and he blinked it away.

Without warning, pain bloomed in his side and he flew through the air. He hit the wall with a thud and slid to the floor, stunned.

"Stop it!"

The girl stood in front of him. She was protecting him from that bully, even after all that had happened. Warmth flooded through him, and he struggled upright.

"That thing needs to be shot!" The man stepped towards Chess and lifted his foot again.

Alice blocked him. "Have you lost your mind? Do you want it to attack you again?"

Hadley scowled down at Chess. Chess stood up and shook himself. Nothing felt broken. He slunk forward, and Hadley drew back, his face white. Chess grinned, and the blond man stumbled back. Hadley tried to draw the girl towards the doorway.

She jerked away. "Don't touch me!"

"You need to get away from that thing. He could attack you next."

Chess watched the violet eyes narrow into slits. "He's not who I'm worried about."

The man loomed over the girl, but the blood dripping off his face and arm ruined the intimidation factor.

The girl lifted her chin and pointed towards the stable door. "I suggest you have those scratches looked at when you get home. They could get infected."

Hadley touched a deep gouge and winced. Then he scowled. "This doesn't change anything, Alice. I'll be back, and when I do, I expect to announce our engagement."

Instead of challenging the man, Alice wrapped her arms around herself. "Just go, Hadley."

Despite his ravaged face, Hadley smirked. The girl turned her head away, and heat rose up in Chess again. He snarled and darted forward. The man squealed and dashed out the door.

Chess stopped at the threshold and watched until the man was out of sight. He couldn't help the purr of satisfaction that rippled out of him.

"I'm not sure if I should thank you or run myself."

The girl watched Chess with guarded eyes. He licked a paw and grimaced. He'd torn a nail, and it hurt like the dickens.

She edged towards him, her voice soothing. "Are you hurt? Hadley kicked you awfully hard." She bit her lip. "If it wasn't for you..." Her voice trailed off and a shiver rippled through her body.

Chess limped towards her. She tensed but remained still. He rubbed up against her leg and purred.

A smile edged up one corner of her mouth, and she reached down to run a gentle hand over his back. He arched into it. Her movements were slow as she crouched down next to him. She examined his ribs with a soft touch, and he winced. She hesitated and then probed harder, even as she watched him.

Chess twisted his head around and she froze. He licked her hand with a sandpapery tongue. A laugh spilled out of her mouth that quickly turned into a sob. She bit her lip, and after a moment, she resumed her careful inspection of his body. She talked to him as she went, though her voice was tight.

"Where did you come from, anyway? I would have remembered you. For one thing, you're enormous. I don't think I've ever seen such a big tomcat—or one with such blue eyes."

He blinked up at her and butted his head against her hand. She scratched him under his chin. He still had to get her to the Rabbit Hole. At least she didn't seem afraid of him anymore. That should make it easier. He hoped.

She turned him over on his side and continued her inspection. A gold necklace swung in front of his face. A pearl dangled from it.

Suddenly, Chess knew exactly how he was going to get her to the Rabbit Hole.

Chapter 6

ALICE KNEW SHE SHOULD still be wary of the huge cat lying at her feet, especially if he was injured. That was difficult to remember with him purring and batting an enormous paw at her necklace like a kitten.

She rubbed a finger along the silky black chin, and the animal's eyes drooped to half-mast. She took the opportunity to study him. He was twice the size of any cat she'd ever encountered.

The cat wrapped one paw around her wrist and pulled it towards his mouth. Hadley's clawed face and shredded suit jacket flashed in her mind. She shuddered, but all he did was lick her fingers. She disentangled her hand. Despite his current sweet demeanor, she reminded herself this animal could inflict a lot of damage. Her lips twisted into a grim smile. She couldn't be sorry, though. For whatever reason, he had come to her rescue, and she was grateful.

Alice was so absorbed in her thoughts, she shrieked and threw herself backwards when the cat lunged towards her throat. Her shoulder hit the stable floor hard.

Pressure pulled at the back of her neck, and there was an audible *snap*. She pushed herself up as the cat bounded out door, her gold necklace dangling from his mouth.

"Blast it!" She scrambled to her feet and pounded after the animal. He dashed down the dirt path that led away from the house and towards the wooded grounds beyond the gardens.

The waving white tip of his tail stayed just out of reach, taunting her. They reached the open field, and Alice knew if he got into the woods, she'd never find him. She put on a burst of speed and lunged at him. Her hands closed on air, and she nearly fell on her face. Was it her imagination, or did the creature grin at her?

She gritted her teeth and barreled after him. Papa James had given her that necklace when she moved in with him and Rommy. It was an exact duplicate of Rommy's. She couldn't lose it.

The cat paused at the edge of the woods, and then he plunged into the undergrowth. Alice followed. The farther she ran, the closer the vegetation pressed in on her until the dirt path she was on became faint and then disappeared altogether. Branches slapped her face, and her skirt caught and tore.

The white tail disappeared. She stopped and bent over, drawing in ragged breaths. Where had the dratted thing gotten to? She straightened and turned in a slow circle. Tears welled up, and she knuckled them away. Crying wouldn't solve anything.

"Here, kitty." She had little hope it would respond to her, but she had to try.

A rustle off to her left revealed a black, whiskered face and two glowing blue eyes. Her body sagged, and she took a cautious step forward. The cat meowed and took a step backwards. Alice took a step forward. The cat tilted its head and took another step back. Alice followed, holding her breath. This went on for several minutes until Alice realized she was so far into the trees she had no idea where she was. She shook her head. She'd worry about that once she got her jewelry back.

Still, this was getting ridiculous. Alice straightened her shoulders. "Now look here, Cat. Just drop my property, and you can run off to wherever you'd like."

The cat's mouth curved and it let out a chuffing breath. Was it laughing at her? Great, now she was imagining things. Worse, she was arguing with a cat in the middle of the woods while her mother and sister were probably wondering what had happened to her. She pressed her lips together. She prayed Hadley had left without stopping at the house.

Alice spread her arms out and slid forward until only a few feet separated them. The cat hissed and leapt back. The look it gave her was almost reproachful.

"If you'd stop being such a git, I wouldn't have to do this." She balanced on the balls of her feet and then launched herself at the cat. This time, her fingers brushed the chain.

The cat skittered away. Then it gave a long, low meow, its ears flattening to its skull. Alice pushed herself onto her haunches. She hoped it wouldn't attack her.

Crouching low, the cat scuttled towards her, and it was Alice's turn to yelp. She leapt to her feet and backpedaled away from the cat. She skipped back just as a paw swiped at her ankle.

"Blimey!" She danced away from the determined creature, scrambling over a fallen log to avoid its menacing claws. The cat jumped onto the log, its back end hitched high and its white-tipped tail waving. Her necklace dangled from his mouth like a prize. Should she make a grab for it? At this height he would have no problem reaching her face if he wanted. The cat wiggled its rump as if in answer to Alice's unspoken concern.

Alice froze, but the cat leapt away from her. He bounded off through the undergrowth, the only sound that of snapping branches. Alice cursed her delicate kid slippers, which weren't made for running through the woods. Branches snagged at her already bedraggled hair, and something sharp caught the edge of her skirt. The ripping of fabric echoed through the air. As she ran deeper, the shadows got longer and darker. It was getting harder and harder to see. Leaves slapped her face as she zigged and zagged around trees.

It didn't take long before she had a stitch in her side and her breath was coming in pants. She sent up a prayer of thanks for her skirt's hemline that only came to her shins. It certainly gave her more freedom of movement than what the women were wearing in the village.

Alice hopped over a fallen branch, and her foot landed in leaf litter. She skidded, trying to regain her balance, but the recent rain had made everything slippery. Her ankle twisted, sending a hot slice of agony up her leg. She tumbled to her hands and knees. She scrambled to her feet and tried to keep going, but her ankle protested. She hobbled towards a large tree. Its roots poked above the forest floor, and its branches spread so wide the ground underneath it was almost empty of vegetation.

Alice placed her back against the tree, the rough bark scratching at her back. The smell of leaves and plants filled her nose. She was deep into the woods of the estate now. The only sounds were the birds twittering and the rustle of tiny animals. How far had she gone?

It took a moment for the silence to register in her mind. She tilted her head. There wasn't any sign of the cat. Had she lost that bloody creature?

She squeezed her eyes shut, and a lone tear leaked down her cheek as she leaned against the scratchy tree trunk. A bit of sunlight glinted through its branches. She swiped at her tears. There was no chance she was getting her necklace back now, and she didn't know how she was going to explain her torn skirts and straggling hair to Mother. She shuddered at the lecture that was sure to come her way.

In the silence, Hadley's threats echoed in her mind. Another tear slipped from beneath her lashes, and she sniffled. She only had a few weeks before she could escape, but what if what he'd said was true? What if Papa James was in trouble? Was it right to just leave him and sail across the ocean to realize her own dreams—after all he had done for her?

Her ankle throbbed, and half her curls hung in her face. She didn't have to look to know her skirt and new shirtwaist were ruined. Her shoes were probably beyond repair, too. She sighed. It was going to be a long walk back to the house.

And that's when she heard it: a faint rustle of underbrush. Her eyes flew open and connected with shining sapphire ones. Hope rippled through her. She searched around for something to lure the cat to her, but she didn't have to worry about that.

Keeping its eerie eyes on her, the cat crept forward. Then, in a blur of motion, it leapt onto a stump and launched itself straight at her.

Alice screamed as it hit her chest, driving the air from her lungs. She staggered backwards, her bad ankle giving way as she fell into empty space.

Chapter 7

ALICE'S SCREAM ECHOED ABOVE her as the air whistled around her face. Her arms flailed as she tried to grab onto anything to stop her descent. Tangled roots and vines blurred by her.

Down and down she tumbled. Her breath ran out, and she drew in another one. Her voice burst from her throat anew, terror clawing at her. Fingers scraped at a vine, slowing her momentarily, but it ripped out of her hand, leaving burning pain in its wake.

And still she fell.

And fell.

And fell.

The vines and roots gave way to fronds of plants and colorful flowers. She opened her mouth to scream again, but a velvet paw pushed against her lips.

The cat. She had forgotten about it. Although, with his bulk sitting squarely on her chest, she didn't know how she could have.

The enormous creature had made itself comfortable, nestling into the fabric of her dress, his paws tucked under him as if they were in some drawing room rather than falling down an endless hole. Her necklace hung from his mouth like a trophy. She wanted to snatch it away, but she was afraid it would go flying and she'd never find it.

"You wretched thing!" She glared at him but he simply stared back with those disconcerting eyes, a smug smile stretched across his whiskered face.

Alice still fell, but the terror had receded. Apparently, you could only be mindlessly terrified for so long. The air whistled by her, and she was still dropping fast enough that the walls of whatever hole she had fallen into were a colorful blur. A strange calm enveloped her.

Alice wondered if she would fall forever. Her mind shied away from a landing. That could only end one way.

The cat, reassured that his perch was safe, unhooked his claws and purred, a satisfied expression on his feline face.

He truly was a beautiful creature, with long, silky black hair, tufted ears, and those blue eyes. The only other color on his body was the white splotch at the tip of his plumed tail.

A sudden gust of wind struck her back. Her dizzying fall slowed, and the walls on either side of her fell away. Before she could process what was happening, she struck a branch and bounced sideways. Her arms wrapped around the cat without thought as she ping-ponged from one tree limb to another. Finally, she landed with a bone-jarring thud in a clump of ferns.

The breath whooshed out of her as the cat's bulk pushed the remaining air out of her lungs. Unfazed, he hopped off her stomach and delicately stretched.

Gasping for air, Alice rolled onto her hands and knees. With a shaking hand, she plucked her necklace from a fern frond. The clasp was broken, so she shoved it into her pocket, and then staggered to her feet. Her ankle gave a throb of protest, but it held her weight when she took a step. She glanced around. She was in the middle of a forest. Not the woods near her home. The trees and plants were all wrong, for one thing.

The cat rubbed up against her leg and purred. She had a powerful urge to kick him, but resisted the impulse.

A loud snort startled her, and a gust of warm air blew her hair forward. Alice's body stilled, the breath frozen in her lungs. A faint tremor took over her legs and arms. She forced herself to turn around. Her gaze landed on an iridescent bronze stump. Scales covered it.

Alice's eyes followed the stump up to a large chest, also scaled. A gust of breath ruffled the top of her head, and she caught a faint whiff of smoke.

Her trembling increased, so she swayed on her feet. Every instinct shouted at her to run, but her feet remained rooted to the earth. Slowly, almost against her will, she tilted her head back. Her gaze collided with mossy-green eyes.

They belonged to a creature Alice had only ever seen in books: a dragon.

Chapter 8

THE DRAGON'S HEAD WAS twice the length of Alice's entire body. Black horns extended from either side, right behind where ears might be. The dragon opened its mouth, exposing teeth the size of swords, and roared.

Alice's bones shook with the sound, and only fear kept her frozen upright. The dragon's wings opened wide, leathery and edged in a coppery gold. With a separate part of her mind, Alice noted that one seemed—stunted, somehow? Still, the movement created such a wind that Alice stumbled backwards.

She tripped, and she sat down hard on the ground, pain jolting up her spine. The dragon lowered its head in her direction, and she skittered backwards, frantically pushing herself with her feet and hands until her spine hit the trunk of a tree.

Was she really going to die this way? Falling down some forsaken hole, only to be a snack for a mythological animal? She'd never see Rommy again, and nobody would know what had become of her. Tears spilled over her lashes.

The dragon drew back and blinked at her, his nostrils flaring. For some reason, she thought of the thing as a male, although for all she knew, it could be a female dragon. Did those exist? They must, or there wouldn't be any dragons eventually, right?

Alice shook her head. She was becoming unhinged, but who could blame her?

The beast swung his head towards the cat and growled. Alice couldn't stop shaking. She hugged herself, trying to hold her body still.

The cat rubbed itself against her hip and then wove in a figure eight through the dragon's legs. The dragon narrowed his eyes and snorted, steam rising from its nostrils in wavy wisps. The cat hissed back, its tail lashing.

Then, it came to sit directly between Alice and the dragon, looking from one to the other, a grin on its face, for all the world like he was introducing them. Alice had observed plenty of cats at home. You could hardly live on a country estate without having a herd of tabbies running around, but she had never seen one smile, never mind grin. There was something decidedly off about this cat.

Of course, she was staring at a dragon, so what did she know?

A deep growl rumbled out of the dragon's chest, and the trembling that had begun to subside took over Alice's body again. She shrank against the tree trunk, trying to blend into its bark.

But the dragon was focused on the cat. The cat yowled at the dragon and began weaving again between the bigger creature's legs.

Apparently, they knew each other. Lovely.

The dragon snorted again and then extended its neck until its giant head was on a level with her body. The scent of brimstone enveloped her, and Alice's entire frame shuddered. She wanted to squeeze her eyes shut, but instead she pulled her feet underneath her and pushed to stand, still pressed against the tree. She refused to meet her end cowering in the dirt. Instead, she lifted her trembling chin and met the dragon's gaze with her own.

Tears sprang to her eyes despite her best efforts, but she blinked them away. Nobody would know what happened to her if she died here. She only hoped Rommy and Finn wouldn't miss their chance because of her.

Alice squared her shoulders and waited. She wasn't sure if she'd rather it blast her with fire or chomp her with its teeth. On the whole, being eaten would probably be the quicker, less painful death. Her knees wobbled at the thought, but she stiffened them.

"Well, what are you waiting for?" she said.

The dragon's expression drooped. He seemed almost sad. As she stared into its eyes, words pressed into her mind. It felt like rocks grinding against her skull. She winced as they took shape.

Won't hurt you.

She squinted up at the dragon, her head aching. Was she going crazy? She shook her head. It wasn't possible it was... talking to her, was it?

Words pressed into her mind again, scraping. She put a hand to her temple and squeezed her eyes shut against the pain.

Return you to your world. Don't worry.

She peeked up at the dragon. Its head was still level with her body, but it wasn't coming any closer. Its eyebrows were pulled low.

Do you understand me?

Some of the tension seeped out of her shoulders and neck. Her stance relaxed. "Are... are you talking to me?"

She immediately felt ridiculous, but the dragon's expression brightened as it nodded once.

Who did you think was speaking, love?

This voice was also male, but it felt more like rough velvet in her mind. She glanced down at the cat sitting at her feet. She couldn't call its expression anything but a smirk. Anger bubbled up in her chest, and she glared down at the creature.

"How am I supposed to know?" she snapped. "It's not as if I have regular chin-wags with any of the animals at home."

Now that she wasn't in imminent danger of being eaten, she took a moment to study her surroundings. Trees of varying sizes and shapes stretched in all directions, but the green of the leaves here was unusual, almost iridescent, their surfaces shaggy with fuzz. Even the bark of the trees was peculiar, shining in metallic golds, bronzes, and silvers. A sweet but sharp scent she couldn't identify floated on the breeze. This decidedly was not the forest on the estate. She wasn't even sure it was the same world. She glanced upward, but the tree canopy blocked all but a sliver of a darkening blue sky. A cold sense of unease curled in her belly as she realized it was late afternoon here. Not the same world, then.

"Just where am I, anyway?" She addressed the question to the cat at her feet.

He grinned up at her and she repressed a shiver. It was unsettling to see such a human expression on an animal. He held out a paw and gestured towards the surrounding woods. *Welcome to the Kingdom of Wonderland.*

Alice looked at the cat and then at the dragon. They were both watching her expectantly. The unease in her belly grew. She might understand them both, and they didn't seem intent on eating or killing her. That didn't mean she should trust them, though. At least, not the cat, she amended. It was true he had saved her from Hadley, but he'd also shoved her down that hole. The dragon, at least, had offered to take her home.

She narrowed her eyes at the reclining feline. "I'm not sure what you expected to get from pushing me into that hole, but I'd really like to go home now."

The cat arched its back and hissed at her. It took a menacing step forward, and Alice pushed her back against the tree, a soft squeak escaping her lips.

The dragon growled again, and his voice sounded sharp in Alice's mind. *Stop acting the rogue, Chess. She owes us nothing. I'm assuming you did not give her a choice about coming here.*

The cat whirled towards the larger animal, his fur bristling and his tail twice its normal size. *Don't be stupid. Of course, I didn't ask—as if I could. But she's here now. She may as well help us as not.* He glanced over his shoulder at Alice. *Besides, she rather owes me for getting rid of her slobbering suitor.*

The growling got deeper, and the dragon tried to move forward, but jerked to a halt. It was then that Alice realized a glistening silver strand was wrapped around the dragon's front leg.

The cat narrowed its blue eyes. *At least get her to release you—or would you rather wait here for the Queen like a gift?*

I wouldn't be in this predicament if you'd only listened to me, but you always have to rush into things without thinking. There was a menacing quality in the dragon's rough voice that sent an involuntary shiver down Alice's back. The cat didn't seem to have any sense of self-preservation, though. He swiped a claw towards the dragon's snout and bared his teeth.

No, you'd rather wait until you're dead or it's too late.

They stared at each other, animosity crackling like electricity between them. She wasn't sure what they were talking about but, frankly, didn't really care. She just wanted to go home, and the dragon seemed the more reasonable of the pair. She'd direct her appeals to him.

While the two continued to glare at each other, she inspected what was holding the dragon in place. It didn't take long to understand the dragon was in some kind of trap. If she helped him, surely he'd help her get home.

Alice straightened away from the tree trunk and spoke into the taut silence. "I can help untangle you." She pointed to where the strands extended into several nearby trees that bent at strange angles.

The cat rubbed up against her ankle and then sat next to her. He turned his triumphant face towards the dragon. *See? She's going to help.* He sniffed. *You don't have to thank me. Once you're free, then we can—*

Alice interrupted him. "I'll help you get free, but I want your word that you'll send me home."

The cat whipped his head towards her, but Alice ignored him. Her gaze was trained on the dragon. His words grated inside her head.

You have my word. He bowed his head. *I am most grateful for your assistance. If I could help you find your way home now, I would, but...* He half lifted the trapped wing, and Alice could see it, too, was caught by the silvery lines.

Alice reached out a hand and rested her palm on the very end of the dragon's snout. It felt both warm and hard, like leather. For a moment, wonder overwhelmed her—she was touching a dragon. Then the cat butted up against her leg, pulling her back to the problem before her. She gave the dragon's nose one last pat.

"Let's see if we can get you out of this."

Alice circled the dragon. He was more entangled than she had first thought. In fact, the thin strands wrapped around one of his back legs and his tail, binding them together.

Whatever the dragon had stumbled into, he was well and truly stuck. Alice tapped a finger on her chin. She touched the string and yanked her hand away. It wasn't string. It was some kind of wire, and it was sharp. There was no way to break it or pull it apart with her bare hands, not without slicing her skin to shreds in the process. A sense of despair welled up. It was obvious the dragon, as big and strong as he was, wasn't getting out of this mess without some help, but she didn't have the faintest idea of how to cut those wires. All she had was what she was wearing.

Her eyes widened, and her hands flew to her hair. If only it hadn't fallen out—! She rummaged through her curls, and there it was. Her hair comb... But it wasn't just any comb. Papa James had made one for both her and Rommy from one of his daggers that had served him during his more adventurous days. If you pulled the decorative part off the top, there was a razor edge. Papa James wanted his girls to have a weapon handy.

She yanked it out of her hair, and the rest of her curls tumbled over her shoulders. She shoved at the mass of hair and hurried to where the dragon was tethered. He kept one large eye trained on her as she bent to cut the strand.

Even with the sharp edge of her comb, it took several long minutes before she was through the wire. She had a nice slice along her palm for her troubles, but at least she could unwind the dragon's leg and tail.

Glancing around, she sliced off two thick leaves, each about the size of her forearm. She used them to protect her hands as she unwrapped the wire from the dragon's tail and leg. Several times, she had to pull the wire out from where it had sunk into flesh between scales. The dragon grunted, but he held very still.

Alice backed up and put her hands on her hips. "There, that's one part done." She frowned at the dark, almost black blood that ran down the creature's leg and tail. "You're going to have to watch that so it doesn't become infected."

Alice turned to her next task—freeing the wing. That was going to be a bit more complicated. For one thing, in order to reach the wire where it was attached to his wing, she was going to have to climb the tree it was fastened to.

Alice didn't think she'd been in a tree since she was about twelve. At least not since Papa James had married Mother. That was five years ago—and she didn't wear skirts back then, either. She sighed and padded to the base of the tree. Fortunately, it had big branches and didn't look too difficult to climb. She kicked off her shoes and reached up. Her toes curled around a rough burl that was conveniently situated as a foothold. She grunted as she pulled herself upward and shook her curls out of her face.

She heard chuffing. The cat was sitting by the dragon's feet, watching her. He smirked.

"I'd like to see you have a better idea," she said.

The cat meowed at her, and Alice rolled her eyes but kept climbing. Once she had pulled herself up to the first branch, it was fairly easy to pick her way to the one that the wire was attached to. Getting out to the end was going to be more of a problem, though.

Alice clung to the trunk and eyed the long, tapering limb. There was no other way to reach the line unless she straddled the branch. If Mother could see her now, she'd be appalled. Alice squared her shoulders. Mother wasn't here, and the quicker she got this dragon freed, the sooner she could go home.

Alice swung her leg over the branch and scooched towards the end, the rough bark tearing her stockings to shreds. It took another several minutes to saw through the wire. She nearly pitched to the ground as the branch sprang upward once it was freed.

The wing was no longer attached to the tree limb, but it was still tangled. Unlike the dragon's leg and tail, there was no way Alice could reach high enough to unwrap the line while standing on the ground. She couldn't reach it from the branch, either.

That left only one option.

Alice scrambled down the tree trunk. When her feet hit the dirt, she walked over to face the dragon while she explained her plan.

He frowned, and his horned eyebrows lowered. Clearly, he wasn't thrilled, but he sighed and extended his front leg for her to climb.

Alice patted his scales. "I'll be as quick as I can. I don't like this any more than you do."

Gingerly, she put her foot on the dragon's leg and boosted herself up. It took some scrambling since his scales were a bit slick, but finally she got herself onto the dragon's back. Crawling on her hands and knees, she inched her way to the wing joint. She had to lie on her stomach to reach it. She frowned at the tangled mess of wire and wing. This was much worse than his leg had been.

In the end, she had to climb on and off the dragon several times. He let out a few hisses as she tugged the strands free from the skin of his wing. Alice cringed each time. She hated causing the creature pain, but there was no other way. So, she pressed her lips together and continued with her task.

She slid back to the ground to work on the rest of the wing tip when a rumbling sounded in the distance.

"What's that?" she asked. "Don't tell me there is a herd of you somewhere?" She laughed, but the sound died on her lips when she noticed the cat and the dragon had gone still.

Grinding stone and velvet crashed into her mind. They both said the same thing.

Soldiers.

Chapter 9

"Soldiers?" Alice's voice rose in a squawk.

The dragon whipped his head around and pushed at her with his snout, almost knocking her to the ground.

Run!

Alice whirled and shoved his nose away from her.

"No! I need to get this wire off!"

The dragon pushed at her again.

Foolish. Run!

"Stop it! I don't even know where I am, never mind trying to run somewhere else!"

She turned back to her task as the rumbling under her feet increased. Alice's fingers fumbled with the wire as she worked it from the leathery skin.

Footsteps thudded closer, and the crackle of branches being trampled became louder and louder. Alice's hands trembled, but she didn't turn around. She had to get the dragon free before—

Something whistled by her head, thunking into a near-by tree trunk. She looked up to see an arrow quivering in the bark.

Just her luck: she had not only fallen down a hole into goodness knows where, but apparently, she had managed to fall into the middle of a war.

The dragon tried to sweep his injured wing over her, but it wouldn't bend. He hissed again as the wire dug in deeper and more blood ran from the many cuts that webbed over the skin.

"Stop that!" Alice snapped. "I'm nearly done."

The ground under Alice's feet shook. She yanked at a wire, but it didn't budge.

The dragon roared, and it echoed in Alice's bones. For a moment, her fingers refused to work, but another arrow whistled by her head. It thunked into the dragon's wing. He grunted in pain.

Alice tugged harder, abandoning her efforts to be gentle. She followed its sharp curve and found it attached to a tree branch.

"Blast it!" There was no time to climb up, not to mention the genuine possibility of being hit by an arrow. Those were flying faster now as the sounds of the soldiers got closer.

The dragon roared again, and Alice felt a blast of heat from the fire as he blew towards the approaching battalion. Alice still hadn't turned to see who was trying to kill them. Her eyes stayed focused on the task at hand.

She pulled out the hair comb again, almost dropping it in her haste. Sweat trickled down her back as she sawed at the trap. The wire bit into her index finger, and she sucked in a breath. Blood welled up and dripped down her hand. The slickness made her grip slippery.

Arrows continued to rain over them, although the dragon's blasts of fire slowed them. A little. Every moment that she worked, Alice was aware of her exposed back. With each second that ticked by, she braced for the pain of an arrow finding its mark.

The wire frayed. Alice bore down on it harder, cutting another finger. With a big exhale, she finally snapped the silvery wire in two, and she dropped the wire bits to the ground. Blood dripped down her arm. She wiped it on her ruined dress as she shoved the hair comb into her pocket and turned to see who was shooting at them.

The surrounding woods were overflowing with men in silver armor. Helmets covered their faces, like so many anonymous tin soldiers. A row of archers continued to shoot at them. Alice grimaced. Arrows stuck out of the dragon's hide like porcupine quills.

Scorched plants marked the perimeter of the blasts of fire. He blasted another hot breath towards the soldiers. To Alice's untrained eye, it seemed weak, almost as if the dragon had restrained himself. The earth shook as he reared back and spread his wings. The injured one didn't quite open all the way, but it was a magnificent display of coppery gold. Fans of scaled horns unfurled on either side of the dragon's head like a spiky mane. The trees rattled with his roar. He opened his mouth and shot more fire that landed just shy of the soldiers. They retreated a few steps, but they kept firing.

One soldier made his way to the front line. He was riding some kind of beast Alice didn't recognize. It had the body of a lion but the head of a hawk. She saw him raise a long sword towards the sky, the jewels in the hilt sparkling in a ray of sunlight.

Something butted against her ankle.

Up! Up! Up!

The cat was pushing at her leg, trying to move her closer to the dragon. She took a few stumbling steps until she pressed against its scaled side.

The cat stretched its body up her leg, asking to be lifted. Alice obliged, but she wasn't sure what she was supposed to do with the thing.

Stupid. Up!

The cat twisted in her arms. She struggled to hold on to it, but he hissed and scratched her. Alice cried out and loosened her hold. The cat sprang onto the dragon's back and glared down at her.

A loud cry made her whirl. The man with the sword lowered his arm, and the men stationed in the trees pushed forward. Alice's heart thundered in her chest, and a wave of dizziness swept over her. Her knees buckled. Something clamped onto the back of her dress and flung her onto the dragon's back.

She slid across the slippery scales and scrabbled until her fingers found purchase on a scale's knobby bumps.

The dragon's wings beat the air, and they lurched into the sky. Alice sprawled in a half-sitting, half-lying position on the dragon's back, and for a moment she just held on, trying to catch her breath. As they rose into the air, the dragon shuddered several times, and twice something whizzed over her head. She pressed herself flatter into the scales, trying to make herself small. The wind whistled along the dragon's body, but this spot at the base of his neck sheltered her.

As they rose higher, the air became colder and Alice shivered, although a reassuring heat rose from the scales. Alice worked her way into a sitting position and looked around. They were high in the sky now, the

occasional puff of cloud the only thing visible. She resisted the urge to peer down, as she already felt rather
precarious.

Twisting around, she spotted the cat. He was lying not
far behind her, sprawled as if in a rocking chair and not
on a flying dragon.

He noticed her attention, and his mouth stretched
into a grin. Alice narrowed her eyes at him, and as if on
cue, her arm where he had scratched her stung.

"You, Cat, are a royal pain," she said.

The cat meowed and seemed to shrug its shoulders.

Saved you.

"I don't think you can make that claim," she said. "You
just saved yourself." She patted the dragon. "This chap
here is the one that actually saved me."

The cat sniffed.

My name is Chess.

Despite feeling somewhat idiotic, Alice placed a hand
on her chest and said, "I'm Alice. I would say it's nice to
meet you, Chess, but so far, it really hasn't been."

So ungrateful.

Before Alice could respond, the dragon suddenly dropped several yards. Alice let out a squeak and
clutched at his scales, gripping the dragon's back with
her legs.

Concerned despite herself, she glanced back at the
black cat. He still lay calmly on the dragon's back, but
Alice noticed his claws were no longer sheathed.

Before she could wonder if that hurt the dragon,
a screech sounded somewhere behind them. Alice
scanned the sky but saw nothing.

The cat behind her swore.

"What is it?" Alice asked.

The cat's expression had turned grim. *It's the Commander. You had better hang on.*

Chapter 10

ALICE LEANED FORWARD ONTO the warm scales. Another scream rent the air, and she risked a look behind them. In the distance, a speck appeared.

"Who's the Commander?" she asked.

Chess's body was no longer relaxed. He was crouched, his fur bristling.

Not anybody you want to tangle with, love.

The dragon dropped again, and Alice swallowed a scream. The injured wing dragged through the air. She looked behind her, alarmed that the speck had grown bigger.

Below them, an expanse of forest spread out. The dragon dropped towards it so fast that Alice's body lost contact with his back for a moment. Her throat closed, and she threw herself forward.

Something hissed above her head, and she popped up to see what it was.

Chess hissed at her. *Keep your head down, girl. Do you want him to put a bolt through it?*

The dragon's voice scraped through her mind and she winced. *Brace yourself.*

Before Alice had time to process the words, they were crashing through the canopy of the trees. Branches scraped at her legs. She hugged the dragon's body and squeezed her eyes shut.

They landed on the forest floor, hard. Alice yelped as she almost lost her seat. The dragon tucked his wings into his sides, and then he was slipping through the forest so fast that everything was a blur. Alice didn't understand how a creature so large could race through the trees without running into any of them. Still, branches caught at her legs and skirt. She tucked in her arms and tried to make herself as small as possible. If she got knocked off, she'd probably break a bone. Or two.

The dragon didn't follow a straight path but wound in a curving pattern. She strained her ears for signs of pursuit, but the wind whipped by her, drowning out any other noise. The dragon ran and ran, his gait choppy from his injured leg. The forest seemed endless.

They burst into a clearing. The dragon skidded to a halt, and Alice jolted against his neck. She sat up and twisted around. The cat was still clinging to his friend's back, but his fur stood on end.

The dragon unfurled his wings. His muscles tensed, and he leapt into the sky. With great effort, they rose above the level of the trees.

Alice looked behind her. The sky was empty, and her muscles unwound a fraction. However, she understood they still weren't safe. She didn't know where the dragon was headed, but it was clear this flight was costing him.

The thought had barely formed when the dragon plunged downward several yards. Alice clamped her lips shut to keep from crying out and clutched at his scales, her knuckles white.

We're nearly there.

Before she could wonder where *there* was, the words *Hang on* flashed painfully into her mind. They plummeted towards the ground at a dizzying speed. For the third time in less than an hour, Alice found herself screaming as a mountain loomed out from the clouds. She squeezed her eyes shut as they arrowed towards it.

The Jabberwock spread his uninjured wing to slow them, but they hit the rocky plateau with such force Chess bounced into the air. He barely hung on.

The girl flipped forward over the dragon's head. She caught herself on Zander's eyebrow. Chess smirked as she apologized and carefully stepped on his friend's cheek before she dropped to the ground.

Chess tensed as the girl wobbled and almost fell, but she steadied herself on Zander's neck. She took a deep breath and straightened her shoulders. Chess's body relaxed. Good, she wasn't getting hysterical. That was the last thing he needed.

He sauntered towards the Jabberwock's head. His friend didn't even look at him.

Zander's eyes were half shut and his breathing labored. His injured wing rested at an awkward angle. Arrows protruded from his hide like porcupine quills, their shafts glistening in the afternoon sunlight. Blood, dark as tar, leaked from various wounds over his massive body. Alice bit her lip and looked at Chess.

He walked over and sat at her feet. They'd have to get those arrows out. He had a bad feeling ithicass poison coated their tips, but only time would tell.

A distant sound made him whirl, his body tensing. The cry came again, and dread pooled in his stomach. He turned back to the girl and butted his head into her leg.

We have to get into the cave.

She looked at the Jabberwock and then back at him, an eyebrow raised.

"But how?" She gestured at his friend.

Chess ignored her and pounced his front paws on Zander's shoulder. A large green eye opened and rolled back towards him.

It's the Commander. He's coming.

Zander's eye drifted shut again. Chess ran to stand in front of the Jabberwock. Chess called his name several times, but there was no response. An urgency he couldn't ignore pushed at him. Hoping he wouldn't regret it, Chess smacked his friend's snout with a paw. Success! Both eyes popped open. Steam rose from nostrils almost as big as Chess's head.

You have to get up!

This time, Zander blinked and his eyes focused. With effort, he raised his head. His great trunk-sized legs trembled as he struggled to push himself to standing. Alice came around and reached for an arrow.

With a hiss, Chess leapt forward and swatted her ankle.

"Ouch! What was that for?"

We don't have time for that now. Didn't you listen? The Commander is coming. If he sees us, we'll have to find a different hiding place. He waved a paw. *Does he look like he's in any condition to do that?*

"I just thought—"

Well, stop it! We don't have time for thinking.

Chess's hair bristled as another cry rent the air. Alice turned, her eyes wide. She pressed her lips together and began encouraging Zander to move more quickly.

Finally! He scanned the sky. Still no sign of the Commander and his griffon, but they sounded closer. He willed his friend to move faster. Every second dragged out until Chess's nerves twanged with tension.

The Jabberwock shuffled forward, stopping to catch his balance between each step.

Chess twisted back and glanced over his shoulder. Was that a speck in the distance?

Hurry! He can't see us.

Alice glowered at him. "He's moving as fast as he can! It won't help us if he falls over." Her tone was tart. She continued to keep a hand on his friend's shoulder.

Chess rolled his eyes. He wasn't sure what she expected to do. If Zander toppled over, she'd be squashed flat. Still, her murmured words seemed to move his friend a fraction faster.

In slow motion, they cleared the threshold of the cave entrance. Zander stopped, his head hanging low. His legs trembled.

Go deeper, Chess urged.

Zander took one more tottering step and then collapsed.

Chess nudged the enormous tail that still stuck out onto the ledge. Alice, seeing what he was doing, ran around and shoved at the tail. Chess placed both paws on the scales and pushed with her. Between the two of them, they got his tail into the cave and out of sight.

And none too soon. Chess looked behind him. The speck was bigger. He hissed. Their only hope was if the Commander hadn't seen Zander. He darted into the cave and butted his head against Alice's leg.

Get back from the entrance. Do you want him to see you?

Alice narrowed her eyes, but she scrambled further into the cave. Zander lay still, his long neck stretched out and his head resting on the stone floor. His eyes were closed, his breathing shallow.

Chess scrunched his face and eyed the arrows still sticking out of his friend. Those were going to have to come out, and the sooner the better.

The scream of the griffon made him jump. It sounded very close. Chess didn't dare peek out. He couldn't let the Commander see him. So far, the man only knew about the Jabberwock, and he wanted to keep it that way.

Alice had settled herself on the floor well away from the entrance, her back against the cave wall.

"Don't you—"

Chess leapt into the girl's lap and pushed a paw on her mouth. *Be quiet. Griffons have excellent hearing.*

Alice's eyes widened, and she opened her mouth, but then shut it with a snap.

They stayed hunkered down in the cave for what felt like forever. Every time Chess assumed the Commander was gone, another screech from the griffon would freeze his insides.

Alice had leaned her head back against the wall. Her eyes had drifted shut, but she wasn't asleep. He had curled up against her leg, and one of her hands was stroking his back. If her body hadn't been so rigid, he would have guessed her relaxed.

After a prolonged period of silence, she lifted her head. "Is he gone?" Her voice was barely a whisper.

Chess cocked a silky ear, straining to hear. He got up and crept to the entrance, keeping his body close to the wall's shadows. His eyes scanned the skies. The sun was sending streaks of purple and gold across the puffs of clouds as it sank below the horizon. The sky was empty. More importantly, it was silent.

He trotted back to the girl. *I think it's safe now. We should still stay inside, just in case, though.*

A sigh gusted from between the girl's lips before she turned her enormous violet eyes on him.

"Good! Now maybe you can tell me how the bloody blazes I'm going to get home if he doesn't make it.

Chapter 11

THE CAT HISSED AT her, but Alice didn't care. She worried about the dragon. His injuries appeared worse than she had realized. While she hoped he wouldn't die for his own sake, she could admit a good portion of her concern was for herself, too.

"I'm sorry about your friend, but I didn't ask to come here, you know." She pushed herself to her feet and straightened her skirt.

The cat leapt onto the dragon's back, winding its way over to an arrow. He sat down and looked at it and then at her. *If you're so concerned, why don't you do something useful, like take these arrows out?*

When she did nothing, the cat let out a meow and rolled its eyes.

You need to pull these out.

A wave of weariness hit Alice. Since she had fallen down that blasted hole, she had plunged from one deadly situation to the next. Not to mention, there was a dragon lying in front of her, and she was arguing with a cat.

As if he'd read her mind, the cat jumped down and began weaving around her ankles. *You can have hysterics later. Those need to come out now.*

Alice lifted her foot to kick the cat away from her, but wobbled on her bad ankle. She exhaled. Besides, he was probably right. Turning, she looked at the dragon.

Alarmed, she noticed his eyes had closed and his breathing had become very shallow. She tentatively reached out and touched the end of an arrow. For a moment, the edges of her vision grew dark, and everything telescoped to the feathered end. Revulsion for the arrows swept over her and she almost gagged. An insistent bumping against her leg snapped her out of it. She gave herself a little shake and braced herself for the task in front of her.

Alice reached for the closest arrow and grabbed the shaft close to where it plunged into the scaley hide.

She placed one hand flat on his side. "I'm sorry about this, but I'm going to have to pull these out."

The dragon's eyelids fluttered open, and one green eye rolled back towards her.

Alice wasn't sure if the dragon understood her. He seemed to go in and out of consciousness, but she wanted him to understand. The last thing she needed was this immense creature lashing out at her in pain.

"Mr. Dragon—"

His name is Zander.

Her gaze flicked down to the cat who was watching her. "All right then. Zander, I'm going to remove these now. If it gets to be too much, let me know, and we can stop for a while. But they have to come out."

The dragon shut his eyes and snorted. Taking that as assent, Alice grasped the arrow as close to the scales as she could and pulled with all of her strength.

The arrow came free instantly. Alice flailed to keep her balance and fell onto her backside with a grunt. A wheezing noise made her snap her head around.

The cat was rolling on its back, paws waving in the air. It was clearly laughing at her.

Anger boiled up in Alice. "You flea-bitten bag of bones." She scrambled to her feet. "I should toss your sorry arse over the side and see if cats really do land on their feet."

The cat rolled back onto all fours and eyed her, as if he thought she might follow through on her threat.

Now, that is not how a lady talks.

The words felt like a bucket of cold water, and her cheeks heated. How quickly her genteel manners fell away. She shook her head. That wasn't important right now. She needed to focus on the dragon. At least getting those arrows out would be easier than she had thought.

Turning her back on the cat, Alice moved around the dragon. With great care, she pulled each arrow out. Even though only two of them had sunk any deeper than the outer scales, she noticed the discoloration on the tips. She reached a finger to touch the sharp end, but a pain on her ankle stopped her.

"What is wrong with you?" she said, glaring down at the cat.

If you want to poison yourself, by all means, don't let me stop you.

Alice's eyes widened as what Chess said sank in. "There's poison on these arrows?"

He shrugged a furry shoulder. *I suspected there might be, but I couldn't tell for sure until you removed the arrows. They shouldn't be that color, even if they pierced Zander's hide.*

Alice made a face and gingerly set the arrows to one side, careful not to get anywhere near the tips.

Once she had taken care of the arrows, Alice inspected the cave they were in. It was roomy, although with the sun gone, the far reaches were only shadows. A few animal bones littered the ground, and she could hear the faint burble of water running outside the entrance somewhere. She was curious to see the plateau they had landed on, since she'd only caught a glimpse earlier. Her attention had been on getting Zander inside.

Her gaze returned to the dragon. His eyes were open now, and he was watching her.

The words rumbled through her mind. *Thank you.*

Alice walked closer and patted the side of the leathery face.

"Your welcome, Zander. Now, we just need to clean out those wounds." She walked around to inspect a gash on his shoulder more closely. She placed a palm on the injury. After a moment, she jerked her hand back. Somehow, she could feel the infection spreading out from the wound. There was warmth in her palm, too, and she looked at her hand, afraid she'd touched the poison. But it didn't look any different.

No. I'll be fine. I heal much faster when I am in this form.

The dragon's words startled her back to the present. She wasn't sure what he meant—maybe the adult form of a dragon? Perhaps dragons started out in a different body, like a tadpole turning into a frog? She shook the thought away—now wasn't the time for a science lesson—and focused on what he was saying.

I'll help you get home... soon. His words slurred at the end, and his eyelids drooped.

Alice did not know what his healing abilities were, but his injuries seemed worse than he realized. She bit her lip.

As if he heard her thoughts, the dragon forced his eyes open again. *You have... my... word.*

Alice smiled at him. "I believe you... Zander."

A soft, smoky sigh escaped the dragon's mouth, and his eyes slid closed again. Alice just hoped he would recover enough to keep his word.

Now that the adrenaline coursing through her was subsiding, a wave of exhaustion swept over her. All she wanted to do was lie down on the hard ground and close her eyes. Perhaps when she opened them, she'd be back home.

But she knew better than that. If this was a hallucination, it was a very detailed one. She didn't think even at her most crazed she would have ever dreamt up something like this. Maybe fairies or mermaids, but not dragons, and definitely not that dratted cat.

As if her thoughts had summoned him, the cat came sauntering out from the back of the cave. He meowed and then stood next to the dragon's side, stretching himself until his paws came to rest just below one of the dragon's wounds. He meowed again and turned those blue eyes in her direction.

"Yes, I was just going to clean those out," she said out loud. "But I need water."

The cat dropped to all fours and ducked around the back of the dragon. After a moment, a clanking sound echoed from the back of the cave. The cat reappeared, batting a soldier's helmet. It looked like a head moving across the ground. When he got closer, he smacked it hard with his paw and it came to rest at her feet.

Alice stared down at it, apprehension twisting in her belly.

For water.

When she didn't move to pick it up, the cat hissed at her. He pushed it with his paw so it bumped into the toe of her shoe.

Alice backed up.

The cat sat on his haunches and glared at her from across the helmet.

Put water inside.

Alice gritted her teeth.

"I know what it's for," she snapped. She bent and grasped the tip of the helmet. "Please don't let there be a head in here, please don't let there be a head in here," she chanted under her breath. She half turned her face away as she lifted it, but it was just an empty helmet. Her whole body unclenched.

The cat was wheezing again, a grin on his whiskered face. Alice narrowed her eyes, but she didn't want to waste any more energy on this irritating feline. She turned on her heel and marched out on the plateau, looking for the source of water she had heard.

She stopped just outside the entrance and took in her surroundings. The ledge was a fairly sizable area of rock that jutted out from the mountain. The cave was tucked into the cliffside, and a stream of water flowed down to a small pool of water. Along its sides, feathery plants grew in sparse clumps.

She walked to its edge and knelt down. It was surprisingly deep. Alice guessed if she got in, the water would come up to at least her chest, most likely deeper towards the middle. She shuddered at the thought. Alice hated the water, and the idea of it being deep enough to go over her head made her chest tighten. She drew in a deep breath. It was okay. She wasn't going in the water. She was just filling this helmet so she could clean the dragon's wounds.

Alice looked around for something to use with the water. She couldn't very well just dump it on the dragon. Her eye caught on some spongy moss growing along the edges. The loamy soil was shallow, so it was easy to pull out several large tufts.

She carried her supplies back into the cave and got to work, washing each gash and tear on the dragon. She was careful to announce her intentions, especially on the deeper wounds, but the dragon didn't even flinch when she cleaned his wing where the worst of the damage was. Anxiety gnawed at the back of her mind, but she pushed it back down. One thing at a time. She wouldn't think about all the what-ifs. She wouldn't wonder how she'd get off this plateau and get back home if the dragon died.

It took several trips to the pool and more tufts of moss, but finally, she had cleaned all the wounds to her satisfaction. By the time she was done, the moon was out and stars twinkled in the sky.

Exhaustion rolled over her until she was swaying on her feet.

She dropped the moss and helmet onto the ground, the events of the past few hours swamping her in a wave of emotion. Her legs buckled, and she plopped onto the rock floor. She drew her knees to her chest and shivered. Although the cave offered shelter from the wind swirling across the mountain plateau, you couldn't call it warm. Goose bumps pebbled across her skin.

She put her head on her knees and closed her eyes. She focused on drawing in one breath after another. It was a trick Rommy had taught her when she first started at Chattingham's School for Modern Girls and things would get overwhelming. Just breathe in and out.

Soft fur brushed against her leg, and then something warm settled against her side. A rumbling purr filled the air. She raised her head. The cat was curled against her. She lowered her knees and sat cross-legged, and he crawled into her lap, turned several times and settled in, still purring.

Alice ran her hands over the sleek fur, finding the warm body and steady purring calmed her nerves. She scratched the cat under his chin, and a sandpapery tongue rasped over her wrist.

"I guess you're not all bad," she said.

Are you calm now?

Alice took a moment before answering, doing a mental check of herself. She was surprised to find that, other than the cuts on her hands from the wire and the scratch from the cat now purring in her lap, she was in one piece. More or less.

She used one hand to push her tangled hair out of her face. Her mind shied away from her predicament. What if the dragon died? How would she ever get down from this mountain or find her way back home? A small part of her wondered if she wasn't still lying in the woods of the estate, knocked in the head, and this was all a big dream. She looked down at her ripped dress. The skirt hung in torn panels, and every time she moved more threads came loose.

The cat nudged her hand with his nose.

You aren't going to get hysterical, are you? He licked her hand again.

"No, I won't get hysterical." She paused. "Although, under the circumstances, who could blame me?"

Alice sighed and slid the cat off of her lap and got up. She was beyond tired, but the cave floor was rock. She didn't fancy sitting on it all night. Her steps dragged as she went back to the pool one more time and picked a large number of the ferns that grew there. She layered them in a spot near one of the cave's walls before she sat back down. She pushed her back against the wall and rested her chin on her arms. Even though weariness tugged at her, Alice kept her eyes fastened on the drag-on, counting each labored breath. Logic told her that keeping watch wouldn't change the outcome, but she was determined to do it anyway.

Chapter 12

ALICE'S HEAD JERKED, AND she opened her eyes to shadowy darkness. For a moment, she thought she was in her own bed, but the rocky hardness underneath her and at her back made her aware that this was definitely not her bed. She wasn't sure what had woken her, but a warm body was curled against her hip, and her fingers found silky fur.

Then it all came rushing back—running through the woods, falling down the hole, landing at the feet of a dragon. As her eyes adjusted, a large lump took shape in the darkness. A rhythmic hissing noise like air leaking out of a rubber hose filled the cave. It was that noise that had woken her. She sat up, jostling the cat. He blinked and yawned.

"Is he supposed to be doing that?" she asked, alarm spiking through her.

Hmm?

The velvety words in her head sounded sleepy, disorientated.

"The dragon—that noise is coming from him."

Alice pushed to her feet and moved towards the creature. The last thing she wanted to do was startle him and get roasted. She dodged around his restless tail and scooted towards his head.

His eyes were closed and his mouth hung open. With every wheezy exhalation, a faint wisp of smoke curled from between his teeth. She laid her hand on the side of his head and jerked it back.

Unlike before, when the scales had felt like warm leather, now they scorched her fingers. She studied his injuries more closely. Dark lines ran from several lacerations on both his wing and back leg. Scales peeled back around the areas, and the flesh underneath looked hot and swollen. A rotten smell wafted from the wounds.

"Chess! Chess!"

The cat was already at her feet, pacing back and forth.

"You have to get some help for him. He's really sick."

You must help him.

"Me? Where am I going to get help? I don't even know where I'm at!"

I told you, the Kingdom of Wonderland.

"Thanks so much. That's not a lot of help. I don't know anyone here or where to go or..." Alice threw up her hands in frustration. "I can't even get off this blasted mountain! Do you think I can just grow wings and fly down?"

I'll take you to Caterpillar.

"I have to find a caterpillar? How is that going to do anything?"

The cat sneezed.

Not a caterpillar. "Caterpillar." He's the apothecary.

Alice stared at him.

Follow me. I'll show you.

Alice crossed her arms. "Someone needs to stay with Zander. He shouldn't be alone in his condition."

Chess hissed and arched his back. *I don't have time to argue with you.*

She narrowed her eyes. "Then don't. You're the one who knows this Caterpillar. Why do you need me?"

The cat tried to swat her ankle, but Alice danced out of his way. "Stop doing that!"

Chess plunked down and licked a paw, running it over his ear. After a moment, he spoke. *Fine. I need you to translate.*

Alice wrinkled her forehead. "Translate?"

Yes, translate. You do know what that means, I trust.

"Of course I do. But I still don't understand—"

Chess growled and stood. *You don't need to understand. What you need to do is come with me and stop asking all these needless questions.*

Alice's glance bounced between the dragon and the cat. Finally, she nodded and followed the cat towards the back of the cave. The further she walked, the darker it got.

"Slow down," Alice protested as her foot hit something hard in the darkness.

Hurry!

"Some of us can't see in the dark," Alice muttered as she shuffled after the cat. She could just make out the waving white tip of his tail, but even that was growing dimmer.

Duck.

The word came just as Alice smacked face-first into a rock wall. She rubbed her sore nose.

"You could have spoken up a bit sooner," she said.

Using her hands, she skimmed her way down to an opening until she was on her hands and knees. She crawled into the black opening, and her chest tightened. She hesitated. She didn't know if she could travel through the dark all the way to the bottom of this mountain. What if the tunnel got smaller? What if she got stuck? Just thinking about it made her skin clammy.

There wasn't enough air to draw into her lungs. The walls pressed in too close, even though she could still sense the opening at her back.

Why did you stop?

"Does this tunnel... does it get any smaller?" Alice choked out the words.

No. It gets bigger soon.

Alice inched forward for several yards in pitch black, wondering just how long it would be before the walls widened. The rocky ground bit into her knees, and the cuts on her hands throbbed. Just when she considered backing out while she was still able, a pinkish glow appeared up ahead. She scuttled forward, eager to be out of the blackness that pressed in like a blanket.

She passed through an archway, and the tunnel opened up into a huge round cavern. Pink squiggles of light spangled the ceiling far above her head. Multiple archways ringed the cavern, presumably leading to other tunnels.

Long, glass-like formations rose from the cavern floor and hung down from the ceiling. Inside each one, speckles of gold moved around in a ceaseless pattern of light, casting weird shadows over the floors and walls.

This way.

Instead of leading her to an archway, Chess hopped onto a stone that stuck out of the wall at a strange angle. Peering more closely, Alice saw that there were a series of stones, almost like steps that led to another opening higher on the wall of the cavern. The cat was leaping from stone to stone, headed for that opening.

Alice clambered onto the first stone. She could just reach the next one, but it was a stretch. She put her hand against the slick wall and prayed she wouldn't fall and break a bone.

The cat meowed down at her.

"I'm coming," she grumbled. "I'm not as agile as you are."

Obviously.

She ignored him as sweat beaded on her forehead. At the last stone, she almost got stuck, but her hand found a small hold on the slick surface of the wall, and she hauled herself the rest of the way to a narrow ledge outside the opening. She looked down. She was at least twenty feet off the cave floor, but the pink squiggles of light looked almost close enough to touch. From up here, she could see that they were small, worm-like creatures that were inching over the rocky ceiling. Staring up at the glowworms made her head swim a bit, and she put out a hand to steady herself. Claws pricked at her ankle.

Come inside and sit.

She stepped into the opening. The darkness leached the glow coming from the cavern and swallowed up the light. Despite the solid rock under her feet, a breeze blew over her. She froze.

Sit.

She forced herself to lower her body into a sitting position. The cold of the cavern floor seeped through her skirt as she crossed her legs.

Straighten your legs.

Alice did as the cat said. Her calf bumped over an edge, and her feet landed on a slick surface. Before her eyes could adjust to the darkness, Chess jumped onto her lap and crawled onto her and pushed her backwards. His paw shot out and hit something. The rock underneath her gave way, and she found herself hurtling down a rocky chute, an armful of cat clutched to her chest.

Chapter 13

A SCREAM RIPPED OUT of Alice as she and the cat careened into the endless blackness. They swirled in loops, and several times passed into even darker openings where she could feel, if not see, the rock press in on all sides. Twice they passed through larger caverns where the pink glow blurred not far above her face.

Alice's fingers gripped the cat's fur, and he was plastered flat against her chest, his claws tiny pricks of pain in her skin.

After several terrifying minutes of flying through the dark, their surroundings lightened. Before she could brace herself, she shot out of the side of the mountain and bounced off something round and rubbery. She flew up in the air and landed on another round rubbery thing before bouncing into a tangle of plants. The cat did an impressive mid-air flip before landing on his feet. Alice glared as she sat up, spitting leaves and flowers out of her mouth.

"You could have warned me," she said, heat rising in her chest.

It was better to show you.

"Better for who?" She scrambled to her feet, dusting herself off.

It wasn't until she straightened she realized the things she had bounced on were giant mushrooms, their caps a deep red with big white spots. There were three in a cluster, each of varying heights, but all of them taller than she was. She wondered if someone had planted them there or if it was a lucky coincidence.

She took a last look at the mountainside, and her gaze caught on a distant flickering light. When she peered closer, she noticed more lights.

She turned to ask Chess about them, but the cat was already trotting away. He stopped when he realized she wasn't following him.

Why are you standing there?

Alice pointed towards the mountainside. Chess let out a string of creative curses.

"What is it?" she asked, but a knot had already formed in her stomach.

Chess stared for a long moment and his tail lashed back and forth. *We have to hurry. I think those are the Queen's soldiers.*

Alice trotted to catch up with him. Chess looked back at the mountain, and Alice did the same. Was it her imagination, or were the lights coming this way?

She scrambled to keep up with Chess as he loped across a meadow of tall blossoms. A strange sound made her stop. It sounded almost like a... snore. She looked around but saw nothing besides her and Chess.

A sharp pain sliced across her ankle.

"Would you stop doing that?" She yanked her leg away from the cat who had come back and was sitting at her feet, glaring up at her.

Do you want an introduction to those soldiers? How many times do I have to tell you to hurry?

"But, don't you hear that? It sounds almost like, I don't know, someone snoring."

The cat rolled his blue eyes, which glowed in the night darkness.

The flowers are sleeping. It IS nighttime, after all.

Ignoring the cat's glare, Alice bent to examine a pink daisy nearby. It nodded on its stem, and at the center was a small face complete with cupid-bow lips and a tiny snub nose. Sure enough, the eyes were closed, and it appeared to be asleep. Perhaps sensing her presence, the little eyes cracked open. It gave a snort and then drifted back to sleep.

"They aren't... carnivorous or anything, are they?" She eyed the chest-high flowers warily.

Carnivorous? Flowers? What kind of place are you from?

Alice shrugged. "You never know."

Chess shook his head and then trotted away again, heading towards the line of trees in the distance. Alice hurried to catch up with him. She wondered why he needed a translator and wished she'd stayed at the cave. She only seemed to slow him down.

Even though the moon was almost full, once they stepped into the shelter of the woods, it got much darker. Alice tripped over a root and landed on her abused hands and knees. She got to her feet, but Chess hissed. She froze, and her voice dropped to a whisper.

"What is it?"

Someone's in these woods.

Alice scanned the trees and almost didn't see it, but then a sliver of light caught her eye. It was still quite a distance away, but it was moving in their general direction.

"More soldiers?"

She felt more than saw Chess shake his head. *There'd be more lights. I think that's the Commander.*

"Isn't one person better than a big group?"

This close, Alice could see the grim expression on Chess's whiskered face.

Not if he has Hesperus with him.

"Hesperus? Like... the goddess?"

Chess narrowed his eyes. No, like the griffon. With a nose like a snark.

"What's a snark?"

Trust me, you don't want to find out.

He stared at the moving light for a moment before he turned back to her. *Let's go. Try to keep low and move as quietly as you can. Even if the Commander doesn't have Hesperus, his Tracking Gift will lead him right to us.*

Alice wanted to ask what that was, but the cat was already trotting through the trees. She hurried after him, afraid she'd lose him in the shadows. The white tip of his tail was a tiny beacon against the darkness.

With the uneven footing of the forest floor, Alice struggled to keep up as she stumbled over roots and other obstacles hidden by the night. Having to crouch low didn't help the situation. Twice, she lost sight of

Chess's tail. He came back for her, but he let her know he wasn't happy about it.

And, always, the light followed in the distance.

Chess finally turned off the overgrown dirt path to a side trail. This one was even more overgrown and difficult to navigate in the dark.

A large root tripped her, and Alice landed hard on her hands. She looked up in time to see the white tail disappear around a bend in the trail.

"Chess!" She pushed to her feet, and her eyes strained at the spot where the cat had disappeared. Only darkness surrounded her, and the tree trunks pressed in on both sides. Something shaggy brushed against the back of her neck. She yelped and whirled around—but it was only a large leaf from a nearby tree.

"Chess!" she said, louder this time.

She looked behind her, and her breath clogged in her throat. The light appeared closer. She scanned the area, but only the shadowy shapes of trees stretched in all directions

A fist squeezed in her chest, and for a moment, she froze. With effort, she drew in a long breath.

All right then. Chess followed a trail. She was still on that trail. She just had to keep moving. Away from the light behind her.

She shuffled forward. Plants crowded on either side and caught at her skirts, but she put her hand on a tree trunk. Using more trunks as guideposts, she crept forward, one step at a time.

A meow sounded off to her left, and then Chess popped into the path in front of her, seeming to appear out of thin air.

Her whole body sagged. "I thought I lost you."

You were right behind me. Why did you stop?

She crossed her arms, her voice sharp. "I didn't stop. I tripped, and then you were just gone. It's not as if I know where I am or where we're going."

Shh, keep your voice down. His head swiveled as he searched the surrounding forest, then returned his attention to her. *I don't know what you're upset about. I came back, didn't I?*

Without waiting for her to reply, he spun back around and loped a few steps before he disappeared again. She stopped and stared at the place he'd just been. Where did he go?

A few seconds later, his head popped into view again. *What are you waiting for?*

"I... You..."

Chess hissed and then walked back to where she stood. He waved his tail at her. *Here, hold on.*

She grasped his silky tail and let him lead her through an opening hidden by a large tangle of vegetation. No wonder she hadn't seen where he went.

They followed a brief downward passage, crowded branches and leaves forming a tunnel. A faint light illuminated a curve in the path, and then they were in front of a round wooden door with a large iron door knocker in the shape of a butterfly. She reached for it, but Chess hissed at her. She froze, her hand hovering over the knocker.

Use the secret knock.

"Secret knock? What? Like a gentleman's club?"

Not all of Caterpillar's customers come through the front door, love. Only a trusted few use this door.

Alice hesitated. "But he doesn't know me. Won't he be suspicious if I show up here?"

It'll be fine. I'll tell you what to say. Now do what I do.

Chess put his paw on the door and tapped it twice, quickly. Alice did the same with the knocker. Then he paused and tapped once, paused, and then tapped twice again more slowly.

Alice copied him. Nothing happened for a long moment. In the silence, something rustled in the surrounding branches. A small square window of light appeared as someone slid back a wooden shutter. A man's face popped into view. His skin was a deep brown, and corkscrews of black hair sprang from his head. A pair of catlike topaz eyes regarded her, their gaze shrewd and assessing.

Alice tried a tentative smile, but the man continued to regard her without speaking. An awkward silence stretched out. She shifted and wiped her palms on her skirt.

When the man spoke, his voice lilted. "I have to wonder why a lovely lady such as yourself is at my door in the middle of the night."

Alice looked down at Chess. He grinned at her.

Tell him Chess Felinas has sent you and is calling in his marker.

Alice repeated Chess's words. The man's eyes opened wide before he threw back his head and laughed, the sound rich. The wooden shutter slid shut, and the door swung open.

Light spilled out and revealed a tall man. The black corkscrew curls fell nearly to his waist. He wore a rough tunic over a pair of soft pants. His feet were bare, and he had a long pipe clamped between his teeth. She wrinkled her nose. The smoke swirled in a sweet, cloying cloud.

His gaze took her in, from the top of her head down to her toes and back again. "Yes, I can believe Chess sent you."

Embarrassment washed over Alice as she realized what she must look like. Her hair tangled around her face. Her clothes hung in tatters. In fact, she was pretty sure she wasn't decent anymore. Her legs were bare, and she had leaves and dirt all over her person.

The man didn't seem to notice. He waved an arm at her and turned back inside.

Chess nudged her leg, and she followed Caterpillar into a cellar, past stacks of wooden crates and up a rickety wooden staircase that ended at the ceiling. Nerves fizzed in her stomach as the man reached up and brushed his fingers against the ceiling. He muttered a few words she couldn't understand. Immediately, a trapdoor became visible, light glowing around its edges. He pushed it open and climbed out before he reached down and offered her his hand.

She hesitated before she placed her palm in his. Without effort, he lifted her into another room.

His white teeth gleamed as he smiled, his eyes crinkling. "Welcome to Caterpillar's Apothecary."

Chapter 14

ALICE GLANCED AROUND. THE place consisted of one large room divided into a living space and his business.

On one side, a hammock hung from two iron loops in the wall. Nearby, a fireplace let out a pleasant minty warmth. On the other side of the fireplace sat a plump chair and a tiny footstool that resembled a mushroom. A small wooden table sat next to the chair, an open book propped there.

Her attention turned to the other side of the round room, where a long counter followed the curve of the wall. Behind it were shelves up to the ceiling filled with herbs, flowers, and things Alice couldn't identify. Above, dried bunches of plants hung from strung lines.

The man moved behind his counter and looked at Alice from across its scarred width. "What remedy can I supply you, dear lady?"

"Remedy?" A surge of panic almost choked her. How did he know? At her surprised expression, the man winked.

"Since we aren't acquainted—most unfortunate—I assume our dear friend Chess sent you for a remedy. One you might not be able to get elsewhere, eh?"

Alice's shoulder loosened as some of the tension leaked out. She glanced down at Chess, waiting for him to answer the man. When the silence stretched to awkwardness, she nudged the cat with her foot and tipped her hand towards Caterpillar.

He can't understand me. I told you I needed a translator.

Alice gave the man behind the counter a tight smile. "Well, I'm not quite sure—"

Don't mention dragons, and whatever you do, don't call me by name.

"But—"

Stop talking to me and ask him for medicine that draws out infection from ithicass vine.

Caterpillar watched her, amusement crinkling the corners of his eyes.

"You can tell old Caterpillar all about it. These are my... private hours for special customers."

She glanced at the jars and containers and rehearsed in her mind what Chess had instructed her to get. It took a minute to wrap her tongue around the unfamiliar words. The man waited, his grin friendly but his eyes sharp.

"Well, Mr. Caterpillar, what I need is something to draw out infection caused by ithicass vine."

Caterpillar's eyebrows drew down, and he took a few puffs on his pipe. "Ithicass poison, you say?"

She nodded. He puffed on his pipe several more times, blowing large smoke rings towards the ceiling, and gave her a long look. Then he turned to his shelves, running long fingers over them. He cleared jars and bottles off part of a shelf and reached towards the back. There was a click, and he pulled the back of the shelf open and revealed a small cabinet. His fingers danced over several bottles until he pulled out a round blue container. He twisted off the lid. Inside was a sage-green salve. A strong antiseptic smell made Alice's eyes water. He reached into a drawer and pulled out a tiny scoop and an empty container.

"How much do you need, Miss...?"

Alice ignored his obvious fishing for her name. She opened her mouth to tell him the amount, and then shut it. They'd probably need the entire container for a dragon, but wouldn't it raise his suspicions if she asked for that much of the goop?

Her gaze sought Chess's.

The cat let out a sigh.

Ask for a smithereen of a pobble.

He said it like only a simpleton wouldn't know this.

Alice tripped over the unfamiliar words as she made the request.

Caterpillar's eyebrows climbed towards his hairline. "That is one big infection." He turned to measure out the salve. "I don't suppose this has anything to do with the news about the soldiers cornering the Jabberwock near the Rabbit Hole, would it?"

Alice gave him a strained smile and lifted her shoulders in a shrug. "I'm sorry, but I don't even know what a Jabberwock is, Mr. Caterpillar."

Caterpillar glanced at her over his shoulder and winked. "I'm sure you don't, Miss." He finished and replaced the blue container in the cupboard and pushed the secret panel back into place. Then he took a clear container with her order in a sack and slid it across the counter.

"That'll be one rubicon."

Alice looked at him blankly.

"I'm sorry... I..." Alice nudged Chess with her foot.

What are you doing? Pay him so we can go.

"What do you mean, pay him?" Only habit kept Alice from shrieking. *A young lady always speaks in moderate tones.* She could almost hear Mother's voice in her head.

Chess blinked up at her.

You don't have any money? Why don't you have any money?

Alice threw her hands in the air. "Because you shoved me down a hole, and I didn't think to bring my coin purse."

Caterpillar puffed on his pipe, a half smile on his handsome face as he watched her yelling a one-sided conversation with the cat. Her face burned. He probably thought she was crazy.

"Is there a problem?" he asked.

"I, well, that is, I seem to have left my money at home." She smiled at him and spread her hands. Her mind scrambled to come up with a solution.

Just grab it and run.

"What? No," she said under her breath. She stared down at Chess. His ears had swiveled backwards. Her eyes darted to Caterpillar, who was still watching her.

Someone's coming, and I don't think it's another customer, love.

"Stop calling me that."

Caterpillar chuckled, and Alice's face flamed even hotter. She was going to kill this cat the first chance she got.

A firm knock on the door had all three of them whirling towards the sound.

"Open in the name of the Queen."

Alice's heart started pounding. She looked around for the trapdoor. In her panic, she couldn't remember its exact location.

Caterpillar quirked an eyebrow before he rounded the counter and headed towards the door.

Sorry, love, but we're out of time.

Before she could understand his meaning, Chess leapt up onto the counter, grabbed the sack in his mouth, and threw himself out the tiny window situated between the shelves.

The sound of voices approaching made Alice whirl around just in time to see Caterpillar gesture towards the man standing next to him. "This gentleman would like a word."

Alice's insides squeezed, making it hard to draw a deep breath.

A tall man in armor strode towards her. Piercing blue eyes gazed out of a stern face with a long aquiline nose.

Alice swallowed hard and took a step back, bumping into the counter behind her.

"I told you, she's just a regular customer." Caterpillar sauntered back behind the counter.

The blond man gave Caterpillar a measured glance. "At this time of night?"

The apothecary shrugged. "I am a registered Alchemist. I help people when they need it." His grin was a bit too wide. "Even if they come to me in the middle of the night, Commander."

The Commander's eyes swept over the shelves behind Caterpillar for several tense moments before he turned to Alice. He gave her a small bow. "You'll need to come with me, Miss." His tone was implacable.

Caterpillar looked between the two of them and took a long puff on his pipe. He blew a large ring of smoke towards the ceiling before he spoke.

"Before you go, I still need that rubicon, dear girl."

Chapter 15

CHESS PAUSED OUTSIDE. THE girl's voice floated through the window. Even from here, her distress was clear. It gave him a momentary pang of guilt, but he shoved it aside.

Zander needed this medicine right away. He couldn't get caught. Besides, if the Commander saw him, it would cause all kinds of complications. The man was all about honor, anyway. She'd be fine.

Probably.

The distinctive sound of a griffon's cry rent the air. A shiver slid down Chess's spine, and he darted under a nearby patch of ferns. He peered through the lacy leaves. The griffon was waiting in front of Caterpillar's mushroom-shaped house. She was lying down, her hawklike face on her giant taloned paws. She had tucked her massive, feathered wings close to her body, but her sharp yellow eyes scanned the area. Her gaze paused on the patch of vegetation where Chess hid. The griffon's feathered head came up. It lifted its nose and its blue tongue darted from between its beak, tasting the air.

Chess shrank deeper into the foliage, his eyes on the other animal's lashing tail with its barbed end. The last thing he needed was Hesperus scenting him out. He didn't want to think what she'd do if she found him.

He needed to leave, and he needed to do it now... yet something held him in place. He glanced at the window. From here, he could see the side of Alice's face. She looked scared, but she had squared her shoulders and lifted her chin. His chest tightened.

Chess shook himself. She'd be fine. The Queen would send her home. It meant he'd have to find someone else, but that was the least of his worries. The curse wouldn't matter if Zander died. The girl wasn't his problem anymore.

His conscience reared up and reminded him the only reason she was here was because of him. He took a determined step backwards, and a branch crackled under his back paw.

Hesperus jerked her head up and pushed to her feet, her eyes trained on the spot where Chess hid. Fear and loathing clawed their way up his throat. His father's griffon had been nasty to him when he was in human form. In this form, she'd eviscerate him, probably while he was still alive to watch. He shuddered.

The voices inside the apothecary got louder, and Hesperus turned her head back towards the door. Chess took a last glance at the window. Alice was following the Commander out of Caterpillar's shop. She'd be fine. In fact, she'd be glad to go home. He had nothing to feel guilty about.

He got a tighter grip on the sack. With a last backward glance, he melted back into the forest. As soon as he had put a patch of woods between himself and Hesperus, he ran. He only hoped he wouldn't be too late.

Chapter 16

THE COMMANDER REACHED INTO a small bag at his waist and drew out a coin. He handed it to Caterpillar. "I trust this settles the young lady's debt."

Caterpillar turned the coin over in his long fingers, the lamplight glinting off its shiny gold surface. He looked up at the other man and grinned. "My thanks, Commander! You've always been a generous man."

Alice cast a pleading look at the dark-skinned man, hoping that maybe he'd help her, but he just winked and made his way across the room to his chair. He sank down and picked up his book, puffing on his pipe. After a moment, he glanced up. "Would you be a love and shut the door on your way out?" Without waiting for an answer, he went back to his reading, as if the Queen's Commander wasn't standing in the middle of his house.

The Commander nodded, his expression impassive. She stared up at him, her mind whirring. Anger at Chess warred with the dread coiling in her gut. She forced herself to meet his gaze.

"What do you want with me?" Her voice trembled.

"I'm to take you to the palace, Miss, to meet the Queen."

"The... the Queen? What would the Queen want with me? I'm not even from here."

"Queen Lyssandra doesn't discuss her reasons with me." He gestured towards the door. "All I know is that I must take you to the palace."

Alice's eyes darted around, looking again for some way to escape. Her expression gave her away because he grasped her arm. "I'd prefer to take you to her as a guest, but you will go, willingly or not." His voice was firm.

The hand on her arm felt like iron, and she didn't bother trying to pull free. What was the use? There was nowhere to go. She lifted her chin and channeled Mother's cool tones. "All right, I'll come with you, but I want you to know I am doing so under duress. I did not come to this world willingly, and I would like to go home as soon as might be arranged."

The Commander's grip didn't loosen as he steered her towards the door. "Duly noted."

Alice allowed him to lead her out, nerves making her stomach queasy. What questions would the Queen have? Would she want to know about Zander? Alice bit her lip. All she wanted to do was go home, but it was obvious Zander and Chess were not on good terms with the Queen or her soldiers. She squared her shoulders. It wasn't her problem. She'd do what she had to in order to get home. It was Chess's fault she was here anyway, and he had abandoned her to her fate. He couldn't complain if she protected herself, now could he?

The Commander stopped her just outside the doorway of the apothecary. "You'll need to wait—"

But Alice didn't hear him. All she could see was the magnificent beast in front of her. It regarded her with large dark eyes. Up close Alice could see the orange-tipped feathers on the griffon's hawklike head. Its feathered wings, folded close to its body, had splashes of blue and purple in them.

She stepped forward, but the Commander stopped her. "You mustn't get close to Hesperus until I introduce you."

Alice shook off the Commander's restraining grip, her eyes glued to the griffon.

She bowed her head and then spoke. "Hello, Hesperus."

A sharp female voice scratched into her mind. *You aren't from here.*

"No, I'm not from here. In fact, I'd really like to go home."

The gold eyes widened. *You have the Creature Gift. Interesting.*

"If you mean I can talk to animals, that's only since I got here."

The creature tilted her regal head. *No, but even in the Mirror World, you would have felt inklings of understanding. Your Gift is strong.* The griffon prowled closer to her, and she heard the Commander's sharp intake of breath. Alice held still as the sharp beak touched the top of her head, and the creature took a large snuffling breath. After a moment, Hesperus stepped back and shook out her feathered wings.

I think you'll do.

Alice wanted to ask for what, but the Commander was right next to her. The creature lowered the front of her body. When Alice didn't move, the griffon shook her head and snorted.

Well, child, what are you waiting for, an engraved invitation?

Alice looked uncertainly back at the Commander. His expression remained stern, but the corners of his mouth had loosened.

"Hesperus rarely takes to strangers, and she's never invited anyone but me to ride her unless I command her." The Commander's deep voice rumbled in his chest, reminding her of Papa James and home. She blinked away tears.

"We should go, Miss. The Queen is expecting us, and we shouldn't keep her waiting."

Alice nodded, and the Commander guided her around the animal's side. A simple leather saddle sat right behind the griffon's wings. She bit her lip, but before she could voice her concerns, the Commander had lifted her onto the front of the saddle. As she awkwardly tried to arrange the tattered panels of her dress over her legs, he vaulted up behind her, reaching around her to grasp the reins. Alice bit back a cry as the creature leapt into the air, its wings outstretched. They soared into the air and headed towards the Red Palace.

The ride to the palace was over before Alice was ready. The griffon touched down in a courtyard without a bump. A giant fountain sprayed rainbow-speckled water into the sky, and a profusion of flowers were a riot of color waving madly around its base.

Alice reflected that this way of arriving was much preferable to her earlier crash landing. To be fair, the dragon *had* been injured. Worry flashed through her. She hoped Chess would get the medicine to the dragon in time to save him. He had looked close to death when they had left the cave. She felt a pang of guilt at the thought of leaving Zander to his fate.

Then Alice shook it off. There was nothing she could about it now. She pressed her lips together. Besides, the cat was the one that had abandoned *her*, not the other way around. He may have gotten rid of Hadley, but now that Chess had dragged her through too many near-death experiences, she considered them even.

While her thoughts had drifted, the Commander had already dismounted and was waiting next to his griffon. Alice paused, unsure how to get off without showing an unseemly amount of her skin. He seemed to understand her dilemma and reached up, plucked her off, and set her on her feet.

Remembering her manners, Alice smiled. "Thank you, Commander."

He nodded, his expression unwavering. "We will go to the Queen's reception room." He grasped her elbow and walked towards the long flight of white steps that led to the palace doors.

Alice was a little breathless by the time they reached the top of the stairs, partly from nerves. A line of soldiers stood at attention on either side of the carved wooden palace doors. When she and the Commander approached, the soldiers hit the end of their spears twice on the ground and then snapped a synchronized salute.

The Commander paused, his eyes traveling along the length of both lines. Not a hint of a smile touched his face. He nodded twice, once at each line. The soldiers closest to each door pulled them open, their bodies at attention the whole time.

The Commander swept into the palace, Alice close behind, and the doors shut behind them with an echoing thud. Just inside the entryway, Alice stopped, overwhelmed by the surrounding beauty. The white marble floors stretched out in all directions towards various hallways. At the back of the cavernous foyer an ornate staircase swept upward, its curved railings intricately carved and glistening with gold, the steps also white marble.

The Commander gave her a moment to gawk before he squeezed her arm to get her moving again. Alice reluctantly walked on, her eyes taking in golden vases as tall as a man, bursting with flowers in a variety of pinks and reds.

The Commander led her to a hallway. A padded red runner ran down the middle, muffling their footsteps. Beautiful paintings in ornate golden frames lined the walls on either side. Interspersed were pedestals with pots of deep, blood-red flowers overflowing. Velvet wallpaper covered the walls in repeated golden swirls from floor to ceiling. She tipped her head up. Every few feet hung small golden light fixtures resembling ornate bird cages with tiny lights that flickered and spun inside. She peered at them only to realize that they weren't lights at all but small flying creatures. They buzzed in circles in the gilded cages. One kept hitting the bars over and over. A dark shiver ran up her spine, and she rubbed a hand over her bare arm and found her skin pebbled in goosebumps.

"Don't let her know you have the Gift." Alice looked up at the Commander, startled. He was looking straight ahead, and for a minute, she wasn't sure she'd understood him.

She stopped moving until he turned towards her. His expression was tight. "Treat her with deference, answer her questions as simply as you can, and whatever you do, don't tell her about your Creature Gift, not if you want to go home." His glance darted to the closest cage, and a grimace ghosted across his face before his expression smoothed out again.

Alice nodded, but her mind felt muddy with weariness. All she wanted to do was go home. She ran a hand through her hair, mortified when a rain of dirt and leaves fell on the plush red runner. She brushed at her torn dress and tugged uselessly at the ripped neckline, trying to at least straighten it into some semblance of the way it should look. Panic bubbled in her chest. How could she face a monarch, a woman who had the power to send her home, looking like this?

"I'm not at all ready to be presented to the Queen," she said, and her voice wobbled. She pushed at her hair again. "Surely, I can take a moment to freshen up."

The Commander's expression softened. "I'm sorry, Miss. She requested I bring you right in. I'm afraid it isn't wise to make her wait."

His voice was low and not unkind. She pressed her lips together to stop their trembling. "Yes, of course."

More soldiers stood outside another set of doors. Their glass fronts were decorated in colorful swirls of flowers and vines. The soldiers again saluted the Commander and opened the doors by their golden handles.

Alice had expected more marble and gold, perhaps an elaborate throne. Instead, the doors opened into a lush garden. Birds flitted in and out of the plants, and the air was warm and steamy. A stone-flagged path twisted around potted fruit trees and tangles of plants of all shapes and sizes. The Commander walked without hesitation, turning confidently whenever the path split. Water gurgled nearby, and Alice heard the tinkle of feminine laughter. Her face flushed at the idea of meeting not just the Queen, but her ladies-in-waiting, too, looking like she'd rolled about in the mud. She smoothed a hand over her hair.

They rounded a grouping of lemon trees, and the room opened up to a small clearing. Rising towards the ceiling, a rock formation stood, swathed in mist. Down its sides a waterfall burbled, falling into a small pool. A group of young girls stood in a cluster around someone seated on a large mound of moss.

Dressed in simple white gowns, the girls chattered and giggled. Shimmery material covered their backs. Alice couldn't help but stare at them. Each one had long, flowing hair in a variety of vibrant pastel shades—but that wasn't the strangest part. Their hair seemed to have a mind of its own, curling and waving around their heads. As she got closer, she realized the shimmering material wasn't fabric at all, but wings. The girls turned at their approach, giggling. Several let their wings flutter open. The top halves of the wings ended in elegant points, but the bottoms of the wings looked strange, as though someone had taken giant scissors and sheared them off. The girls' skin tones ranged from the milky white of an opal to the brown of an oak leaf. Each one had enormous eyes the same shade as their hair, but the most disconcerting part were their pupils, which were vertical slits. Although they were beautiful and seemed harmless, Alice shuddered as all those alien eyes looked in her direction.

She turned to the Commander, who released her arm and dropped to one knee, placing his fist over his heart. "Your Majesty."

Chapter 17

CHESS STEPPED INTO THE back of the cave, his eyes adjusting to the light coming from the front entrance. The sun was just coming up, casting a warm, orangey glow. He dropped the sack and stretched his jaws. He missed having hands.

It was then that he noticed the silence. A cold ball of ice formed in his stomach, and he rushed over to the Jabberwock. The horrible hissing sound had stopped, but that didn't reassure Chess. Quite the opposite.

The large body was still and unmoving.

Zander!

The Jabberwock didn't stir.

Chess moved around to the large snout and leaned in close. For an endless moment, he felt nothing. His heart hitched in his chest. He couldn't be too late.

Then the faintest wisp of steam curled from a nostril. Chess dropped onto his haunches and closed his eyes. But only for the briefest of moments.

He didn't have time for the emotions that bubbled just under the surface.

Instead, he fished out the container from the sack and grumbled as he tried to twist off the top. Blast his lack of opposable thumbs. After much fumbling, he got it open. He stared at the strong-smelling goop, his eyes watering. Then he looked at Zander.

With a deep sigh, he stuck a paw in, scooped up some ointment, and smeared it on the closest gash. Again and again, he came back to the container until he had dug out every dab. When he was done, Zander glistened like an overly large basted turkey. Chess only hoped it was enough.

Out of habit, he raised his paw to his mouth. The antiseptic odor slapped him in the face, and he wrinkled his nose.

He padded out to the pool and stuck his paw into the cool water, swishing it back and forth until it no longer felt greasy. He shook it, sending water droplets flying.

Back in the cave, he walked over to the bed of ferns Alice had made. He turned in a circle several times before settling himself on the soft greenery, and the faint aroma of lavender and vanilla filled his nostrils.

There was nothing to do but wait now. Either Zander would get better or... Chess wouldn't think about the alternative.

His eyes grew heavy as he watched the patch of sun at the front of the cave inch along until sleep pulled him under.

Chess jerked awake and ducked just as the tip of a spiny tail hit the wall behind him. The Jabberwock was no longer still. His legs thrashed, and a low moan came from his throat.

Chess stood and slid along the perimeter of the cave until he was no longer in danger of being bashed in the head. He circled in closer to get a better look at his friend, his eyes watchful for any sign of fire behind the bared teeth. Fever glazed Zander's eyes. They looked at Chess without recognition. Without warning, the enormous jaws snapped in Chess's direction. He danced back and darted into the shelter of one of the cave's back tunnels.

He watched helplessly as his friend's body fought to rid itself of the poison. Dark liquid bubbled from the many wounds and dripped down his scales, landing with a hiss on the cave floor, leaving scarred indents as they evaporated in a puff of steam. Chess wished there was something more he could do, but even getting close risked bodily injury or poison by proxy.

His gaze landed on the helmet. A smile tugged at his mouth as he remembered Alice and her worry about picking it up for fear a head would be inside. He had an inexplicable longing to see her again. She'd help Zander, not just watch his struggles. He stared down at his black paws and the smile faded. He was useless to his friend in this form.

Zander wasn't just his cousin and built-in best friend—he was like a brother. It hurt Chess that there was nothing else he could do to help when Zander needed it the most. His friend had been there for him in his darkest moment.

Fourteen-year-old Chess pelted into the house. The door banged shut behind him. It surprised him that Zelda, their only servant, didn't chide him about it. Mother, being one of the flower fae, liked few people around, so the older woman was cook and maid and nanny all rolled into one.

For a moment, he wondered where everyone was, and then shrugged. His mother was most likely wandering around outside. She didn't just love the outdoors; she needed it like air. Over the years, his father had expanded the gardens and the wooded areas to accommodate her needs.

His foot was on the first step when Zelda appeared in the entryway, wiping her hands on an apron. He reversed direction and darted over to her.

"I don't suppose you made any of those strawberry tarts I like so much, did you?" He grinned and dropped an affectionate kiss on her cheek.

Instead of teasing him or calling him a scallywag, as she usually did, her expression remained somber, her eyes red-rimmed.

"Yer father wants to see ya in the library."

Chess's eyebrows rose. "What's *he* doing home?" With his duties as the head of the Red King's armies, Chess couldn't remember the last time his father had been at home in the middle of the day. Unease settled in his stomach, but he pushed it away. His tutor had probably complained that Chess had disappeared during his lessons—quite literally. He grinned at the memory of old Saxton calling his name and searching for him, with no luck. Until recently, the only thing he'd seemed to inherit from his mother was her smooth, dark-brown skin. That had changed right around the time his voice had started to, a few months ago. He'd yet to tell anyone about it.

Zelda sniffled, snapping him back to the present. Her voice wobbled when she spoke. "He's... he's got something to tell ya." She cleared her throat. "And don't ask me what. That's all I can say, but you'd best hurry along."

The unease in his stomach curled into a hard ball, and he swallowed, regretting the meat pie he'd snitched from the palace kitchens.

Chess turned down the hallway, his feet dragging with each step. The sun slanted through mullioned windows on either side of the front door and cast diamond-shaped patterns across the floorboards. For once, he hoped that he was in trouble for something.

Outside the door, he stopped and stared at the knob. His arm didn't seem to belong to him as it rose and reached for it. The round surface was cool under his fingertips. He let his hand rest there for a long moment. He didn't know how long he would have stood there if he hadn't heard the squeak of a floorboard that announced Zelda's presence.

When he went in, his father was standing by the window, his back to the room. "Come in and shut the door, Chess."

Chess did as his father commanded. Everyone did. Except Mother. Where was she, anyway? She lost track of time when she was outside, but his father was home. It was unusual for Mother not to be here when he was.

His father turned and came around to stand behind his desk, his fingertips braced against the surface. Chess watched as his father straightened the already neat pens and lined up the letter knife that sat at a perfect right angle to the blotter. Chess began drumming his fingers against his thigh and made himself stop. After a long drawn out minute, he shifted his weight onto one leg and crossed his arms.

His father's face was smooth, with no hint of why he had called Chess here, but Chess noticed his father's golden hair looked like he'd raked his hands through it several times. Instead of his uniform, he wore trousers and a loose linen shirt. When was the last time he'd seen his father out of uniform?

The silence stretched between them like a dare. Chess broke it. "Zander's waiting for me. We're supposed to head out soon so we can make camp before it's dark."

His father's gaze flicked up to meet Chess's. The blue eyes, just like Chess's own, pierced into him, and Chess steeled himself to hold the gaze.

"Your mother's left."

The words dropped like rocks in Chess's chest.

Before he could ask, his father answered the question burning inside him. "She went back to her people."

"But... we're her people," Chess blurted.

His father shook his head. "No, Son, we've never been her people, not really."

"But... but we need her, I need her. She can't just leave. Mothers don't just leave."

His father's piercing gaze met his. "You're not a child any longer, Chess. You're a young man."

Chess shook his head, his mop of black curls flopping. "I... I don't understand."

The sigh that came from his father sounded weary. "I know you don't, Son. The truth is, she's never been happy here, away from the Faelands. You know she can't go to the palace anymore since she refuses to get her wings clipped."

Something hot and dark rose in Chess's throat. He clenched his fists. "I don't believe you. You made her leave. You're the one who wouldn't let her go to the palace because of your precious rules. Nobody would have cared. You're the King's brother. She wouldn't leave me without saying goodbye." His voice cracked on the last word.

A spasm of emotion rippled over his father's face before his expression smoothed out again. "It was too painful for her. She stayed longer than most of her kind would have. Perhaps if you'd manifested her fae powers..." His father's voice trailed off and his jaw clenched, his eyes shiny. He swallowed several times before he spoke again. "You should be grateful she stayed as long as she did."

Chess backed away until his back hit the door. His hand fumbled for the knob. He saw his father reach towards him, concern wrinkling his brow. He heard his name and a strange keening sound. Shoving the door open, he whirled and ran—past a startled Zelda, out the front door, and down the steps. The words rang in his ears as he ran. *Your mother's left. Not her people. Fae powers.* The last words pounded in his brain with each footstep. Finally, his lungs about to burst, he stopped deep in the woods, bent over at the waist, hands on his knees, dragging in great gulps of air, sure that his heart had cracked in two.

That's where Zander had found him. Instead of saying something stupid like it would all be okay, Zander settled down next to him and handed Chess his handkerchief. He sat with Chess while ugly sobs threatened to tear him in half. He stayed throughout that long night of grief and pain and bewilderment. He was a steadying presence while Chess's childhood shriveled and died on the forest floor, and the polished, carefree adult rose in his place.

When the sun had come up, Chess's tears were spent. Zander handed him the bag Chess would have packed himself, enough to camp out in the wilderness for the next three days.

He'd looked Chess right in the eye when he asked, "Do you want to go after her?"

For one wild moment, Chess considered the idea, but only for a moment. Then he shook his head no. Zander had clapped him on the shoulder and nodded.

For the next three days his friend had kept him so distracted with hunting and shooting and climbing that by the time night fell each evening, Chess was so tired, he'd collapse into his makeshift bed. By the time they headed home, Chess was able to pack away the unbearable pain and function again.

Zander never brought up those three nights, not even when his own mother died some years later. Chess had sat with his friend while Zander grieved, but it was a different kind of grief because, unlike Chess's mother, Zander's mother hadn't wanted to leave.

When he returned home, his father didn't ask where he'd been and never mentioned Mother again. Not even when it became clear that Chess *had* inherited her Fae powers, including the ability to change forms. It was like she hadn't existed and it had only ever been just the two of them.

Chess.

The voice, ragged and weak, brought him back to the present, to the cave. Zander was looking at him, his gaze lucid again.

Chess felt his throat tighten, and he had to pause a moment before he spoke. He forced a grin onto his face and sauntered over to his friend.

Welcome back to the land of the living.

Zander groaned. *I'm not sure if that's good or bad.*

Chess chuckled. *Trust me, it's definitely good.*

Zander's eyes drooped. *How long was I out?*

Chess grimaced. *Just over a day.* He cleared his throat. *I wasn't... that is, I'm glad you're awake.*

Zander's reptilian face softened into his version of a smile. *Me too. I think.*

He lifted his head with effort and looked around the cave. His horned eyebrows furrowed as his gaze returned to Chess.

Where's Alice?

Chapter 18

ALICE STARED WHEN THE group of giggling girls separated to reveal a young woman who looked only a few years older than Alice herself. This tiny doll of a woman was the Red Queen?

The woman bounced up from the moss cushion, gathering her skirts, her deep-red nails looking like dried blood against the whiteness of the fabric. Her long white-blonde braid swung off her shoulder as she rushed across the space to stand in front of Alice and the Commander.

She put a delicate hand on the man's shoulder and gave him a warm smile when he raised his head. "Commander Felinas, do get up and tell me all about this darling creature you've brought me."

She turned her large chocolate-brown eyes up to Alice. They sparkled with curiosity and friendliness.

Alice hastily dropped into an awkward curtsey. Her heart thumped faster, and she chided herself. She should have curtsied immediately. What would the Queen say? She braced herself for the Queen's anger.

Instead, the woman let out a surprisingly throaty laugh. "Come, come, my dear, none of that now." She grabbed both of Alice's hands in her tiny ones and held Alice's arms out from her sides.

Her dark eyes traveled from Alice's rat's nest of hair down to her ruined shoes. She frowned, and Alice wanted to shrink into the lush grass at her feet.

Seeming to read her mind, the tiny Queen squeezed both of Alice's hands with surprising strength. "I can see just what you're thinking, and I want you to push that worry right out of your head. We'll get you all cleaned up in no time, and your beauty will shine just like all the lovely things in my garden."

"Thank you, Your Majesty. Please, do not trouble yourself on my behalf."

"Nonsense, it's no trouble at all." She pulled Alice to the moss cushion and patted the spot next to her. "You must tell me all about yourself."

Alice lowered herself to perch next to the Queen. Her eyes flicked to the Commander who was standing at attention. His blue eyes stared somewhere over their heads. There was something familiar about his features, but she couldn't put her finger on it.

The Queen grasped Alice's hands again, interrupting her thoughts. Alice fought the urge to yank them away from the tight grip. A small voice in the back of her mind wondered why this woman was acting like Alice was her long-lost friend. Shouldn't the Queen at least be asking a few uncomfortable questions? Alice bit her lip, unsure where to start.

The Queen must have had the same thought because she turned her body towards Alice and leaned in. A delicate crystal pendant swung forward on a rose-gold chain. Inside, a ribbon of red swirled like a drop of blood in water. The Queen noticed her gaze. She clasped the necklace in her hand and smiled. "Do you like it?"

"It's quite lovely, and unusual."

"It's not as spectacular as some of my jewels, but it has sentimental value. I always keep it close at hand." Her gaze sharpened. "Now, why don't you tell me your name, darling?"

A flutter of nerves danced in Alice's stomach, but she pulled her manners around herself. She gave the Queen her best dimpled smile. This woman could send her home, after all. She remembered what the Commander had told her. If the Queen wanted to treat her as a friend, Alice would go along with it. She'd answer just enough of the woman's questions to keep her happy.

"My name is Alice Cavendish, Your Majesty, and I must thank you for your warm welcome."

"Oh, you darling thing! Of course, you're welcome here. Now, how did you get here? Pardon me for saying so, but your appearance would suggest your trip to our Kingdom has been a bit... difficult." One dark-blonde eyebrow rose.

"It wasn't much of an adventure," Alice said. "I was pu—er, I fell down a hole in my world and landed here." Alice let out a light laugh and shrugged. "I'm not at all sure how it happened."

The Queen's gaze sharpened, and her smile dimmed. She tilted her head and studied Alice. "How very odd. You must have come through the Rabbit Hole." After an uncomfortable moment, she shrugged. "Ah well, it's unusual, but not completely unheard of. We've had a few lost souls who have found their way here by accident."

"It was a shock, I can assure you, Your Majesty."

The Queen patted Alice's hand, her attention turning to the Commander. He still stood at attention, his face devoid of emotion, but he was watching Alice from the corner of his eye.

The Queen waved her hand in his direction. "You may go, Commander Felinas. This girl talk must bore you to tears." She leaned forward and tapped his arm. "And goodness knows, Alice here is no threat, are you, dear?" Her voice was light, but Alice felt the weight of the other woman's stare. She resisted the urge to shrink away and forced another laugh.

"Of course, not. I only wish to go home, Your Majesty."

The Queen turned back to the Commander. "See, Commander Felinas? Alice is an absolute darling, and we are getting along famously. Why don't you run along and do... whatever it is you do."

While the Queen's tone was light, there was something prickly about her words. The Commander bowed low again.

"As you wish, Your Majesty." With a last glance at Alice, turned on his heel and left.

Alice wanted to call him back—but that was silly. She barely knew him. He was obviously loyal to the Queen, but she felt adrift without his steadying presence.

The Queen tapped one long finger against Alice's cheek. "You've left us, Alice. The Commander *is* quite handsome, but he's far too old for you, my dear."

Alice felt her cheeks heat. "I didn't—that is, I'm not—"

The Queen threw back her head and let out another laugh. "You are too adorable with your blushes. I was only teasing you." She glanced over her shoulder at the path where the Commander had disappeared. "Just between us girls, we can admit when we see a deliciously handsome man, no matter what his age." She gave Alice a playful wink.

"Now, you were saying you fell down a hole, and you landed in the Kingdom of Wonderland? That *is* a fantastical tale, my dear." She chuckled. "I can hardly countenance it. You must be from the Mirror World?" She tilted her head.

Alice frowned. "The Mirror World? I'm not sure what you mean by that, Your Majesty. I live in Somerset, England."

The Queen clucked her tongue. "Aren't you quaint? No, darling, the Mirror World lies on the other side of this one."

Alice wrinkled her forehead.

"I can see you still don't understand, but that's all right. Most of the humans in the Mirror World have no idea about our Kingdom, but we grow up knowing about your world."

Alice nodded, wondering how she could bring the conversation around to going home again. Before she could broach the subject, the Queen leaned forward again.

"Now, tell me—how in the world did you fall down the Rabbit Hole? Wherever did you land?"

Alice scowled, just thinking of Chess knocking her into that hole. He had caused all this mess. The Queen noticed her expression and her own turned to one of delight.

"I can see you have a tale to tell." She looked at the colorful young women fluttering around her. "Come closer, girls. Alice is going to tell us a story."

The girls drew in, their eyes now all trained on Alice. Alice swallowed. "Well, it's rather silly. I was—well, it's a long, boring story." She waved a hand. "I'm sure you don't want to hear it."

The Queen's smile took on a razor edge. "Oh, but we do, dear. *Do* go on."

Alice glanced around and saw that several of the girls had stopped giggling and turned serious. Another one with pale-yellow hair caught Alice's gaze and gave a tiny shake of her head.

"Well, if you truly want to hear it..."

The Queen raised both eyebrows, and several of the girls nodded and clapped their hands.

"Yes, well, there was a young man." Alice glanced down at her hands, gathering her words. She needed to make this a good story. "He was handsome and wealthy. He offered me a proposal of marriage." She paused and the girls bent closer. "But, I told him no."

The Queen frowned. "Is he not suitable?"

"Oh, no, everyone thinks he is a marvelous catch."

The girls all held their breath. The Queen leaned in, her voice dropping to almost a whisper. "Then why in the world don't you return his affections, my dear?"

Alice wrinkled her nose. "Well, *he* rather knows he's a marvelous catch, if you know what I mean. His favorite topic is himself."

The girls giggled behind their hands.

The Queen frowned. "Don't your parents insist you accept him?"

"You want the truth?"

All the girls nodded, smiles hovering on their faces. The Queen's smile had faded away. "Yes, I think I do, Alice."

Alice took a breath. "The truth is, Papa James rather thinks he's a twit. It wouldn't bother him at all if I don't marry Hadley." Alice's voice caught on her father's name, and Hadley's threat loomed in her mind. It all seemed so far away here in this fantastical place. Alice brought her attention back to the present. She couldn't afford to lose focus when her goal was so close.

She continued to spin her tale. "Mother's another story, of course. She would be very pleased if I accepted Hadley's offer, but she'll follow Papa's lead, and he wants me to be happy." Alice's throat tightened at the thought of her family so far out of reach.

"No wonder you're so eager to go home, darling." Something in the Queen's tone made Alice look up. For a moment, pain seemed to shadow the other woman's eyes, but it was gone so fast, Alice wondered if she had imagined it.

"You must have had quite an adventure since you landed here. The Commander said you were at Caterpillar's little shop when he found you. You never said how you ended up at the Rabbit Hole to begin with."

Alice gave a light laugh, but her instincts told her not to mention either Chess or the dragon. "Oh, that. I wanted to get away from Hadley, and he was quite... persistent. I wasn't watching where I was going, and the next thing I knew, I was falling down a hole and landing here."

"All by yourself?" The Queen tapped a finger to her chin. "How very curious that you ended up at Caterpillar's little shop in the middle of the night."

Cold prickled along Alice's skin, but she smiled. "I suppose I was lucky. When I landed in a strange forest, I wandered around until I stumbled upon Mr. Caterpillar's place of business. As kind as everyone has been, I have to admit, I am more than ready to go home."

The Queen tapped her playfully on the arm. "Everyone? Come, tell us more. Don't be afraid." She gestured around her. "I'm aware that to someone from the Mirror World, some of our denizens might seem strange or even frightening."

Alice nodded. "Well, the Commander's... I think he called it a griffon? She was terrifying at first, but once we, erm, were introduced, she was quite friendly."

The Queen lifted a blonde eyebrow. "I don't think I've ever heard anyone call Hesperus *friendly*. In fact, she doesn't let anyone but the Commander near."

Alice's mind scrambled. "Oh, well, maybe *friendly* isn't the right word. She was quite magnificent though, and she seemed devoted to the Commander."

"I see." The Queen looked at Alice for an uncomfortable moment. Then a smile bloomed across her face again. She stood, dragging Alice up with her, and clapped her hands. All the flower maidens turned their rapt attention to the Queen.

"I'm going to get Alice settled and"—her gaze swept over the group before her eyes settled on the maiden with butter-yellow hair—"Buttercup is going to serve as your lady's maid."

The girl gazed at Alice with a shy smile before she lowered her pale-yellow eyes. "I will be happy to serve you, my lady." Her voice was soft and musical with an odd, lilting accent.

Alice smiled at her warmly and tried to ignore how the other girl's curls floated around her head. "Thank you for your willingness to help me."

"Come along, then." The Queen reached up and looped her arm in Alice's and led her along one of the stone paths. It twisted away from the clearing, into the tangle of the garden.

Chapter 19

IT TOOK ONLY A moment before Alice was standing before a rock-covered wall. Plants and flowers twined over its surface, but a door was outlined in the wall. Alice wondered how the Queen planned on opening it, though, since there was no handle visible.

The Queen reached for the smooth surface and, with deft movements, touched several places near the edge, and it swung open.

They stepped into a flagstone corridor. The walls were also stone, but a series of intricate tapestries hung on them, interspersed with portraits. The Queen strode towards the staircase at the end of the hallway, but Alice's steps lagged as she stared up at the portraits.

She came to a stop in front of a picture of a young man. His bronze-colored hair hung to his shoulders in thick waves. He was standing straight as an arrow, his hands clasped on the top of an ornate sword. Striking rather than handsome, he had a hawkish nose and a firm mouth.

Serious green eyes stared out of the picture as if the world was a puzzle he was trying to solve.

The Queen paused with Alice and looked up at the portrait. A gentle exhalation escaped her red, cupid-bow mouth. "This is—was—my stepson."

Alice looked at her in surprise. The young man in the picture appeared to be about the same age as the Queen.

"Oh, I see your surprise." She pointed at another portrait. The man in it was clearly the younger man's father. They shared the same bronze-colored hair, moss-green eyes, and hawklike noses. "That was my husband."

She pulled a lacy handkerchief from her pocket and dabbed at her eyes. "I lost them both within a short time of each other. It's the tragedy of my life." She twisted the handkerchief in her hands.

"What happened?" The words were out of Alice's mouth before she could stop them. She grimaced. "Please excuse me. Of course, you don't have to share anything if you don't want to."

The Queen gave a sad smile. "No, it's all right, my dear. My husband died of a strange ailment. I sent for the best healers in the Kingdom of Wonderland. None of them could save him." She shook her head and stared up at the older man's face. "Oh, I realize he was much older than I was, but he honored me when he asked me to be his wife." A wistful tone crept into her voice. "He was so kind to me." She lifted a finger and ran it along the bottom of the frame. "And so handsome."

With visible effort, she pulled herself away from memories of her husband and turned her gaze to her stepson. "And his son was made of the same cloth—handsome, kind, responsible." She sighed again. "He would have made a great king after his father, and Zane was so proud of him."

"Did the same ailment kill his son, too?" Alice shuddered as she remembered the horrible influenza that had swept through England a few years before. It hadn't discriminated, taking old and young alike.

"Oh, no, it wasn't an illness that took the prince." She pressed her lips together and her brows drew down. When she spoke again, her tone was hard and had lost all of its warmth. "It was the Jabberwock." Her hands clenched, and Alice saw tears in the other woman's eyes. "He was leaving on a trip to another part of the Kingdom. Things were so hectic at the time, we weren't able to say a proper goodbye so I flew out on my griffon before he could get too far. He was so kind after his father died, always checking on me, and we had grown close."

She dabbed at her eyes again. "We had no warning. It swooped down, like a flying devil, and attacked us. The prince was a fair warrior, but he was no match for the great beast. It blasted us with fire, but the prince protected us with his shield. He made me run into the shelter of a nearby stand of trees. He fought so bravely, but in the end..." She pushed her fingers against her mouth and drew in a shaky breath... "In the end, the creature was too much for him. The last I saw, the horrible thing had my stepson clasped in his claws and was carrying him away, his wings looking like copper fire."

A rock formed in the pit of Alice's stomach. She may not have known what a Jabberwock was, but she had a horrible sinking feeling it was a lot like a dragon.

"I'm afraid I've never heard of a Jabberwock," she said as they moved away from the portrait and continued down the hall. She had the creepy feeling that the doomed prince watched her go.

They reached the bottom of the stone steps, and the Queen turned to her. "I suppose in the Mirror World, you'd call a Jabberwock a dragon."

Alice faltered and almost missed the step, and the rock in her stomach grew to a small boulder. "A... a dragon?" She gave a weak laugh. "I thought those were only in stories."

The Queen reached out to steady her. "Oh no, darling, they are very real." She tilted her head. "Although, in the Mirror World, there aren't very many left, and certainly, there aren't any in your England. They may still lurk in remote mountain caves or forests." She gave a tinkling laugh. "One could hardly blame you for not knowing what kind of nature they have."

The Queen continued up the steps, but Alice stood paralyzed, the rock in her stomach weighing her down. The Queen must know. She knew Alice had helped this Jabberwock, this creature that killed the prince.

"What happened to the prince?" she asked, her voice uneven. "Did you ever find him or...?" Alice trailed off, not sure how to ask if they'd found a body or not.

The Queen glanced back over her shoulder and her eyes gleamed in the dim light of the stairwell. "Nobody knows. He's disappeared, but it's the general belief he's dead, and that the reason nobody has found him is that the Jabberwock"—she gave a delicate shudder"—feasted on his remains."

They were halfway up the winding staircase, Butter-cup still trailing some distance behind them, when the Queen stopped on the step above her and turned to Alice. The Queen gripped her arm. Her long crimson nails made Alice wince.

"The Jabberwock is an enemy of this Kingdom, and anyone helping him would also be viewed as an enemy both to the Kingdom and to me personally."

Alice swallowed hard. "I... that is to say..."

The Queen pushed one finger against Alice's lips. "Shh, my dear. One cannot be blamed for what they do not understand." Her teeth flashed and, for a moment, it seemed they were too long and sharp. "But that changes once we have the knowledge. Then, we are accountable. Don't you agree?"

Numbly, Alice nodded. "I... I just want to go home," she said, her voice a whisper.

The Queen straightened, her tone warm again. "Of course you do, darling, and I'm going to see that you get your chance."

Alice exhaled and followed the Queen up the last few steps to a large wooden door. The Queen pushed it open into another long hallway, this one almost as lavish as the one Alice had entered with the Commander.

The Queen flitted ahead of her, pausing at several doorways before stopping at one about midway down the hall.

Alice stopped beside her and clasped her hands in front of her to stop their trembling. The Queen grasped the curved crystal handle and turned to Alice.

"Here's your room, dear," she said. "Please, make yourself at home and rest. I want you to be ready for the afternoon festivities."

"Festivities? But I thought—"

The Queen gave a tinkling laugh. "Oh, my dear, I can't let you leave Wonderland without experiencing one of our afternoon tea parties."

"But—"

The Queen wagged a finger. "I realize you want to go home, but I would be terribly hurt if you didn't come to my party." The other woman pouted , but her eyes twinkled.

There didn't seem to be much choice. Besides, how could a few more hours hurt? Alice smiled. "Then of course I accept, but..." Alice looked down at her ruin of a dress.

The Queen waved her hand. "Don't worry about that. I'll make sure you have something appropriate to wear, but first—" She pushed open the door, and Alice gasped as a swirl of butterflies filled the doorway. "First, you must get cleaned up and rest." She gave Alice a gentle push into the lush room. "And remember, don't be late." With a whirl of skirts, the Queen disappeared down the hallway.

Chapter 20

ALICE BLINKED OPEN HER eyes, unsure where she was at first. A tiny, jewel-encrusted butterfly fanned its purple wings on her pillow. She turned her head to get a better look, and it fluttered away. Through the filmy curtains around the bed, she could see a blurred view of other butterflies, their wings sparkling in the sunlight peeking through the window.

A soft voice made her start. "Miss Alice, I must help you get ready now."

Buttercup pulled back the draperies that enclosed the four-poster bed, securing them to the sides.

Alice sat up and brushed the hair out of her eyes. She hadn't meant to fall asleep, only to rest her eyes for a moment. "How long did I sleep, Buttercup?"

The girl's lips curved into a gentle smile. "Most of the afternoon. You looked so peaceful. I didn't want to wake you, but Her Majesty will expect you for the afternoon lawn party soon."

Buttercup pushed a cup of something into her hands. Alice took a tentative sip, and it fizzed in her mouth. She looked into the cup. The blush liquid bubbled in creamy froth.

"What is this?" she asked.

"It's passionberry water. It clears the mind and helps you to wake up." Buttercup pushed the cup back towards Alice's mouth.

Alice downed the drink in several long swallows. She swung her legs out of bed and put her bare feet on the floor. Buttercup held out a soft robe and Alice shrugged into it. She padded into the washroom connected to her bedroom and glanced at the large soaking tub set into a marble dais in the middle of the room. As much as she had wanted a bath, putting herself into such a vulnerable position in this strange place made her uneasy. In the end, though, getting rid of a day's worth of dirt was too much of a temptation. A chair wedged under the door handle eased her mind enough to take the chance.

After Alice had washed her face in the basin and cleaned her teeth, she returned to the bedroom. Buttercup pulled out a stool in front of a gilt dressing table.

"Come, I will fix your hair," she said.

Alice sat on the rounded cushion. When she looked down, delight rippled through her. There, on the glittering surface of the dressing table, lay her hair comb, and next to it, her pearl necklace. Someone had repaired the clasp.

Buttercup was running her fingers through Alice's black curls. Alice touched both the items before she twisted around. "I forgot all about the hair comb. I'm so glad I didn't lose it."

"They fell out of your pocket. I thought you would want them."

Alice nodded and held up the necklace. "Did you fix this?"

The girl smiled and ducked her head. "I hope I did the right thing."

Alice resisted the urge to throw her arms around Buttercup. Instead, she clasped the other girl's hand. "Thank you! This necklace means the world to me. I can't tell you how much I appreciate you fixing it for me."

Buttercup's brown cheeks flushed at the praise. "You are welcome. It was a simple thing." She watched Alice for a moment before she put her hands over Alice's. "Here, let me help you."

Alice felt her chest loosen once the necklace was around her neck again. She reached up and clasped the single pearl. She met Buttercup's eyes in the mirror and smiled.

The flower maiden once again gathered Alice's hair into her hands. As her hands deftly worked, Alice studied her in the round mirror. The girl was tall and thin in that oddly stretched way that seemed to characterize all the ladies-in-waiting. Buttercup glanced up and caught Alice watching her. She tilted her head, her hair waving like tentacles.

"Did you need something else, Miss Alice?"

"No, I..." Alice's face grew hot, but her curiosity clawed at her for answers. Was Buttercup human? She couldn't very well ask that, though, so she tried a different tack. "How long have you lived at the palace and served the Queen?"

Buttercup continued working on her hair as she answered. "They inducted me into the palace on my fifteenth birthday, as is the custom for those who choose this life. I'm nineteen now."

"Are there a lot of, erm, girls who want to serve here?"

Buttercup paused, her fingers resting in Alice's hair. "It is a great honor to serve the Queen, but not... all are willing to sacrifice what is necessary."

"You mean leaving their families?" Alice felt a pang at the thought of her own family, and her muscles tensed. Hadley's sly smile when he had mentioned her father's debt flashed through her mind. She forced herself to relax her shoulders. The Queen would send her home, and then she'd worry about Hadley's proposal.

Buttercup's lilting voice interrupted Alice's thoughts. "Yes, it is a sacrifice to leave our families, but it's not unusual for us to leave home at that age. We are considered adults then. It's more because of—" She paused, and the girl's wings fluttered in the mirror's reflection.

Alice frowned, confused. Buttercup pushed several long pins into Alice's hair to anchor the intricate topknot and then slipped the hair comb so it twinkled at the base. When she was done, she turned sideways and stretched out one wing so the shorn part was visible.

"Some of my people, they... they don't agree with our having our wings clipped."

Alice's stomach gave a queasy lurch. "Clipped? You mean, like a bird?" Unthinking, she reached to touch the gossamer edge of membrane closest to her. Her fingers hovered for a moment, and then she snatched her hand back, worried she had overstepped herself.

Buttercup didn't seem to mind. She frowned down at her own wing. "Yes, I suppose it is a little like that."

"Did it... hurt?"

Buttercup smiled, her slit-like pupils almost disappearing, and shook her head. "Oh no, not really. It's more about..." She paused and looked around. When she spoke again, her voice was low. "Clipping our wings mutes our magic."

"Magic? But how—" Alice knew this place was different. After all, cats didn't talk and dragons didn't exist, at least not in her world. However, her mind balked at the very idea of magic, even though deep down she realized she was probably using magic herself every time she talked to Chess or Zander.

"All the different fae have innate magics. The ladies who serve in the courts are flower fae. We can do many things, not like the one or two Gifts of the humans." She lowered her eyes to her hands. "We make humans... uncomfortable, so we have to agree to have our magic muted before we come to the palace."

Alice tucked away the fact that Buttercup had just confirmed she wasn't human, but rather some kind of fairy. Instead of commenting on that, Alice looked again at the clean-cut edge of the wing closest to her. "Is it... permanent?"

"Oh, no. No fae would permanently mute her magic. Although some..." A hard look flickered over Buttercup's face before it settled back into her normal placid expression. She waved a hand in the air. "But you don't want to hear about me, Miss Alice."

Alice opened her mouth to disagree, but then she caught sight of Buttercup's reflection. Her face held a closed-off tightness. It seemed Buttercup didn't want to share anymore. She reinforced that idea when she turned Alice back to the mirror, adjusted a few pins in the topknot, and then fluffed the rest of Alice's hair so it hung in loose curls over her shoulders. "I'll get your dress. We can't keep the Queen waiting."

It didn't take long until Alice was ready. The gown that the Queen had sent up for her was a soft periwinkle, almost the same shade as Alice's eyes. A softly shirred bodice ended in an empire waist marked by a band of velvet in a darker shade of blue. Short, fluttery sleeves draped onto Alice's arm. The rest of the dress floated in soft, shimmering waves to just above her ankles. A pair of leather slippers in the same shade as the velvet band completed the outfit.

Alice smoothed a hand down the silky skirt and smiled at Buttercup. "Thank you for your help."

The girl ducked her head. "It is my honor to serve you, Miss Alice."

Alice put her hand on the other girl's arm. "No, really, you've been so kind, answering all my nosy-parker questions and all. You didn't have to do that."

Buttercup blinked large yellow eyes at her, a strange expression ghosting over her features before she tilted her head. "I enjoyed helping you, and your questions were... That is, most see us as pretty decorations of court, not someone to ask questions."

Alice rolled her eyes. "They're the daft ones, then."

They shared a smile before Buttercup turned towards the door. "We must go. The Queen is waiting for you."

Alice followed Buttercup out into the hallway and down the winding staircase.

As they walked along the stone corridor with all the tapestries and portraits, Alice's steps slowed in front of the doomed prince.

She looked up into his face. He stared down at her. She tilted her head, trying to envision this young man fighting the dragon. It didn't make sense to her. The dragon had seemed reluctant to hurt the soldiers that were trying to kill him, so why would he try to kill their prince?

Alice had the distinct feeling she was missing a large piece of this story.

"Miss? We must go." Buttercup touched her elbow, her smooth forehead wrinkling.

"Yes, of course, I'm sorry." Alice stared up at the picture for another moment.

Buttercup sighed beside her. "Prince Zander was a good man," she said.

It took a moment for Buttercup's words to sink in. When they did, Alice whipped her head in Buttercup's direction. "What did you say his name was?"

Buttercup wrinkled her perfect brow again. "This is Prince Zander. His father was King Zane."

When Alice continued to stare at her, Buttercup touched her arm. "Are you all right, Miss?" Worry shone out of her eyes.

Alice shook her head. "I'm... fine." She walked numbly after the flower maiden, glancing behind her as she went.

The prince's reproachful gaze followed her through the gloom of the hallway. Her mind raced as she realized why the prince had seemed familiar. His eyes were the same shade of green as the dragon's. The dragon named Zander.

Chapter 21

BUTTERCUP LED ALICE DOWN another long hallway and out onto a large terrace at the back of the castle. Alice paused just outside the doors of the palace. She stared, only dimly aware that Buttercup had melted into the throng of people. Festooned with flowers and swags of white filmy material, the tiered terrace led out to the vast lawn. Waistcoated footmen circled among the guests, offering flutes of bubbly drinks in a pastel rainbow of colors.

Square tables covered in white cloths formed a loose circle around a larger round table, on which sat a fantastical cake. It rose towards the sky in a swirl of looping icing and sugared flowers.

On the lawn, someone had set up a game of croquet, and a flock of tall, vibrantly pink birds stood huddled on the far end of the course. A young man stood next to them, apparently their keeper.

A small group of musicians played softly off in one corner of the lawn.

The colors and noise swirled around Alice as her head reeled with her new knowledge.

What did it even mean? How could the dragon and the prince be the same? She shook her head. No, that was impossible. Besides, the Queen had said that the Jabberwock carried the prince off. She rubbed her forehead, trying to calm her thoughts.

Someone touched Alice's arm, and she jumped, almost spilling her drink.

The Queen's laughter rang out. "Goodness, darling, I didn't mean to startle you." She lifted a lock of Alice's hair and smiled. "You look stunning. I knew that color would be perfect for you."

The Queen had changed into a petal-pink dress that set off her delicate coloring. It bared her shoulders and ended in a skirt of frothy tulle and chiffon. A delicate gold crown nestled in her pale blonde hair. She beckoned to Alice.

"Come, you must sit with me at my table. They'll be serving the afternoon tea soon."

The Queen grabbed Alice's hand and towed her through clusters of people. As they passed, people stopped what they were doing to drop into bows and curtsies. The Queen sailed past them without even a nod, and Alice was left with an impression of well-dressed lords and ladies. The women wore candy-colored frocks, all in the same loose style, while the men wandered about in white linen.

A man sidled into their path. The Queen jerked to a halt, an eyebrow raised almost to her hairline.

"Lord Alivaras, what an unexpected surprise!" Her smile didn't flicker, but her tone was frosty.

The man bowed low, giving Alice a perfect view of the bald spot on the top of his blond head. "Your Majesty." He straightened and tugged at the edges of his perfectly cut linen coat. His middle-aged face wasn't quite handsome, but Alice had lived with the Cavendishes long enough to recognize money and clout when she saw it. His next words confirmed her suspicions.

"I wouldn't miss your little afternoon gathering. As the King's cousin, I wanted to show my support, even if my invitation did get waylaid." He turned his mist-grey eyes to Alice, and she fought the urge to shrink away. His lips curled into a smile. "And I'm so glad I did. Who is *this* ravishing creature?"

Alice wanted to hide from the gaze that slid over her. Instead, she lifted her chin. The Queen spoke before Alice could, her smile showing too many teeth. "She's my special guest, Dane. "

The man gave a low chuckle, his smile oily. "Of course she is. I've just never seen her before. I'm sure I would have remembered if I had." His eyes wandered to Buttercup, who had been following them through the crowd, and she stiffened beside Alice. Even though her expression remained serene, her hair lashed back and forth. The tension in the air thickened and stretched. Alice's scalp prickled with a warning, though of what, she wasn't sure.

Then, the Queen let out a low, musical laugh and, standing on tiptoe, reached up and patted the man's cheek a bit too hard. "You have the most amazing memory in that head of yours. Try to keep it on your shoulders, Dane."

Without waiting for the man's response, the Queen grabbed Alice's hand again and pulled her back into the throng of people. When Alice looked back over her shoulder, Lord Alivaras was watching them go, his eyes narrowed and his face pale.

They stopped in front of a longer table on the far side of the terrace. The front of the table sported large swags of tulle and flowers. The Queen glided around to the middle chair and gestured for Alice to take the one next to her. Several of the flower maidens were already in the other seats.

Once Alice sat down, the Queen climbed onto her chair and clapped her hands. Alice raised both eyebrows, but nobody else seemed surprised. In fact, despite all the chatter and clinking of glasses, silence descended with startling swiftness.

A wide smile split the Queen's face as she looked around at her guests who stood in a frozen tableau, staring up at her.

"Welcome, welcome!" She tapped Alice on the top of the head and waved for her to stand up. Alice got to her feet as everyone's eyes swiveled to her. She pasted a smile on her face even as her palms grew damp. All she had to do was get through this party, and she could go home. Even if the prince was the dragon, there wasn't anything she could do about it.

"This is my special guest, Alice." There was a pause and then a pattering of polite applause. "She is from the Mirror World and will be returning home shortly. I wanted her to enjoy one of the Kingdom of Wonderland's spectacular afternoon tea parties first, though. Please make her welcome."

A murmur of voices rippled through the crowd. Alice's smile felt stiff as she looked out at the sea of faces. Inside, she wished the ground beneath her feet would swallow her whole.

The Queen held up both her hands. "Our lovely servers will bring the tea around, so please find a seat and enjoy!"

Grasping her skirts in one fist, the Queen clambered down from her chair and plopped into her seat.

"Goodness, you haven't even taken a sip of our special punch," she said. She tapped the stem of Alice's flute with a long nail.

Alice obediently brought the glass to her mouth and took a swallow. The sky-blue liquid fizzed down her throat, and a bubble of delight floated into Alice's head. She smiled at the Queen.

"This is delicious."

The Queen's eyes sparkled. "Yes, it's lovely." The Queen raised her hand and snapped her fingers. Within moments, another tray of drinks appeared at Alice's elbow. "Try another color. The spring green is one of my favorites."

Alice picked up a flute, this one full of mint-green punch, and set it on the table.

The server carrying drinks had barely gone when another server appeared and placed before her a scalloped plate piled high with delicate tea sandwiches.

Alice searched the area around her plate for silverware, but there wasn't any. She glanced up and down the table and saw the flower maidens picking up their sandwiches and taking dainty bites, so she did the same. Flavor burst over her tongue. She had never tasted anything so delicious. They had a wonderful cook at home, but the food here was a whole other level of good.

A creamy, sage-green soup followed the sandwiches. The Queen only took a few spoonfuls, but Alice finished her own bowl.

A few moments later, thick slices of cake were brought out on delicate china plates accompanied by ice cream in crystal bowls. A set of dainty forks and spoons were set down next to the desserts.

Alice was already full, but the cake looked so good, she ate it and the ice cream, anyway.

The Queen gestured to a server. "Here, dear, your glass is getting quite low. Try the lavender this time."

Her glass was whisked away and replaced by a lavender one. She took a sip before turning to the Queen.

"This is amazing, Your Majesty."

The Queen waved a hand. "Oh, it's nothing, darling." She nudged Alice's hand so her glass was closer to her mouth. "Now, drink up. We're almost ready to play croquet."

Servers swarmed to the tables with wheeled carts which they piled high with plates and bowls. The people stirred restlessly.

The Queen stood and clapped her hands again. "Let us all convene to the lawn for our game. Who is feeling lucky this afternoon?"

Several young men and a few young women moved towards the far side of the lawn where the flock of pink birds stood. Alice stood up, and the Queen looped her arm through Alice's.

"I do hope you know how to play croquet," she said.

Alice nodded, but she didn't want to play. A headache had started behind her eyes, and her mind felt fuzzy.

As they walked towards the stairs leading down to the lawn, the Queen leaned in. "I've been wondering something."

Alice looked at her.

"Weren't you quite frightened of the Jabberwock? Whatever made you want to help him?"

Alice blinked several times. Her mind raced. The Queen's earlier warning had been oblique. Alarm made Alice stiffen, and a distant part of her mind was screaming at her to be careful.

Instead, when Alice opened her mouth, she found words pouring out about how she could understand the cat and the dragon, and she had discovered the poor thing's injuries, and she didn't even know if he was alive anymore or not.

The whole time she was talking, it was like part of Alice was floating above herself, horrified, but helpless to stop the words from spilling out. She abruptly shut her mouth and blinked at the Queen.

The Queen patted Alice's hand. "I thought you might have the Creature Gift. I am rarely wrong about these things."

Alice's face must have shown her alarm because the Queen laughed. "Oh, don't look like that, darling. What you've shared has been quite informative."

Somehow that didn't make floating Alice feel any better, but her mouth smiled as she slurred, "Thank you."

They had crossed the lawn and were standing by the flock of tall pink birds. Several other players had moved off, each with their own bird held by a short tether.

Alice noticed that one bird kept shuffling away from the front of the group, but as the group kept dwindling in number, his tactic was getting less effective. There were only three birds left by the time the Queen and Alice stepped up. The Queen's eyes zeroed in on the evasive bird and she pointed a long red nail at it. Pulling the bird forward, the keeper handed the tether to the Queen.

The bird balked, and the Queen's cupid-bow mouth twisted in annoyance. The bird fluffed up his feathers and leaned away from her. She gave her tether a vicious tug, making the bird's neck bend at an awkward angle. The bird pecked at her hand.

All movement halted, everyone holding their breath as a perfectly round drop of blood welled up on the Queen's white hand.

The Queen's lips lifted into a snarl, and the bird shrank into itself, its long neck seeming to retract into its small round body.

The Queen's eyes narrowed into two dark slits, and she passed the tether in two pinched fingertips to the guard.

"Deal with this creature," she said.

The keeper took the tether, reached to his belt, and pulled out a long, wickedly sharp knife. Without a word, he swung it, and the bird's head fell neatly from its neck onto the ground. It was so fast, the bird blinked once before going still. The long legs supported the body for several heartbeats before slowly crumpling to the ground.

The Queen's gaze turned to the guard. "I trust the rest of your birds are better behaved than that one is."

The guard's face turned a chalky white, and his Adam's apple bobbed up and down. He bowed low.

"My most humble apologies, Your Majesty," he said. "I don't know what got into him. You will find the rest of my birds to be perfectly behaved."

As if to prove his point, the two remaining birds presented their tethers to the Queen and Alice without even being asked.

The Queen's face transformed again. Her smile bloomed across her face, and her eyes widened with pleasure. "Thank you. I knew I could count on you." She turned to Alice. "Well, don't just stand there, darling, let's go play our game!"

Alice followed behind her on numb feet, disturbed by the other woman's wildly changing mood. Alice knew she should be afraid, but the fuzziness in her brain made the fear distant and muffled.

They reached the first wicket. Everyone had waited so the Queen could go first. A small creature trundled over to where she stood and rolled itself into a ball. The tall pink bird bent over and extended its foot backwards towards the Queen. She grasped one leg, and the bird stiffened its whole body, raising its other leg so she could grab it, too.

To Alice's complete amazement, the Queen turned the bird upside down, and using its large beak, she hit the rolled-up creature through the wicket.

The Queen turned to Alice. "It's your turn."

As they moved through the course, the waitstaff continued to circulate with the flutes of punch. Thirsty from the activity and sun, Alice drank another glass. Everything the Queen said made her laugh, and she stumbled a few times.

The Queen pulled Alice into the shade with her. Alice watched her stroke her pink bird's head.

"How can you just chop off one bird's head when you seem to like them so well?"

The Queen smiled. "I'm the Queen. I can't show any weakness, or nobody would listen to anything I say. You saw that idiot man earlier. He thinks just because I am young and a woman, he can bully me." Her mouth thinned. "He'll soon learn differently."

Alice swayed on her feet.

"Is that what happened to the prince? Did he try to tell you what to do?"

The Queen's gaze sharpened. "Whatever do you mean? I told you the Jabberwock carried the prince off." She gave Alice's arm a playful tap. "I think you've had a bit too much punch, my dear."

Alice shook her head, making the lawn waver. "No."

The Queen's nails dug into Alice's arm, and her voice lowered to a hiss. "You need to get ahold of yourself and stop making a scene."

Alice tried to pull her arm away, but the Queen's grip was surprisingly strong. "Can't make a scene. That would be rude." Alice stumbled and caught herself against the trunk of the tree. She reached out towards some moss. "They're the same color, you know."

"Goodness, I believe you are drunk," the Queen said more loudly this time. A few nearby players tittered.

"It was the eyes. Their eyes are the same color." Alice continued in a singsong voice, "Dragon Zander and Prince Zander have green eyes." The sky spun overhead, and Alice leaned on her bird, who squawked in protest. "It's why I know you're... lying."

The sky tipped sideways, and Alice felt herself falling, but she couldn't stop. The grass flew up to meet her face. Then the world went black.

Chapter 22

CONSCIOUSNESS HOVERED JUST BEYOND Alice. She reached towards it, swimming up through the murky darkness. She broke the surface and cracked open her eyes. Then slammed them shut again.

The weak light burned. There was an insistent pounding in her head, and her mouth tasted like something small and furry had crawled inside and died there.

As she came more awake, various places on Alice's body complained—her right hip and shoulder, in particular, were sore, as well as the right side of her face.

She forced her eyes open and looked around, confused. The room was dark, with only dim light filtering in through a window high in the wall. Strange lines of shadows lay on the concrete floor. This wasn't her room in the palace.

Alice used one hand to push herself gingerly into a sitting position. She closed her eyes again as the room swung crazily for a moment. She peeled one eye open and then the other. The room stayed put. She drew in a sharp breath and wrinkled her nose. It smelled dank, with an underlying odor she couldn't identify and wasn't sure she wanted to.

As her eyes adjusted, an icy chill settled in Alice's stomach. She was in a prison cell, and from the placement of the window, she wasn't in the palace. She was under it.

Alice drew her knees up to her chest and put her head on her arms, closing out her surroundings.

What had she done to end up here? The memory of the tea party was hazy. They had been playing croquet. She shuddered, remembering the Queen's transformation from warm and friendly to deadly and angry, the bird's head lying on the ground.

Was the Queen going to do that to her? What had she said or done to make the woman angry enough to throw her in here? Alice squinted, trying to remember. They had been standing by a tree, and there was something about moss...

A clank of a door sounded beyond her cell. Footsteps echoed on a stone floor. The sound stopped in front of her door, and a small slot in the bottom opened and someone shoved a tray inside.

Alice jumped to her feet, ignoring the pain in her head, and ran to the door, pounding on it.

"Please, wait! Please don't go!"

The footsteps paused, and a small panel slid back at the top of the door. A face she didn't recognize appeared. It was a young man, not much older than she was. His face twisted into a scowl of suspicion.

"What's you want?" He squinted into the darkness of her cell, and Alice shifted so he could see her better.

His expression softened when he caught sight of her face. Relief made her sag. "I... I... thank you." She blinked against tears. "Please, I need to know. Why am I in here? Did you hear anything?"

"I don't rightly knows, Miss. Don't nobody tell me nothing, but..." He looked over his shoulder and lowered his voice. "They's settin' up the trial boxes on the south lawn." Sympathy shown in his eyes. "There's some bloke as going to trial tomorrow. They'll probably put you on trial right after. Saves time that way."

Alice drew her head back, bewildered. "But I didn't do anything or... at least I don't think I did. One minute I was playing croquet with the Queen, and the next I woke up in this cell. How in the world will I defend myself if I don't understand what I did?" Alice slapped at the door.

The boy shook his head. "It's usually that way. Most of the poor sots don't even know what they did."

"Are you saying this happens all the time?"

"It does now, Miss."

"But, I didn't do anything," she repeated, shaking the bars. "I just want to go home." Her voice cracked on the last word.

The boy's mouth tipped into a sad smile. "Miss, it don't matters."

"What do you mean?"

His mouth drooped. "Ain't nobody left one of the Queen's trials with his head attached, not since the King died anyways."

"What?" Alice's knees turned to liquid, and her stomach dropped.

The rattle of metal on metal made the boy jerk his head around. He looked back at her. "I'm sorry, Miss, but I have to go. It'll be me own head if they catch me talking to you." He gave her a last sad smile and slid the panel shut again.

Alice walked back to the thin cot on numb legs and dropped on its edge. She put her face in hands. Tears slid down her cheeks. She was going to die in this forsaken place. Her family would never learn what had happened to her. A hand squeezed her chest as she thought of Rommy and Finn, America, her chance to start over. All gone because of some power hungry queen.

A surge of emotion pushed Alice to her feet. She reached into her topknot and poked around. Her fingers brushed the hair comb. While she might be able to use it as a weapon, it wouldn't help with what she had in mind now. She reached back up and found one of the pins Buttercup had used to secure her hair. It had been a long time, but she'd known how to pick a lock once upon a time.

She pushed the tray of food aside and knelt in front of the door, pushing the pin into the tiny keyhole. As she worked, she reviewed what she remembered from the tea party. Things had started getting fuzzy right about when they started playing croquet...

The pin slipped in her hand. "Blast it!" She shook out her fingers and then pushed the hairpin into the opening again.

She pressed her lips together as she concentrated, the pin catching and then slipping off a mechanism in the lock. Alice gritted her teeth and tried again, while her mind strained to remember right before she had passed out. The Queen had told her not to make a scene, and then she had proclaimed Alice was drunk. Alice snorted.

Yes, drunk on that stupid punch the Queen kept pushing on her, so whose fault was that? Then there was the moss on the tree.

Alice sat straight up, the pin falling to the floor.

She had called the Queen a liar.

Bollocks. She was in the stew now.

What had she been thinking? She rolled her eyes. Well, it was clear she hadn't been thinking. She'd been more than a little tipsy, and even though most people would have ignored her slurred ramblings, the Queen couldn't, not when Alice knew her secret.

The Jabberwock *was* the prince, and now, the Queen knew that Alice knew.

She leaned her head against the door, coldness seeping through the skirt of her rumpled dress. Despair weighed down her limbs.

There was no way the Queen would let her go now. Alice was involved, whether or not she wanted to be. The Queen wanted the Jabberwock dead. It was why she had blamed the creature for the prince's supposed death—which, Alice admitted to herself, was very clever. The prince would be taken care of, and the Queen's hands would never get dirty.

Alice's mind scrabbled at workable solutions. If she couldn't get this lock picked, maybe she could talk to the Queen. Alice wasn't a threat, not if the Queen sent her home. It's wasn't like she'd be coming back ever. Her conscience twinged, but she pushed it aside. She felt sorry for the prince, but what could she do to help him? At the moment, she couldn't even help herself.

A sob rose in her throat as she thought of her family again, and she swallowed it down. She'd been so close to going home.

Their faces flashed through her mind. The memories were a hot knife through her heart. How many years would they spend looking for her? Would Papa James be ruined if she wasn't around to marry Hadley?

Alice banged her fist against the door, anger bubbling up next to the despair. It wasn't her fault the Queen was a deceptive piece of baggage. She'd never asked to be drawn into their bloody politics. And that stupid cat. It was all his fault. He was the one who had pushed her down that hole. If not for him, her biggest problem right now would be Hadley Beechworth. Compared to losing her head, he seemed a mere trifle.

Her hands groped around on the floor until she found her hairpin. She picked it up, determination burning in her chest, and poked it back in the keyhole. If the Queen thought she'd just curl up and die, the bloody woman was in for a big surprise.

Chapter 23

WHAT DO YOU MEAN you left her with the Commander?
Zander's roar ricocheted off the cave walls.

Chess forced himself not to cower. Instead, he gave an
elegant shrug of his furry shoulders. *She'll be fine. The
Commander's not in the habit of harming young women.*

The same cannot be said of the Queen. Zander let out
a low growl. *And we both know the Commander is loyal
to my stepmother.*

Chess sat down and examined one paw. *I still don't
understand what you're so upset about. So what if Alice
meets the Queen? She'll probably just send her home,
which is what the girl—and you—wanted, anyway.*
Chess licked his paw and washed one ear. *You and I both
know Lyssandra's not sent one woman to the block.*

Zander stretched his wings out and stomped his massive front leg. *Yes, but that doesn't mean Alice is safe.
How long do you think the Queen will keep Alice around
once she realizes the girl has the Creature Gift? Do
you think I want one more death on my hands? Alice
wouldn't even be here if you hadn't brought her.*

Chess stopped what he was doing and looked up at the dragon. *Don't shove this on me, Zander. You might be willing to curl up and die, but I'm not! I have a life, and may I remind you, I risked it willingly, trying to block that blasted curse.*

Zander opened his mouth, but Chess wasn't done. *I don't regret it. You're like a brother to me, but you'd given up. I had to do something, which is always better than nothing.*

The growl had gone out of Zander's voice. *Don't think I don't realize what you've done for me, but Alice is an innocent. She doesn't even understand what's happening here, and she has no idea what the Queen is capable of, how charming and sweet she can appear. It's like offering a lamb to a wolf.*

You're underestimating the girl. Chess paced back and forth, his tail lashing. *There were real soldiers with real arrows shooting at her, but she kept a cool enough head to get you out of the quicksilver trap. There's more to Alice than meets the eye.*

Zander snorted. *I'll give you she's good under pressure, but Lyssandra is another story. The woman is a witch—literally.*

Chess shook his head and snorted. *Don't be melodramatic. Your stepmother has the Alchemist Gift, without a doubt, but she's unregistered, not some Baba Yaga in the woods.*

I know what that woman is capable of, and Alice has no idea. She's from the Mirror World, for goodness' sake. They don't even have the Gifts there.

Chess shoved down a pang of guilt. Zander was right, but he'd had no choice. Besides, he believed what he'd said to Zander. Alice was tougher than she looked. He'd been around a lot of society girls and women. Heck, he'd wooed and charmed many of them. There was something different behind Alice's veneer of propriety. Even if he couldn't quite put his paw on it, he recognized in his gut she wasn't helpless, even against the Red Queen. He turned back to the Jabberwock.

Look, Zander, what did you want me to do? You needed that medicine. You would have died without it.

Maybe, but now a young girl will die instead! A ruler doesn't ask his subjects to die in his place.

Steam rose from the prince's nostrils, and Chess could feel the anger rolling off the Jabberwock in waves. He didn't care. He padded over until he was toe to toe with his friend.

Get off your high horse. The Commander escorted her to the palace, not to the chopping block.

Zander shook his head. *It's only a matter of time, Chess. You know what the Queen's like!*

Yes, she's quick to make heads roll, but she's never executed a woman. She guards those flower maidens of hers like a dire wolf with her cubs. You are worrying about nothing.

Zander snorted again. *And you're trying to salve your conscience. Keep lying to yourself if it makes you feel better.*

Chess's temper snapped. *You and your high-and-mighty morals! You no longer have that luxury of remaining pristinely upright—not with half the Kingdom trying to kill you. Do you want Wonderland to fall permanently into Lyssandra's hands? How about your prized subjects then?*

Chess's tail had puffed to twice its normal size, and his eyes dilated until the pupil almost swallowed the blue. A rush of fire heated the air over his head, but Chess's anger burned away any fear. He wasn't afraid the prince would actually hurt him. It was that blasted nobility of his—it was both his greatest strength and his greatest weakness.

Not for the first time, Chess wondered where they would be if Zander hadn't clung quite so tenaciously to his ideals. Would it have killed him to let his halo slip a bit and put aside some of that chivalry? Chess sighed, knowing the futility of wishing for something that would never happen. Zander would never change.

Still, Chess didn't have to like it. He stalked out of the cave before he said something he'd regret. He had grown up with Zander, and their friendship was solid enough to withstand what was, for them, a regular argument. Zander wasn't the only one who wasn't going to change. Chess sat on the edge of the ledge and looked out at the misty fog that blanketed the world below.

He felt the prince's footsteps before he heard them. It was difficult for a Jabberwock to sneak up on him with his heightened feline senses. Chess didn't turn his head or acknowledge the prince's presence.

A loud sigh came from over his head, and Zander slid down until he was lying on the rock next to Chess.

Don't think I'm not appreciative that you saved my life—again. And I admit, you have a point about the good of the Kingdom. There was a long pause.

Chess glanced over at the prince. *I sense a "but" coming.*

The dragon curled his mouth into a smile and tilted his head. *Of course there is.* Chess rolled his eyes. *I can't just leave the girl in Lyssandra's clutches. If she finds out the girl has the Creature Gift after spending time with us, she won't be able to let Alice leave. Lyssandra's too close to her plan's success.*

The prince paused, but Chess didn't speak. The dragon sighed again, his breath ruffling Chess's fur.

You weren't the only one who saved my life, Chess. If it wasn't for her, my own soldiers would have killed me. He nudged Chess with his snout. *You know I have to see if she's all right. I couldn't live with myself otherwise.*

Chess stood and stretched. *Nothing I say is going to stop you, is it?*

The dragon's eyes drooped, but he shook his head. *No, it's not, but I won't take any unnecessary risks. I'll sneak in, see that she's okay, and then I'll go. You're probably right, and Lyssandra has sent her home already.*

Chess snorted. *Yes, it's so easy to stay out of sight when you're the size of a small cottage!*

The prince nudged Chess again. *It's not like I plan on landing on the front lawn.*

Chapter 24

ALICE WOKE AS THE first rays of dawn crept across the floor of her cell, even though she had stayed up for hours trying to get the lock open. She stood and tried to freshen her appearance. If she didn't keep herself busy, the hopelessness of her situation would overwhelm her.

Alice ran her hands over her hair, straightening it as much as possible without a mirror. Then she patted at the crushed gauzy fabric of her dress, trying to get the wrinkles out. As Mother always said, a girl should present her best self to the world. That probably applied triple to being on trial.

Once she had freshened up as much as she could, given her circumstances, Alice paced the small cell. She rehearsed various strategies in her head from denying any knowledge of the prince to simply making a run for it. She'd save that as a last resort, though.

Maybe she could coax the griffon over and escape that way. The Commander seemed to keep the creature near him, and he'd surely be at the trial. Alice twisted her hands together. No, she couldn't count on that.

She was so focused on her thoughts, the scrape of the tray on the floor startled her. Alice scuttled over to pick it up, determined to eat every bite to keep up her strength.

She almost dropped her breakfast, though, when the panel in the door slid open and the Queen's voice floated through the small square.

Alice stared at the opening.

"Alice, darling, don't let me interrupt your breakfast. It'll probably be your last one." The sugary tone that accompanied the words made Alice grit her teeth. She put her tray down on the cot and strode over to the door.

The Queen stood just on the other side, and Alice glared down at her.

"Oh, don't look like that," the Queen said. A small sigh escaped the woman's red lips. "I suppose you want to know why you're here. Most of the time I'd just let someone in your position wonder. It increases the mental terror, but I like you, Alice. I truly do. So, I thought it was only right that I come down here and tell you why you're going to die."

Alice wrapped her fingers around the bars. "You weren't ever going to send me home, were you?"

The Queen waved a chiding finger at her. "Now, now, don't be bitter. I said I was, didn't I? I'm not in the habit of going back on my word." She shrugged. "Even after I learned you had the Creature Gift, I was planning on sending you home. As I said, I like you." She looked away and her mouth drew down. "But I had to find out what you knew, and I was right, wasn't I? Really, darling, it would have been far better if you weren't clever. As they say, ignorance is bliss."

Alice opened her mouth and then snapped it shut. She wrinkled her nose instead. "I don't even remember what you're referring to, Your Majesty." Alice rubbed at her forehead. "That punch made me so muzzy-headed, I don't even remember what I said or did. Whatever it was, I sincerely beg your pardon." She turned innocent eyes down at the Queen, willing the woman to believe she had no idea what the Queen was talking about.

The Queen looked at her for a long moment and then gave Alice a look of begrudging respect. "That was quite an impressive performance, darling. If I didn't know everyone was drinking my special veritas punch that encourages people to tell the truth, I might have actually believed you were innocent." The other woman let out a sigh. "I wish that was the case. I do. We women need to stick together." There was real regret in the Queen's voice. "I hope you don't think I make a habit of sending women to lose their heads. I've used my position to protect women like you."

"Well, goody for you."

"I wish you wouldn't be like that, Alice. It's not my fault you're in this position. If I'm not mistaken, you can blame that on a man, too."

Alice was tired of the other woman's excuses. "I don't think you can blame someone for being cursed."

The Queen's eyes lit with glee. "That's not who I meant. After all, you didn't just stumble into Wonderland all by yourself, now did you?"

Alice forced herself not to roll her eyes and reeled in the hot words on the tip of her tongue. There might still be a chance. The Queen sounded regretful; she would work with that.

Alice rose on tiptoe and gripped the bars tighter, pressing her face against the metal. "Just send me home. If I'm in the Mirror World, I can't tell anyone about your secret. Please. My family won't even realize what happened to me." Her voice broke on the last word. The Queen's mouth curved into a sad smile.

She shook her head. "You're breaking my heart, Alice. You truly are, but thrones can't be usurped by leaving loose threads. They have to be snipped. For what it's worth, I am sorry about this."

Alice's stomach dropped with a sickening lurch, and her chest burned. She squeezed the bars, her control gone. "I don't give a bloody shilling about yer buggered politics."

The Queen drew back, a frown on her face. "I know you don't, dear, but rulers don't have that luxury." She turned to go.

Alice knew she'd lost, knew she should just shut up, keep what dignity she had left, but the hot words spilled over her lips anyway. "It's not fair! I didn't even want to come here." Her voice cracked and tears leaked out despite her desperate attempt to blink them away.

The Queen's expression softened as she swung back around. She reached up and gently tapped Alice's fingers where they still clenched the bars. "If you lived longer, you'd learn that life is many things, but it's rarely fair." She turned to leave.

"Don't I even get a trial?"

The Queen glanced over her shoulder, a frown marring her porcelain features. "Yes, of course you do." She lifted one shoulder. "It just won't make any difference."

Before Alice could reply, she swept out of view. Alice's feet sank flat to the floor. She slid down the wooden door and started to cry.

Chapter 25

It was close to noon, at least as near as Alice could tell from the way the sunlight had moved across the floor of her cell, when two young soldiers arrived to escort her to the trial. Despite her earlier fit of crying, she had composed herself. A strange calm descended on her as they walked through the twisty hallways and up several sets of stairs.

As they passed through the doors onto the terrace, Alice blinked in the bright sunshine. The two guards led her down the steps flanked by more soldiers. The Commander stood with his men. She caught his eye, and he gave her the faintest of nods. A flicker of hope sprang to life.

They had almost reached the bottom of the staircase when the guards drew to a halt. Alice glanced around. Someone had transformed the lawn from the last time she had been out here. A squat man in black robes perched behind a large lectern that dwarfed him. He was banging on it, his oversized powdered wig in danger of falling over one eye. Obviously, this was the judge, who was none too happy, based on his scowl. The source of his unhappiness was the scuffle taking place somewhere off to the left in front of the Queen who rested on an elevated throne in her own covered gazebo.

Alice couldn't quite see what was happening because the rows of spectators that filled the benches blocked her view.

Suddenly, a man came hurtling towards the Queen. He threw himself at the railing in front of her, his eyes wild, his face red. "You can't do this! I'm the King's cousin! You don't even have the Council here!"

The soldiers standing behind the Queen lurched forward, but she held up a hand to stop them. Unruffled, she raised one eyebrow. "That attitude is why you're here, Dane. You don't seem to understand that I am the Queen, and I can do anything I choose."

Now Alice recognized the oily man from yesterday's tea party. The man fell to his knees, still gripping the rail. "I'm sorry. I know you're the ruler here." As his shoulders heaved with sobs, he babbled, "I'll do anything you want."

The Queen tilted her head. After a momentary pause, she leaned forward and put a hand on his clenched fingers. He peered up, tears and red blotches marring his face, hope in his posture. The Queen smiled gently.

"Men like you don't deserve mercy. You not only accosted one of my flower maidens, but you've done everything possible to undermine my authority." She sat back and folded her hands in her lap. "Now you will serve as a warning to others in the court. Besides, the truth is, I've never liked you, Dane, and to be quite frank, neither did the King."

She waved a hand at the soldiers that were hovering nearby. Several stepped forward and grasped the man under his arms, dragging him back towards a distant spot across the lawn. Alice stood on tiptoe to see what awaited the prisoner, but she could only make out a hulking man with—she swallowed—an enormous ax over his shoulder. Flat black eyes were the only thing visible under his leather mask. She shivered.

The jury, an even dozen, made up of a mix of both men and women, sat glued to the tableau in front of them. They all leaned forward against the waist-high wall that enclosed their seats and watched as the prisoner was dragged, screaming and sobbing, towards his doom.

Alice studied the jury more closely and recognized several guests from the tea party. Others appeared to be of more humble origins.

"No, no, please." The man's head and shoulders bobbed into view as the soldiers towed him in front of the executioner. He was forced downward and disappeared from view again. He continued to yell and plead. Turning, the executioner raised his ax. Sunlight gleamed off the blade before it fell in one smooth arc. The pleading voice cut off abruptly.

As one, the onlookers let out a collective sigh. After a moment, all eyes turned towards Alice.

Alice lifted her chin, straightened her shoulders, and followed the soldiers on shaking legs down the aisle next to the spectator benches.

Two tables were in front of the spectators, facing the judge. Behind one was a tall, thin man. His spectacles perched on the very end of his long, narrow nose. He sat ramrod straight, his hands folded on the table. On the other side was a short, round gentleman. He had a monocle fitted into his left eye, and while he sat, he never stopped fidgeting with the papers in front of him.

The guards led her to the seat next to the round fellow. Once she sat down, they turned on their heels, snapped a salute towards the Queen, and then marched back down the aisle to join the contingent of soldiers standing at the foot of the terrace.

Now that Alice was past the benches of spectators, a plain wooden block became visible. There was a slight indention in the middle. and red stains glistened around the dent.

A whirring started in Alice's ears, and the noise behind her telescoped to a distant ringing. The block filled her vision, and her body swayed. A touch on her elbow anchored her.

"My dear, are you quite all right?" The portly man next to her spoke up for the first time.

Alice put a hand to her temple. "No, I don't think that I am, sir."

The fellow wrung his plump hands. "Oh dear, oh dear. You're not going to faint, are you? Last week, one of my clients fainted dead away, and it set the trial back by over an hour. I didn't get lunch until almost teatime."

The ridiculousness of his response snapped Alice back to the present.

"I'll try not to interfere with your meal plans." Her tone was dry.

The man blinked up at her. "I do appreciate it, my dear." He took out his monocle and polished it on his jacket. "Now, what did you say your name was?"

"I didn't."

"Yes, yes. Quite good." After a moment of shuffling the papers in front of him, he glanced up at Alice, who was a head taller. His monocled eye bulged up at her. "Oh, oh, well, I say..." He tapped his fingertips together.

Alice took pity on him and introduced herself. "I'm Alice Cavendish."

The man nodded, his head bobbing up and down. "Good, good. Quite regular."

"And you are?"

He blinked several times. "Oh yes, how remiss of me. Bartleby, Anther Bartleby at your service."

He shuffled his papers and again and squinted up at her. "It says here that you conspired to kill the prince." He tsked and shook his head. "Not much I can do with that. You'll have to throw yourself at the mercy of the court, not that they have any, mind you." He shrugged round shoulders, and his coat buttons strained.

"But I've never even met the prince," Alice protested.

"Then you shouldn't have conspired to kill him. Most foolish of you, my dear."

"But—"

The gavel came down with a loud *bang*. A uniformed young man blew a long horn and intoned in a nasal voice, "All rise for the Honorable Pettigrew Foghorn."

The judge rose about three inches. He barely cleared the lectern, the only thing visible from her vantage point his enormous nose. Alice stifled a hysterical snicker. She rose to her feet with everyone else.

"You may sit," Judge Foghorn said, his voice high-pitched and squeaky. Again, Alice swallowed an inappropriate giggle as the judge tried to hop onto his seat, but missed. A few of the jurors did laugh, and he shot an angry glare in their direction as he clambered into his chair. He banged his gavel several times. "Quiet in the gallery!" he said.

He turned his gaze onto Alice. "You are charged with conspiring with the Jabberwock to kill the prince. How plead you?"

"Not innocent," Bartleby said.

"What are you doing?" Alice asked.

"Well, you said you aren't guilty, but you're obviously not innocent either."

Alice turned towards the judge. "What he meant to say is not guilty. I am not guilty."

Loud murmurs rose behind her. The jurors shifted in their seats, and one young man elbowed an older woman who had nodded off. She yawned as she sat up straighter in her seat.

The judge banged his gavel again. "Quiet, I say."

He lowered his spectacles and peered at her. "I must say, the defendants are usually much more meek than you appear to be, but let the record show that the guilty party says she's not guilty." He gestured at a slight woman who sat at a miniature desk off to the side. Alice hadn't even noticed her. The woman licked the nib of her pen and scribbled in a tablet.

"But I'm not the guilty party."

"Strike the *guilty party* part," said the judge.

The woman let out a huff but dutifully crossed something off her paper.

The judge turned to the jury. "What say you? Based on the evidence, do you find the defendant guilty or not guilty?"

The jurors glanced at each other, confusion written on their faces. Nobody said anything for several minutes, until finally, an older gentleman dressed in overalls stood.

"Your Honor, we haven't heard any evidence yet," he offered, shuffling his feet.

"What? Oh yes, evidence." The judge gestured to the gaunt prosecutor across the aisle from Alice. "Do get on with it, Higgsby."

Higgsby stood to his full height. He towered over everyone else, but he was so thin, Alice wondered how he could hold himself up.

Moving in a languorous slouch, he rounded the table. "I will call my first witness, Eleanor Chathbottle."

A woman Alice recognized from the tea party sailed towards the witness box. She stepped into the box and sat with a rustle of silk, her gloved hands clasped primly in her lap.

"Tell the court what you saw at the tea party," Higgsby instructed.

"I was immediately suspicious of the girl. Everybody knows those from the Mirror World are up to no good, and I could tell she was, as well." She took out a handkerchief and sniffed into it. "It only reinforced my low opinion when she made a complete cake of herself during croquet."

"Can you explain for the jurors what you mean by 'make a cake' of herself?"

"Well, if you can believe it, the girl was plainly"—here Eleanor Chathbottle leaned forward and lowered her voice to a whisper—"drunk." She sat back and nodded her head decisively. "If that doesn't cast suspicion, I don't know what does. She was obviously so overcome with her treacherous deeds, she had to numb her conscience with spirits."

"Quite condemning," Higgsby agreed.

Alice clenched her teeth together to keep from speaking. If she remembered correctly, this Chathbottle woman had been weaving all over the lawn the last time she saw her.

"Thank you, ma'am. Your testimony has been most helpful."

Higgsby gestured towards Alice's lawyer.

Bartleby stood. "No questions from us," he said and then dropped back into his seat.

"How can you not have any questions for her?" Alice protested. "Nothing she said has anything remotely to do with what I'm being charged with."

Bartleby shushed her. "Questions take so much time, my dear, and I have my own witness." He patted her hand. "Just you wait."

Alice subsided, but her eyes drifted to the block. The executed man's voice echoed in her mind. Resolutely, she pulled her gaze from it and considered the jurors.

Several stared back at her, and she met each gaze squarely in return.

Her attention returned to the proceedings as Higgsby called another witness to the stand. She didn't recognize this one.

"Please tell the court your name and credentials," Higgsby said, leaning against the witness box, his eyes on the jury.

The man cleared his throat and ran a finger around the collar of his shirt. "My name is Dr. Weetle, and I am the foremost expert on Mirror World residents and culture in the Kingdom of Wonderland."

Higgsby tapped the edge of the witness box before pushing off and slouching across the lawn, his hands clasped behind his back.

"And what can you tell us about the young lady, based on your expertise?"

The professor glanced at Alice and then shifted in his seat again. "People from the Mirror World lack a general sense of right and wrong. They have a desire to cause chaos wherever they go, and it would not be unheard of for a visitor from that world to take it into her head to try to kill a sitting ruler in the Kingdom of Wonderland. It's not the young lady's fault, necessarily. It's just her nature."

Rustling and loud murmurs rose behind Alice, and the jurors whispered amongst themselves.

The judge banged his gavel. "Quiet! Quiet!" He turned to the "expert." "Thank you, Professor, for that enlightening information. You may go now."

Alice jabbed Bartleby in the side. "You need to question him," she said. "What he said isn't true at all."

"Now, my dear, he's the expert. Not you."

"But I am *from* the Mirror World," she said.

"And that's why you wouldn't have any idea how you act or think."

As the witness stepped down, Alice shot to her feet, unable to contain herself any longer. "With all due respect, Professor, you are very mistaken in your assessment of people from the Mirror World."

The professor paused in mid-step and stared at her, his squinty eyes blinking. "I assure you, I've studied quite extensively."

"Have you even met someone from the Mirror World?" Alice asked.

"Well, no, but I have it on good authority—"

"How can you be an expert if you've never even met someone from the people and culture you claim to know so much about?" she demanded.

The judge banged his gavel again and popped up from his seat. "Quiet! Quiet! I demand the defendant be quiet!" He swung his gavel at the professor. "And you, go sit down. You've had your turn."

Alice turned to Bartleby. "Aren't you going to do something?"

The man shrugged. "You heard the judge. He wants you to sit down and be quiet."

"But—"

Bartleby grasped Alice's arm and dragged her down to her chair. She yanked her arm away and pressed her lips together to keep herself quiet.

Higgsby sauntered back to his seat, rounded the table, and sat down.

"I'm done now."

The judge turned to the jurors. "Now that you've heard the evidence, what is your verdict?"

There was a long pause as the jurors whispered furiously amongst themselves. Finally, the same older man pushed to his feet. "Begging your pardon, Your Honor, but we've only learned the one side. I think we're supposed to listen to the young lady's view of things."

Annoyance flashed across the judge's face, and he let out a loud, gusty sigh. "Oh, all right, then." He gestured with his gavel towards Bartleby.

The portly barrister stood and straightened his purple waistcoat. Then he polished his monocle. Finally, he cleared his throat. "I call Miss Alice Cavendish to the stand."

A sense of relief washed over Alice. Now she could tell her story and straighten things out. She stood and made her way to the witness box. She sat very straight on the edge of her seat, her head up.

Bartleby came to stand in front of her. "Please tell the jury where you are from."

"I am from Somerset, England, in a place you refer to as the Mirror World." Alice articulated each word.

"And how did you come to be here in the Kingdom of Wonderland?"

"I fell down a hole in my world and landed here. It was quite by accident, I assure you."

"So, you came here by accident? Can you explain to the court why you wanted to murder the prince?"

Alice reined in her temper and stated her answer. "I didn't want to kill the prince, or anyone for that matter. I've never even met the prince. Didn't he go missing months ago, anyway? I only just arrived here a few days ago."

"Then, can you tell the court how you conspired to get rid of the prince while still in the Mirror World?"

Alice took a deep breath and blew it out before answering. "I have never met the prince. I had no idea the Kingdom of Wonderland existed until I arrived here, accidentally, two days ago." She turned to the jurors and met several gazes. They were all leaning forward. "This is all a big misunderstanding."

She looked out at the sea of faces, and clasped her hands. "I'm very sorry about your prince. I hope you find him in good health, but I had nothing to do with whatever happened to him."

Alice cut her eyes towards the Queen. The other young woman met her gaze and one side of her mouth tipped up.

Bartleby moved towards his seat without another word, and Higgsby approached her. He stared down his nose at her. Alice shivered as his colorless eyes swept over her without blinking.

A smile curled across the prosecutor's pale face. "That's an interesting story, Miss Cavendish. I would almost believe you if I hadn't heard the esteemed professor's testimony. How can you explain that?"

"Explain what, exactly?" Alice asked, bewildered.

"How you killed the prince." Higgsby pointed at her dramatically, and a gasp went up from the crowd.

Alice threw up her hands. "I didn't kill the prince. I don't know the prince, and neither of your witnesses even came close to proving that I did."

"Aha!" he said, again pointing dramatically and again soliciting a gasp from the audience.

The judge pounded his gavel. "You are excused, young woman."

"But—"

The judge interrupted her. "I will have none of your defiance in this courtroom. Go sit down!"

Alice reluctantly got to her feet and moved back to her seat.

The judge turned to the jurors. "Now, have you learned enough? Can you please deliver a verdict?"

The jurors put their heads together, talking in hushed tones. The people behind Alice shifted in their seats while the jurors continued to talk.

After several long moments, the older man stood up again. "Your Honor, it seems that the young lady hasn't done anything, so we find her not guilty."

Alice sagged in her seat, the knot in her stomach unraveling.

The judge nodded at the jurors. "Thank you for your service." Then he turned to the Queen. "The verdict has been rendered. What is her sentence, Your Majesty?"

Alice bolted upright. The Queen's dark gaze held Alice's, and a smile ghosted over her crimson lips. With a glance back at the judge, the Queen stood and lifted one hand before bringing it down sharply.

"Off with her head!"

Chapter 26

ALICE JUMPED TO HER feet. "That's not fair!" She pointed her finger at the jurors' box. "They said I wasn't guilty! You can't behead me for no reason!"

The judge banged his gavel. "I demand you sit down and control yourself!"

"Or you'll what?" Alice folded her arms across her chest. "She's already sentenced me to death! What else are you going to do?"

The judge opened his mouth and snapped it shut again. He scowled and banged his gavel again. "Sit down!" he said again. His voice cracked as it rose to a loud squawk.

"I will not sit down!" Alice swung her gaze towards the Queen. "If you think I'm just going to go meekly put my head on that block, you're balmy on the crumpet."

Bartleby plucked at her sleeve. "Miss, you must calm yourself," he said. "Please, sit down."

Alice jerked her arm away, glaring down at the rotund man. "And you! Why don't you go have your bloody tea. You've certainly proved yourself utterly useless."

Bartleby pulled his head back as if someone had slapped him. "If my best isn't good enough for you, I'm sure I'm very sorry, but I'm not going anywhere." He straightened his cuffs. "My duty lies with you, even if you are ungrateful." Under his breath, he added, "Besides, they won't let me leave until they carry out the sentence."

Alice growled, her hands curling into fists, but before she could speak, the Queen gave her a brisk nod. "I admire your spirit, my dear, but I don't have time to listen to your hysterics." She clapped her hands. "Carry out the sentence."

"But—" the judge sputtered, gesturing towards Alice who was still standing in defiance of his order.

The Queen waved her hand in the air. "Surely, it makes no difference if she sits down first or not."

The crowd had risen to their feet behind Alice, and their voices rose and fell with excitement as their heads swiveled between Alice and the Queen.

Two soldiers approached from either side, and the anger that had held Alice up dissipated and left her trembling. It was only by holding onto the table edge that she stayed upright. Her gaze darted from side to side, but before she could make a run for it, two sets of hands gripped her arms. She had hesitated too long.

They dragged her from behind the table, even as she fought their iron grips. Alice dug her heels into the grass, but the two men simply lifted her so her feet no longer touched the earth.

Alice twisted to peer at the jury and the spectators. "I'm not the guilty party. The Queen is the one who is guilty! She lied about the Jabberwock. It didn't carry off the prince. It—"

"Oh, do cut off her head so the child will be quiet already." The Queen's languid tone was at odds with the glare she directed towards Alice.

Alice hardly noticed. She twisted and bucked between the two soldiers. Her eyes darted around the gathering, trying to catch anyone's eye, but everyone avoided her gaze. Were they just going to watch the Queen kill her for no good reason?

The block loomed ahead of her, each of the soldiers' steps bringing her closer to death. Rommy. Finn. Papa James. Their faces flashed in her mind. A sob rose in her throat.

Desperate determination flooded through her. She bucked and kicked. Her foot caught one soldier in the stomach. With an *oof*, his grip loosened. Alice yanked her arm free. Without thinking, she hauled back and punched the other soldier as hard as she could. Her fist connected with his nose with a satisfying crunch. Pain streaked through her knuckles, but she ignored it.

"Stop her!" The Queen's voice roared across the lawn. Alice risked a glimpse back and almost tripped. The Queen had left her gazebo and was racing towards her. A snarl contorted her face, and her hands curled into claws as she ran across the grass. It almost looked as if steam was coming from the other woman's nostrils. Alice jerked her head back around as she nearly lost her footing. She darted past the the jurors and around the judge's bench, aiming for the open lawn beyond. Everyone's heads snapped around to watch her escape.

Footsteps pounded behind her. Her breath came in gasps, but she pushed harder. In front of her, the lawn was wide and open. The welcome embrace of the woods seemed impossibly far away.

As the footsteps got louder, she risked another glance behind her. The Commander had joined in the chase and was outpacing everyone else. Alice put on a spurt of desperate speed, even though she knew she would not make it.

A loud roar shook the air, and Alice tripped and fell to her knees. Air whipped by her head, and a pair of bronze legs the size of tree stumps landed in front of her as a hand gripped her arm, pulling her to her feet.

The dragon loomed over her, coppery-gold wings stretched wide. He roared again, and fire blasted over her head. Alice's bones felt like jelly and her knees buckled. The Commander shook her. Alice's gaze flew up to his. His nod was terse.

"Hit me," he said.

"What?" Alice blinked at him.

"Hit me. It can't appear like I helped you."

"Oh, yes, thank you," she gasped out. Still, she hesitated.

"Do it!" he said.

She pulled her arm back again and hit the Commander in his jaw, making his head snap back.

The dragon roared again, and his voice scraped in her mind.

Hurry!

She wheeled away from the Commander, who had fallen to one knee. She doubted it was her punch that had done that. The dragon reached down, grabbed the back of her dress, and threw her on his back. She slid across his scales, and before she could get a grip on anything, the creature beat his wings and they lifted into the air.

Alice's body swung sideways, her legs kicking into empty air. Her scream sounded thin as she scrambled to find anything to hang on to. The dragon banked the other way, and her body slid back onto his back, her hands finally finding purchase on the slick scales.

For a long moment she lay there, the dragon's scales warm under her cheek.

Are you hurt?

The words scraped the inside of her skull.

Her teeth chattered as she tried to answer. "N-no, I'm okay. I... I just want to go home."

I know.

Alice pressed her face into the warm, leathery scales and let the tears run down her cheeks as the dragon flew them to safety.

Chapter 27

BY THE TIME THEY landed on the outcropping outside the dragon's cave, Alice had cried herself out. The flight had been a silent one. After Zander's first question about her welfare, he had let her be, for which Alice was grateful.

The dragon glided to a stop on the cave ledge. Alice swung her leg over and hopped down before he had even folded his wings. She came around the front and looked up at the creature who had rescued her.

"Thank you," she said, her voice hitching. "I'd be dead if you hadn't come for me."

The dragon snorted.

You saved my life first.

Alice put a hand to her temple, but she noticed the dragon's words weren't as painful any longer. Perhaps, she was getting used to her Creature Gift, as the Queen had called it.

"Yes, but you didn't have to come, especially since you can't be fully recovered yet, and... and I know the Queen wants you dead, too." She paused and then blurted out, "You're the prince, aren't you?"

The dragon bowed his head.

Yes.

"Then I'm doubly grateful for your help."

The dragon lowered his head and nudged her with his nose.

Alice placed a hand on his snout and let her forehead rest on its ridge, her breath shuddering in and out.

If you two are done fawning over each other, maybe we should talk about the fallout of all this derring-do. You realize the Queen will command everyone to look for the girl now.

Chess sauntered out of the cave, his tail waving in the air.

Alice whirled in his direction and pointed a shaking finger. "You! If you hadn't abandoned me, this would have never happened."

The cat sat on its haunches, licked one paw, and began washing his ears.

It's not my fault you neglected to bring money with you. Who comes to a new place without so much as a myder on them?

Alice stepped in the cat's direction. "Maybe someone who gets shoved down a hole against her will!"

If you want to be nit-picky, you tripped and fell down the hole.

"Your big arse hitting me in the chest had nothing to do with that, right?" She gripped her hands together to stop their shaking.

Chess shrugged a furry shoulder. *We needed help.*

"Ever hear of asking? Instead, you led me on a wild goose chase through the woods and then pounced on me!"

Yes, explain how I would have asked, since you couldn't understand me.

Alice put her hands on hips. "But I have the Creature Gift!"

The cat rolled his blue eyes. *It doesn't work like that in the Mirror World. Tell me, did you chat with animals a lot before you came here?*

This brought Alice up short. "Erm, no—at least not recently."

Chess tilted his head. *Recently?*

Alice waved her hand. "Never mind about that." She glared down at him. "Why can't you just admit this situation is your fault?"

The cat sniffed. *Because it's not.*

Alice let out a growl. "You are the most annoying creature I've ever met."

Chess stood and rubbed up against Alice's ankles. *Most young ladies love me.*

Alice shoved him away with her foot with more force than was strictly necessary. "I guess I'm more of a dog person."

A rumble sounded from the dragon.

Chess, you may as well admit you're at fault. I don't think you're going to charm your way out of this one.

"I can't imagine that anyone finds him charming."

The cat sniffed, turned his back to both of them, and sat near the edge of the overhang. The dragon shook his enormous head and then turned his gaze to Alice.

Chess is right, though. The Queen isn't going to just forget that you learned her secret. We need to get you home.

A fierce longing welled up in Alice's heart, and she nodded. "The sooner, the better."

We can't send someone back using the portal you arrived through. The Looking Glass is much easier to use, if a little finicky. My father always had it well guarded, though. It would surprise me if the Queen hasn't continued that practice or, at the very least, that she wouldn't send her men there to intercept you.

What are you talking about? We can't send her back yet. Chess had turned around and was facing them.

Of course, she needs to go back. You said yourself, the Queen will look for her.

But she's one of the few people who can understand you. If she goes home, we'll be back to square one and—

The dragon cut him off. *Alice wants to go home.*

Chess let out a hiss. *Well, I'd like a lot of things, but it doesn't mean I get them.*

Alice snorted, but Chess ignored her and stalked up to the Jabberwock.

Will you let go of that nobility of yours for just a moment? It's your precious high ideals that left us with a ticking clock. She's our best chance. Or do you want Lyssandra to take over the Kingdom?

Soldiers were dragging her to the chopping block, Chess. The dragon closed his eyes. *It was still wet with my cousin's blood.*

Chess sat back on his haunches, and his whiskers twitched. *It's not like I'm happy about what happened.* His gaze darted to Alice before he focused back on the Jabberwock. *But your birthday is less than a week away, Zan. There isn't time to let your finer feelings get in the way.*

"I'm still here, you know," said Alice. She glanced between Chess and Zander.

The dragon shuffled closer to her and curled his tail around Alice's feet. *It's too dangerous.*

Alice held up her hand. "I don't understand what either of you is talking about," she said. "What I do know is my family is probably frantic with worry, and I want to go home." She pointed at Chess. "Tell me one good reason that I should stay here."

How about more than one? Chess got up and paced back and forth. *You already learned that the Jabberwock and the prince are one and the same. The Queen cursed him, and if we don't break it—by midnight on his next birthday—she'll keep the crown... permanently.*

Alice rolled her eyes. "Obviously, someone cursed him, and only a nitwit wouldn't realize she was after the throne. But how does any of this pertain to me? I mean, I can see why you needed my help to untangle Zander from that trap." She shot Chess a look. "Although you still could have *asked*." She held out her hands. "I can't see what help I'd be now, though. I know nothing about curses or how to break them. Not to mention, the Queen has most likely put a bounty on my head."

For one thing, there aren't many people with the Creature Gift, so nobody we trust can understand him. Except Citrine, who he refuses to see. It makes it almost impossible to search out a way to break this curse without someone trying to kill him. For another—

Chess, stop it. Zander's voice was a rumble of warning. He turned his large reptilian head towards Alice. *If you want to go, I'll take you to the Looking Glass. You should be able to get home through there.*

Chess opened his mouth, but Zander shot a stream of fire, scorching the rock near Chess's feet. He jumped, his back arching and fur bristling. He crouched down, and his tail lashed back and forth.

Alice laid her palm on the dragon's nose. "Thank you, Zander. For what it's worth, if I thought I could help, I'd think about staying." She shrugged one shoulder. "But I need to get back to my family."

Chess hissed. *She deserves to understand the whole truth before she decides, Zander.* He leapt up onto a large rock so his whiskered face was almost even with Alice's. *If you leave, we'll never break the curse, and that's the truth. The entire Kingdom will be under the rule of the woman who tried to chop your head off. Both of us will be cursed in these forms for the rest of our miserable lives. The longer we stay like this, the less human we'll be.* His laugh was bitter. *Of course, we probably won't live very long since everyone will be hunting us.*

"Both of you are cursed? But aren't you... I mean, I thought..."

That's right, love. The prince and I are cousins. He snorted at Alice's look of surprise. *What, did you think I was the prince's pet talking cat?*

Alice felt her cheeks heat. That was exactly what she had thought, but anger flickered to life at the unfairness of the whole situation. "How was I supposed to know? It's not like we have talking cats at home."

So you have talking Jabberwocks instead?

Zander snaked his head out between them. *Knock it off, Chess. She doesn't owe us anything, even if she could break the curse. And we don't even know that for sure.*

Chess's blue gaze bore into her. The sun glinting on the ax blade flashed through her mind, and the terror of those moments burned through her. Her knees suddenly wobbled. She put a hand out and steadied herself on Zander's shoulder.

She shook her head. "I'm sorry about what's happened to you, both of you, but I don't belong here."

Chess flattened both ears to his head and pointed a paw at Zander. *You know as well as I do she can break the curse.*

Zander snorted. *You only have Lyssandra's word for that, Chess.*

You know I'm right. You just don't want to ask anyone for help. Well, good luck to you both. I'm not going to wait around for the clock to strike midnight. He whirled and bounded into the cave. Alice watched him go, her chest tight. A puff of steam warmed her cheek.

I'll take you home once it gets dark. Chess was right about one thing—the Queen will be looking for you.

The Jabberwock turned and slunk into the cave, leaving Alice standing on the ledge alone. The wind whipped through her hair, and she wondered if she was making the right decision.

Chapter 28

ALICE EVENTUALLY FOLLOWED ZANDER into the cavern. He was already curled into a ball, asleep. Although she was anxious to get home, it was probably best if they waited until dusk fell. It wouldn't hurt either of them to get some rest, either. Alice guessed Zander's wounds still bothered him.

She laid down on her bed of ferns, positive she wouldn't be able to sleep, between all that had taken place and the excitement of leaving. However, the longer she lay there, the heavier her eyelids became, until exhaustion pulled her under, too.

Almost immediately, she was back at the palace. The guards' fingers bit into her arms. Onlookers loomed on either side, their voices loud and overwhelming. The block drew nearer and nearer.

Blood gleamed on its surface.

She couldn't move, her body paralyzed. Fear crushed her chest as they approached the heavy square of wood. Hands pressed her down, and her legs buckled beneath her against her will, even as she strained to stiffen them.

The sunlight glittered off the executioner's ax before the guards shoved her head downward. Instead of grass, she came face to face with the severed head of Dane Alivaras. She recoiled in horror.

Suddenly he opened his eyes and smirked. "Better run, you ravishing creature."

Alice jerked awake with a scream. She gulped in great gasps of air, her chest heaving as if she'd raced a mile.

Zander's neck snaked towards her, and his eyes darted around the cave. *What's wrong?*

She tried to slow her breathing and offered a perfunctory smile. "I'm all right. It was just a bad dream, I guess." Her breath shuddered. "I'm sorry I woke you."

He nudged her with his snout. *Don't worry about it. After your dreadful ordeal, it's not surprising you're having nightmares.*

Alice shrugged, embarrassed. "I'll be fine. You should go back to sleep. You need your rest."

Zander didn't move. *You do, too.*

She scrubbed at her eyes and laid down. "You're right. We should get some sleep while we can. Who knows what we'll turn up when we arrive at the Looking Glass?"

After a minute, Zander laid his head down. It didn't take long for his breathing to slow. Alice stared at the shadowy ceiling. She was afraid to go back to sleep. Every time she shut her eyes, the doomed man smirked at her.

Lying there wouldn't help, so Alice got to her feet and walked out to the overhang. The wind buffeted her this high, but it drove the last fragments of her dream away. She wandered closer to the edge and lowered herself until she sat with her legs kicking out into empty air.

The sun was low in the sky and its long rays bathed the surrounding peaks, turning them pink and blue. She must have slept longer than she realized. It was just as well. She'd never been good at waiting.

She hugged her arms, and Chess's words kept running through her mind. Why did he believe she was the one to help? She had the Creature Gift, it was true, but there were others right here that did too, so why her?

She bit her lip. Maybe she was making a mistake. If they needed her help... She pushed the thought away. This wasn't her problem. It wasn't even her world. Yes, the Red Queen was a nasty piece of work, but what could Alice do?

A warm breath on her neck startled her out of her thoughts, and she twisted to discover the Jabberwock looming behind her.

May I? He jabbed his nose towards the spot beside her, and Alice nodded.

He sank down next to her, his face towards the setting sun. He watched it in silence for several minutes before he spoke.

You don't owe us anything. You're making the right decision, going home.

Alice glanced up at the imposing creature beside her. A part of her wanted to agree, to go home and forget this place, but another part of her knew she'd always wonder what had happened to Zander and Chess.

She leaned against his shoulder. "What if Chess is right? If you need my help..."

It wasn't right of Chess to drag you into our mess. His sigh reverberated over the empty space. *Don't mistake me—Chess has been a loyal friend, but consequences aren't something he considers. He acts before he thinks, and... these stakes are too high for that.*

"Then maybe I should stay." The words tumbled out, almost against her will.

Zander dropped his head so he could see her eyes. *No, you shouldn't, Alice. The Red Queen, as much as I hate to admit it, has us outnumbered and outmaneuvered. The chances of us making it out of this alive are poor, never mind taking my crown back.* He shook his head. *You're brave and clever, but I expect you realize how nasty this can become. I'm just sorry a gently reared young lady like yourself had to experience the ugliness of human nature.*

Alice bit her lip. She was tempted not to say anything. After all, she was returning home, and she'd never see him again. In the end, though, it felt dishonest not to tell him who she really was. She stared out at the mountains, now flaming with pinks and reds.

"It's a good thing that I'm not a gently reared young lady, then."

Zander's head drew back. *What do you mean?*

Alice got to her feet and gestured down at herself. "I only seem like a proper young lady, Zander. The truth is, this"—she waved a hand towards her face—"the manners, the posh accent, it's something I learned."

I don't understand. Chess said your father was a gentleman.

Alice shrugged. "I'm adopted. When my sister Rommy found me, I was six years old, living in the back alleys of London, fighting for every tiny scrap I got. In fact, if she hadn't intervened when she did, a gang might have beaten me to death, or close enough. I've learned how to maneuver in society and push that street urchin down deep." She gave a wry smile. "Although occasionally, she pops back out to embarrass my family. No matter how hard I struggle to eliminate her, she's still there."

The dragon tilted his head and studied her for several long moments. Alice refused to look away from him, but inside she squirmed. His reaction was hard to read. Dragons didn't have expressive faces. Perhaps he was pleased she was leaving now—or, worse, he assumed she had deceived him. She lifted her chin. Fine, let him believe what he wanted. She was so tired of trying to be someone else.

Maybe you should stop trying to get rid of her then. Your family adopted the six-year-old, so they must have loved her, not just the person you've grown into. She's part of who you are now. He blew out a chuckle. *After all, there aren't very many ladies who can throw a right hook. I think you took the Commander by surprise.*

Alice exhaled a startled laugh even as her eyes over-flowed. She swiped at the tears, mortified at her weakness.

"What do you know about it? You're a prince. You were born knowing the correct way to talk and act."

The dragon nudged her with his muzzle. *I spent a good portion of my life attempting to be something I wasn't. Out here, I'm in my element. Even when I'm not in this form, I can hunt and track just about anything, but those things don't translate well in the sparkle and glamor of court. All the things that come naturally to Chess—flattery, charm, dazzle—I'm rubbish at. I tried to be that person, but it's just not my nature. In fact, I despise all the games and backstabbing. When my father died, I finally realized that I couldn't lead this Kingdom as anyone but myself.* He snorted. *A lot of good that did me.*

Alice glanced up at the dragon, who was watching her with serious eyes. She reached out a tentative hand, and he pushed his snout into her palm. "Thank you," she said, her voice soft. "I'm not sure how you managed to say what I needed to hear when you barely know me."

Time doesn't always have a lot to do with knowing someone.

Their gazes held for several beats, and then the dragon blinked and straightened away from her. *The sun's set. We should go.*

Alice jumped to her feet and dusted off her skirts. There wasn't anything to pack. All she had was the dress the Queen had given her. The clothes she'd arrived in were back at the palace, probably in the rubbish pile. She gave a last glance towards the cave. Her heart pinched at the thought of never seeing Chess again, even though she still wanted to shake him. Then she shrugged off the feeling. It was time to go home.

Chapter 29

GOOSEBUMPS PRICKLED ALONG ALICE'S arms, but the scales beneath her were warm. She and Zander soared over deep gorges and wove around walls of rock to the neighboring mountainside. The air was cold and thin, but nestled at the base of the Jabberwock's neck, Alice wasn't uncomfortable. She was determined to enjoy the ride since this would most likely be the very last time she ever rode on a dragon. Her heart gave a pang at the idea of never seeing Zander, or Chess, again. She shook the knowledge away. She was going home, and based on what Zander had told her about the trip, they should be at the Looking Glass soon.

They'd been flying a little more than a quarter of an hour when Zander started circling lower, past the bare upper peaks and down towards the tree line.

Alice peeked over the dragon's side. She trusted Zander, but the trees looked so thick, she didn't know how he'd be able to land, never mind check for the Red Queen's men.

Before the thought fully formed, a clearing opened up below them. Zander glided down and landed in the tall grass. Alice looked around. Ringed in long, slender trees with silver and gold leaves that chimed like bells, wildflowers as big as saplings filled the scooped-out bowl of forest. Alice considered the place very pretty. It was also very empty.

"Is the mirror... invisible or something?"

The Jabberwock shook his head. *No, but this will give us a chance to circle around and check if any of the Queen's guards might be lurking about.*

Alice swung her leg over, but Zander put out a wing to stop her. *No, it'll be faster and safer if you ride.*

Alice settled herself back on the leathery scales, and Zander slid into the surrounding forest at a speed that made the breath catch in her chest. She clung to his neck as he twisted his way through the trees. Once again, it surprised her how such an enormous creature moved through the crowded trunks without a ripple.

Before long, the trees thinned, and Zander slowed down. His voice whispered through her mind. *Stay silent. If anybody is waiting for us, we don't want to let them know we're here.*

Alice patted his neck to let him know she understood. As they moved forward, she glimpsed another clearing and parts of a broken-down building. Zander crept in a loose circle, scenting the air like one of Papa James's hunting hounds, until they returned to where they had started.

Alice's chest tightened. She was almost home. It was time to say goodbye.

Finally, Zander deemed there was no danger, and they stepped from the cover of the trees. He paused again, his serpentine body half in and half out of the forest. Alice scanned the clearing. This one was large and irregular. At the very center was a dilapidated stone building. It looked a lot like the abbey ruins close to the Cavendish estate where they often took guests on picnics.

She swung her leg over and slipped down to the soft grass. With Alice keeping one hand on Zander's shoulder, together they walked towards the building. The dragon stopped and sniffed every few feet. Alice appreciated his caution. Even though this clearing was larger, there was nowhere to hide, and they had already circled the surrounding forest.

Despite how much Alice wanted to see her family again, she found she didn't mind the slow pace. The Jabberwock stopped several yards from the building, and Alice got her first glimpse of what she assumed was the Looking Glass.

The mirror wasn't impressive. Attached to one of the stone walls, the dull glass was a rectangle enclosed in a plain wooden frame.

She looked up at Zander. "What do I do?"

Zander wrinkled his snout. *The steps are simple. You just stand in front of the mirror and envision where you want to go. When the glass reflects where you want to go, you just step through. It usually works.*

Alice's head snapped around. "What do you mean, *usually?*"

Zander scuffed a huge foot on the ground and lifted one of his shoulders. *The mirror has a reputation for being a bit... temperamental.*

"You've got to be kidding me. Why isn't anything easy in this place?"

There's no reason to believe it won't work.

"What happens if it doesn't? Will I end up in some in-between place?" The idea horrified her.

Zander shook his head. *Oh no, nothing like that. It's just sometimes, the mirror doesn't take you where you want to go.*

"I thought you said the mirror was a portal. Aren't those supposed to be like doorways or something?"

This isn't exactly a portal. It's more a travelling device.

Alice had the overwhelming urge to yank on her hair, but instead, she clasped her hands in front of her and kept her voice even. "All right. But if I want to go back home, why wouldn't it take me where I want to go?"

I shouldn't have mentioned anything. I just didn't want you to be startled if you popped out somewhere else in Wonderland. Phineas Sacklepenny created it, but he was rather eccentric himself.

"Can he help us, since he's the creator and all?"

Oh, that was hundreds of years ago. He's been dead for at least a couple of decades now.

Alice didn't comment on the fact that meant the man had to have lived several hundred years.

He was an Alchemist. His Gift was powerful but sometimes got away from him. He created the Looking Glass to make travel easier in Wonderland. His original intentions weren't to make a way into the Mirror World. It's one reason Alchemists have to register now.

I can't decide if you're trying to talk her to death or if you're just putting off saying goodbye.

Alice whirled around at the velvety voice. She couldn't help the grin that spread across her face at the sight of Chess as he sauntered out of the ruins, his tail waving in the air. She resisted the urge to run over to him.

He winked. *You didn't expect I'd let you leave without saying goodbye, did you, love?*

Chapter 30

CHESS SAUNTERED OVER TO Alice and noted the wide grin on her face. A glow of satisfaction warmed him as he wound around her legs. Just as he had intended, she leaned down and ran her hand over his fur. He wasn't sure if it was the Creature Gift or what, but she gave the best scratches. He leaned into her palm and let out a rumbling purr.

Zander interrupted the blissful moment. *What are you doing here, Chess?*

His friend's voice was heavy with suspicion, and Chess pushed down the pang of hurt. Instead, he swished his tail and shot a slit-eyed glance at the Jabberwock. Alice paused in her petting, her expression tight.

You don't listen too well. I just said I came to say goodbye to Alice. He butted his head against her shin and she resumed petting him.

Hmph. That's all?

Chess's fur bristled. *Why do you always assume the worst? Alice has become my... our friend. We'll never see her again. Even you can understand why I didn't want our last words to be angry ones.*

"Can you two please wait until I'm gone before you start fighting?" Alice straightened and looked between them. "Chess is right. We probably won't ever see each other again. I'd like to say a proper goodbye." Her voice wobbled on the last word and Chess bit back a smile. He'd been right. Whether or not she realized it, she wasn't eager to leave.

He widened his eyes and looked up at her. *Zander can be an uptight stick-in-the-mud, but he's right about one thing. I shouldn't have dragged you into our mess. I can't be sorry that I found you, but I should have given you a choice.*

Alice's eyes turned shiny, and she sniffed. To his surprise, she bent, scooped him up, and pressed her face against his fur. Warmth spread through his chest, and he nuzzled against her chin, his purpose forgotten for the moment.

"This has been a... an adventure I'll never forget, even if it did almost kill me." She gave a half sob, half laugh. "I... I hope you break this curse and beat the Red Queen. She deserves it."

Chess made his voice soft. *You don't have to leave, you know. With your help, we can defeat her.*

Alice's arms tightened around him, and he felt her heart speed up. He pressed his advantage. *Without your help, I don't think we have a chance in... well, any chance, love. Zander doesn't want to ask, but I'm not too proud. I don't want to die never being a man again.*

Alice inhaled. He'd hit his mark. He upped his purr. He was so close.

Zander bent down and nudged Alice's shoulder. *Stop using that fae charm to sway her, Chess. That's not fair.*

Chess gritted his teeth. If only he was bigger, he'd punch Zander in his princely nose. *It's not polite to insert yourself into private conversations. I'd think a prince would recognize that.*

Alice's body stiffened, and she set Chess down on the grass. She crossed her arms, and his hopes plummeted. "Fae charm?" One black eyebrow rose, and her violet eyes sparked. "Were you trying to magic me or something?"

The only charm I was using was my own, love. You can't blame me for making my best plea before you leave.

Hurt rippled over her face, and Chess felt like a heel. He tried to rub against her leg again, but she moved back. Determination settled over her face, and she looked at both of them. "I do wish you both the best, but I need to get home. My family, Papa James—they need me, and they're probably worried sick."

Zander nodded his big, stupid head. Sometimes, Chess thought his friend didn't truly want the crown. If Zander's fate wasn't tied to his own, Chess would be tempted to let him do what he wanted. But Chess, for one, had no desire to die as a feline. He looked back at Alice. No, he definitely wanted to be a man again.

Alice walked towards the Looking Glass. Despite the look of purpose on her face, her steps were slow and hesitant. He scampered after her. They entered the old Alchemist's pavilion, the stone cold under his paws. The electric crackle of the mirror's magic rippled over Chess. He narrowed his eyes. Something was off. He couldn't quite put his paw on it.

Alice hesitated before she stepped in front of the mirror. Then she bit her lip. She glanced back at Zander, who gave her an encouraging nod. "What do I do now?"

The off-balance quality of the magic increased. *Alice, I don't think you should—*

"Look, I know you don't want me to leave, Chess, but this is my choice."

No, it's not that—

He heard a whistle, and his body reacted before his brain caught up. He leapt at Alice, and she staggered sideways as an arrow flew out of the window and slammed against the wall. Her scream pierced Chess's eardrum as he whirled back towards the mirror just as a soldier erupted from the surface.

Zander's roar shook the crumbling stones, but Chess knew his friend dared not blast fire at the mirror for fear of destroying it.

Alice scrabbled backwards, away from the Looking Glass. Another arrow narrowly missed her head as a second soldier pushed out behind the first.

Get up, get up!

Fear closed his throat. He was too small to shield her. If she didn't move, she'd be dead. It would be his fault.

He launched himself at the nearest soldier's head, claws out. The man flailed and stumbled backwards, hitting the soldier behind him. That man's heel hit the edge of the mirror and he toppled backwards, disappearing from view.

Good. The men could only come out one at a time. He'd use that as an advantage. Alice scrambled to her feet and grabbed a broken piece of wood. She hefted it in her hand and stood at the ready.

What are you doing? Get out of here. Chess pushed off the man's face, and Zander's jaws snapped close enough to wave the hairs on Chess's back. The man screamed and backpedaled towards the mirror, just in time to run into another soldier climbing out.

Get her out of here.

Zander hesitated but swung his head in Alice's direction.

She shook her head. "No, we can't leave Chess."

Go. Go. Don't worry about me.

Chess bunched his back legs and leapt at the next person coming through. An iron fist collided with the side of his head, and he flew. He had enough time to brace himself before his body hit the stone wall with a brain-rattling thud. Pain streaked through him. He heard Alice's scream, Zander's roar, felt the rush of wind from Zander's wings.

As darkness crowded in, the last thing he saw was the Commander's familiar blue eyes, wide with shock. "Chess?"

Chapter 31

ALICE STEPPED TOWARDS CHESS, but before she knew what was happening, she found herself sprawled across Zander's back. At this rate, she was going to need a handle sewn in the back of her dress. With one powerful stroke of his wings, they were airborne.

And then they were dropping towards the earth again.

A scream stuck in her throat as the Jabberwock braked his dive, kicked off the ground, and shot straight up into the air again.

Feeling sick, Alice struggled upright. "What are you doing? We can't leave Chess!"

I've got him.

"But... he... you... how?"

The Jabberwock's wings beat the air, and wind rushed by his big body. *Talons sometimes come in handy.*

Alice sagged against Zander's neck. "Is he..." She swallowed, unable to say the words.

Zander's voice was grim. *He's alive. It's a good thing he's got a hard head.*

Alice blinked her eyes to get rid of the sudden moisture and found she couldn't speak past the lump in her throat. She patted Zander's shoulder instead.

I don't think they'll follow us, but just in case, I'm going to take a different way back.

The Jabberwock's route took them twice as long as the flight to the Looking Glass. Instead of the ledge she'd become used to, Zander banked towards the face of a cliff.

Duck down.

The voice scraped across Alice's mind, and she threw herself forward as Zander stretched out his wings to slow them, arrowing towards what looked like solid rock. Alice squeezed her eyes shut as he slid into a narrow opening and skidded to a stop, his landing awkward as he balanced on one foot. The cave was shallow, but tunnels branched out from it, twisting into blackness.

If I give Chess to you, can you hang on to him? We're still visible here if someone is looking hard enough, so I'd rather get to a more protected place.

"Yes, of course."

When Zander twisted around, Chess hung limply in his jaws. Alice bit back a cry of alarm, then chided herself. This wasn't the time for hysterics. Instead, she held out her arms and took the lump of black fur.

I'm sorry, but you're going to have to stay low. This tunnel will be a tight squeeze for all of us, but it opens up to a larger cavern not too far from here.

Alice placed Chess in front of her, careful not to jostle him too much. He had hit that stone wall hard, and she didn't want to injure him any more than he already was.

The dragon slithered through a tunnel opening. He'd been right. It was a tight fit, and Alice's breath hitched in her chest as the walls closed in on them. The ceiling was so low she had to press herself almost in half, even as she tried not to crush Chess.

Zander pushed into the blackness, and Alice hoped he knew where he was going. The idea of getting lost down here made her aware of every ounce of the mountain above them.

They'd been walking for what felt like hours when the bundle of cat underneath Alice squirmed.

As delightful as I find being pressed up against you like this, love, I can't breathe.

Alice felt her face heat, and she scooted back to give Chess more room.

"Is your breathing better now?" Alice kept a steadying hand on the cat's body, and gnawed at her lower lip. She hoped this wasn't a similar case to what had happened at home when a horse had kicked one of their farm dogs. It had broken the poor animal's ribs, which was bad enough, but the bone had pierced a lung. By the time their coachman, Tom, had realized what the problem was, it was too late.

Now that you're not smothering me, yes.

"Are you in pain?"

Well, I can't say that I'm comfortable, but there's not anything we can do about it now.

The furry body's tremors belied Chess's casual words, and Alice's heart twisted for him. Her fingers twitched to check his injuries, but Chess was right. She'd have to wait until they were somewhere with light and space.

As if he could read her thoughts, his voice sounded in her mind.

I'll live. It's not that bad.

Alice snorted. "I'll believe that when I see it."

They lapsed into silence as the Jabberwock continued to push his way through the winding tunnels. After endless turns, they passed into a cavern, its ceiling illuminated by a writhing glow of pink. The dragon stretched his wings with a sigh. Alice slid from his back, her legs so stiff, she staggered. She put a hand on a large rock to steady herself. Chess didn't move from his place on the dragon's back. There was a grimace on his feline face.

Alice walked back over to him. The pink light of the cave gave her hands a faint glow. She looked up at the ceiling. The glowworms' constant movement made weird shadows and light patterns. She shrugged and turned her attention back to Chess. She ran her hands over his body and gently probed along his ribs and then his spine. On her second pass, she pressed harder and Chess snarled at her.

"Where does it hurt?"

Where doesn't it hurt? He shifted away from her.

She ran her hand back over his spine. It was almost like she could visualize the bones there. Chess growled, his ears pinned back, when she pressed harder on the lower portion just above his tail.

Are you trying to get back at me or something?

"I'm sorry. I know this hurts, but I need to see how bad it is." She paused before her shoulder muscles relaxed. His spine was only bruised, not broken, as she had feared. She wasn't sure how she knew with such certainty, but she did.

Chess tried to get to his feet but collapsed back down with a yowl.

"Can't you wait a minute?" Concern sharpened her tone. She ran a hand over his right shoulder, and he snarled.

Are you trying to kill me?

Alice rolled her eyes and turned to Zander, who watched with a furrowed brow. "I think he's knocked his shoulder out of place. The good news is, I think I can fix this." She paused.

What's the bad news, love?

She wrinkled her nose. "It's going to hurt like the dickens."

Chess hissed. *Are you sure you can do this? I don't much fancy being a failed experiment.*

Alice spread out her hands. "I've done it before, but the coachman was helping me. I've never done it alone before, but if we don't put the leg back in the socket, you won't be able to walk on it. Worse, if we wait, it could swell and make it much harder to fix."

Let her try, Chess. If you can't walk, you'll be helpless.

I'm not helpless. As if to prove his point, he attempted to stand, only to fall back down with a cry. He tried again with the same result.

Alice didn't comment. Zander wisely didn't either. They waited in silence.

Finally, Chess let out a loud huff.

Fine. Fix it, but you better not make it worse... He let the words trail off.

Alice bit back her smile, but her face soon turned serious again. She grasped Chess's back and took hold of his paw on the injured leg.

"On the count of three, I'm going to put it into place, all right?"

Just do it.

"One, two..."

A loud popping sound echoed off the cavern walls, followed by a yowl. Chess slumped onto the dragon's back, his eyes sliding closed.

After a moment, the rough velvet voice spoke with more than a hint of reproach. *You said on three.*

"It works better if you don't tense up as much," Alice said. "Let me make sure everything is as it should be."

Chess hissed at her.

"Don't be a baby," she said. "The worst is over."

Why don't I believe you?

Alice ignored him and slid her hands over the cat's shoulder. "It'll be bruised, but you should be all right now."

The dragon twisted his head in her direction. Even in the cavern, it was tight for him to maneuver. *Did you train as a healer?*

Alice shook her head and her mouth twisted. "Oh no, nothing formal like that. Tom, the coachman, has worked with animals all of his life. He's been kind enough to let me help him occasionally."

The dragon titled his head. *That seemed like more than—*

Much as I'd love to continue this discussion on the fascinating differences between our world and Alice's, I'd like to remind you we still have a curse to break. He gingerly got to his feet and stretched. *We also have a small complication.*

Zander leaned his head to one side. *What's that?*

Chess glanced at Alice and then back at Zander. *He saw me.* The two shared a long look.

Alice frowned. "Who saw you? The soldiers?"

No, the Commander.

"So? Surely, he's seen you before. Why does that matter?" Even as she said it, Alice realized Chess had managed to be absent every time the Commander appeared. Something tickled at the edges of her brain, something she should know.

Chess shook his head. *Look, it's not important.*

Alice snorted. "Well, you're the one who brought it up." She tapped her foot on the stone floor. "You may as well explain yourself."

There was a long pause and then Chess huffed. *He's my father.*

Alice felt her eyes widen. How had she not put two and two together? Chess Felinas. Commander Felinas. Still, she could hardly believe it. "You're joking."

I can assure you, love, it's no joke being the Commander's son.

"I don't see why..."

No, you don't, and you don't have to. Suffice it to say, now that he knows I'm around, it'll make things more... difficult. Chess leapt up onto a stony ledge and turned his back on her.

Heat rose up Alice's neck into her cheeks, and she crossed her arms. Zander glanced between them and sighed.

His father swore an oath to the King, that he would protect his wife after he was gone. It puts my uncle in a bad position.

The tickle in her mind came into focus. Alice glanced at Chess. "You're trying to protect your father."

Chess shrugged a shoulder. *It was just better that he didn't know I was cursed too, that's all.* He flicked his tail. *The important thing is breaking this curse, and there's only one person who would probably know how to do that. Now that we have Alice, we can talk to him.*

Steam rose from Zander's nostrils. *Don't start this again. Just because she can't go through the Looking Glass doesn't mean Alice should put herself in danger.*

Chess rolled his eyes. *She's got just as much vested in this as we do now. We need someone with the Seer Gift.*

Alice raised her eyebrows. "Seer Gift?"

I know your Gifts don't work the same way in the Mirror World, but surely you know what a seer is. Chess flicked his tail.

Alice didn't, but she wasn't about to admit that. Her confusion must have showed on her face, though, because Chess sighed deeply and he spoke very slowly, as if she was a bit simple. *Someone with the Seer Gift can see things, magical things.*

Zander blew out a hot breath. *Stop being a git, Chess. Besides, the Queen will know that's where we're headed. It's too dangerous.*

I'm not the one who's being a git, Zander. You—

"Oh for goodness' sake! You two are like an old married couple, constantly bickering." She held up a hand when Zander tried to speak "Look, I'm stuck here. Breaking the curse is the only way I'll get home. Of course I'm going to help." She turned to Chess. "Now, who is this you need me to talk to?"

Rough and velvet voices spoke at the same time. *The Mad Hatter.*

Chapter 32

SEVERAL HOURS LATER, ALICE stood at the edge of the clearing, wondering what she had gotten herself into. The small wooded alcove was quite beautiful, ringed with silver birches. The area dipped in the middle like a bowl, and a riot of wildflowers carpeted the grass, their blossoms glimpses of silver in the dark hours just before dawn.

In the middle of the clearing, a small shack leaned drunkenly to one side. Despite the dilapidated condition of the tiny house, the front door was a gorgeous swirl of carved wood. Just in front of the building sat a long table covered in a moth-eaten lace cloth. Haphazardly stacked plates and cups sat all along its length. Between the stacks, cobwebs glistened in the dim light of the stars. The place looked deserted except for a large black crow that was stalking up and down the table, spearing its beak at the dirty plates and tablecloth. The whole thing gave Alice the creeps.

He's probably sleeping inside. Chess butted his head up against her ankle.

"Are you sure there's anyone in there? It looks deserted."

You won't find that out cowering here in the shadows.

Alice raised her chin. "I'm not cowering. I'm checking the area out. Zander said that someone would likely watch the place."

Chess hissed. *Why do you think that crow is walking around?*

Alice wrinkled her nose. "You mean to tell me the crow is the lookout?"

Birds observe everything and nobody notices them.

"Well, he's being rather obvious. Besides, I can't just march up there if that bird's going to go tattle to the Queen."

Chess shrugged his furry shoulders. *By the time the crow reports back to the Queen and she sends her men out here, we'll be long gone.*

"Do you think so?"

The longer you stand here, the less time we have.

Alice hated to admit it, but the cat was right. She drew in a deep breath and took a cautious step out from the shelter of the trees. A low huff came behind her. She looked back over her shoulder. She could just make out the glint of Zander's eyes from where he hid deeper in the trees.

They had all decided that a Jabberwock showing up on his doorstep would not predispose the Mad Hatter to answer Alice's questions.

Alice nodded to Chess. Okay, it was time to get some answers. Without letting herself think about it anymore, she scurried across the empty meadow. When she reached the table, she gave it a wide berth, keeping one eye on the crow.

It stared at her with beady black eyes, tilting its head.

Hesitating in front of the door, she felt the crow's eyes drilling into her back. She lifted her hand to knock and found it was trembling. She closed her eyes, pressing her lips together.

A raspy voice made her jump.

Yes. Yes. Black hair. Violet eyes. The troublemaker has arrived.

With a loud caw, the bird lifted off the table with a flap of its large wings. He swooped low over her head.

Run, little girl, while you still can.

He arrowed off towards the trees.

Alice straightened her shoulders. The clock was now ticking. She didn't hesitate this time and knocked firmly on the door.

Nothing happened, so she knocked again, louder this time.

She heard someone moving about inside. Footsteps came near the door and stopped. She could feel someone looking out the peephole. She waited, trying to look friendly.

After a moment, she lifted her hand again just as the door swung open. She checked herself before she hit the person who had opened it.

"Banging, banging on my door, whatever for?" said the man. Alice blinked. His violently orange hair was styled in a huge pompadour. Perched on top sat an elaborate nightcap in an unfortunate shade of pea green. Alice didn't know quite how he held his head up straight, what with the pompadour and the hat. He wore a blue checked robe with a white fur collar. On his feet were slippers, also white and furred. He blinked pale yellow-green eyes at her.

"Answer me or off you be." He made a shooing motion with his hands.

"I beg your pardon?" said Alice, not quite sure what he had said.

The man shook his head and closed the door. Alice stuck her foot out to stop it. "No, please, Mr. Hatter, I need your help."

"Help from me, whatever can it be?"

Alice looked around the quiet clearing again and lowered her voice. "It's about the prince. You see, he's alive, but he's been cursed. You're the only one who can help him."

The man pulled his head back, and his eyes widened. "Why send you iffen he could say it too?"

Alice was beginning to understand the strange cadence of his words. "Well, that's part of the curse. He's... maybe you should come look for yourself."

After a pause, the Mad Hatter took a tentative step onto his stoop. She turned and waved towards the woods. After a moment, several trees rocked, and then the Jabberwock stepped out into the clearing.

A shriek sounded behind Alice, and she turned just as the Mad Hatter crumpled to the ground in a dead faint.

Chapter 33

"OH, NO!" ALICE DROPPED to her knees next to the prone man.

I hope his curse-breaking abilities are better than his looks. Chess sniffed at the Mad Hatter's hat where it lay next to the pompadour which had rolled off to the side. His exposed head was as bald as an egg.

"Oh, do be quiet," Alice snapped at Chess. He turned his back and sat on his haunches.

A rustling caused her to look up. Zander was creeping back into hiding. Maybe that was for the best. The Mad Hatter might have the Seer Gift, but he didn't have strong nerves.

She shook his shoulder. "Mr. Hatter, Mr. Hatter, please wake up."

He moaned and rolled his head, and was still again. She reached over and patted his cheek. "Come on now, Mr. Hatter. You need to wake up."

He didn't move, but after a moment, one of his eyes slitted open and winked shut again. In her mind, Alice heard the clock ticking. She didn't know how long they had, but she didn't want to spend precious minutes on a faker.

"I know you're awake, Mr. Hatter. You may as well open your eyes."

Instead of opening them, the man squeezed them shut more tightly. Alice blew out a breath. What was she supposed to do now? Before she could come up with a solution, the man yelped and sat straight up, grabbing for his ankle.

Chess stood near the man's feet, flexing his claws. He grinned at her. She should scold him for being so rude, but she had to admit, his method was effective. She turned her attention to the Mad Hatter, who was trying to hide behind her, his strange eyes scanning the clearing.

"Gone he be, so eaten not me?"

It took a moment to untangle his words before Alice nodded. "Yes, he's gone, and he won't hurt you. He's the prince. I told you, the Queen cursed him, and you're the only one who can help us."

The poor man shivered, but Alice pushed down her sympathy. Time was trickling away. She didn't have time to be polite. "Mr. Hatter, get ahold of yourself," she said, her voice stern. She stood and held out a hand to him. "Come now, stop shaking in the grass."

He glared at her as he scrabbled around for his wig. Jamming it on his head, he ignored her hand and stood on his own. One of his slippers had flown off, and he limped towards the door.

Afraid he'd disappear inside, she ran after him. She tried to grab his shoulder but, surprisingly agile, he evaded her grasp. She yelled after his retreating back,

"Where are you going? Are you really going to go hide in your house when you could save this Kingdom? I thought you had a Gift, but I guess everyone was wrong about you. You aren't a Seer. You're just a scared little man hiding in the woods."

The Mad Hatter paused in mid-stride and spun on his heel. His eyes sparked, and he lifted a hand, pointing a finger in the sky. "Tea must be for you and me!"

"I don't think—" But before she could finish the sentence, the man had dashed into his house and slammed the door.

Alice's shoulders slumped. She had made a right cake of things. She stood for a moment until a soft head butted against her leg.

Why are you standing there? That bird is almost at the palace by now.

"What would you like me to do?"

Go after him. I would think that's obvious. Chess tilted his head in her direction.

Alice heaved a sigh and marched back to the front door. Before she could even raise her hand, the door swung open again. She stared.

The Mad Hatter had exchanged his robe and slippers for an old-fashioned suit of brilliant purple. He wore an acid-green waistcoat that complemented the black-and-white checked stockings that disappeared into his breeches. On his feet, heeled shoes sported large sparkling buckles. A pair of spectacles sat on his button-shaped nose. Perched on his head was a large silk top hat, the exact pattern of his waistcoat and socks. The brim sported a tiny forest, complete with miniature squirrels scampering around and minuscule birds flitting among the trees.

Alice leaned in closer to get a better look, but the Mad Hatter clapped his hands and shouted, "Teatime!"

He held out his elbow and bowed his head in Alice's direction. "We shall to tea and all will be as you see."

Not knowing what else to do, Alice took his arm. She almost tripped over her own feet when she caught sight of the table. The dirty dishes and cobwebs were gone. Instead, plates and silver glistened in the moonlight. A large pot of tea steamed in the middle of the table, and delicate tiered plates held finger sandwiches and petit fours. Alice allowed the Mad Hatter lead her to the table and seat her.

Alice noticed that there were three place settings, not two. Chess leapt into a chair, answering her unspoken question. The Mad Hatter poured hot tea into all three cups. Alice wondered if a cat even drank tea. Then she gave herself a mental shake. She had to focus and get answers. It wouldn't be a straightforward process to get them from this man.

She took a sandwich from the offered plate. "Thank you, Mr. Hatter. This is lovely... and unexpected."

The man beamed at her. "Teatime all the time." He lifted his cup and slurped. She took a sip of her own tea. Ignoring the tiny sandwich on her plate, she set her cup down.

"Now, Mr. Hatter..."

"Alistair Baggins, I be."

"Pardon me," said Alice. "Mr. Baggins. As I mentioned before, we need your help, and I'm afraid we don't have a lot of time."

"Teatime, any time. Teatime before the sublime."

Alice opened her mouth, but Alistair held up a plump hand. He crammed an entire sandwich in his mouth and slurped more tea. Her shoulders sagged. She wasn't getting anything out of him until he'd had his tea. Resigned, she took a bite of her own sandwich, her eyes straying to the surrounding woods.

A velvety chuckle pulled her attention to Chess. He grinned at her. She narrowed her eyes. He had known all along what this would be like. He could have warned her.

The cat lapped at the tea, spilling some into the saucer. He used a paw to snag a sandwich and took a delicate bite. Alice shrugged. She was rather hungry. It had been a long time since she had eaten anything.

For a while, the only sounds were the clank of silverware and the sounds of chewing and, with Alistair Baggins, slurping.

Finally, the man sat back, burped, and put both hands on his stomach. He smiled at Alice, and she pushed her own plate back.

"Now that we've had our tea..." Alice began, but stopped as the Mad Hatter stood from his chair and climbed onto the table, his hat tipping to one side. He crouched over the large teapot and threw the lid over his shoulder.

Alice sat transfixed as the man took the tea pot and shook it first one way and then the other, peering into it as he did so. She exchanged a glance with Chess. He raised his eyebrows and shrugged a shoulder.

When he was done, Baggins looked up at her, his eyes glowing yellow. He dropped the tea pot and crawled over until he was right in front of Alice. She wanted to pull away, but she forced herself to meet his eerie gaze.

He pulled a tarnished gold pocket watch from his waistcoat pocket and looked at it. He shook it, put it to his ear and gasped. His gaze swung back to Alice's. He spoke in a singsong voice that made the hairs on the back of Alice's neck stand up.

Time, time ticks away
Flower red-and-white holds sway
Pluck at midnight
Blooms so bright
Breath of fire on the nectar
Melds the before and the after
Take them all to smear
Evidence of royalty will appear
None of Wonder the glass to take
Or the darkness will not break
Find the circle close at hand
Break it before falls the last sand

Before Alice could ask him to repeat the strange poem, a cry rent the air. She looked up and saw a blur in the distance. Chess leapt to his feet.

It's the Commander or the Queen. Either way, we have to go.

"But shouldn't we write that down?"

There's no time.

Alice shot to her feet, but the Hatter grabbed her wrist in a painful grip. She tried to pull away, but his fingers tightened. He pressed some pink and blue cubes into her hands and closed her fingers over them.

Pink, pink, pink
Eat to shrink

Chew the blue

Oopsie, you grew

He let her go just as quickly as he had grabbed her. The glow disappeared from his eyes and he sat back on his knees, a gentle smile on his face.

"Will you be okay?" she asked as she shoved the cubes into her pocket.

He nodded, his eyelids drooping. "Fine, I be, for not even the Red Queen can touch me."

A sharp pain on her ankle broke the spell.

If you want to stand here and wait for the Queen, go right ahead. I'm leaving.

Chess took off across the clearing. Alice gave one last glance at the strange little man curled up on the table, already asleep, before she whirled and followed Chess into the forest.

Chapter 34

ALICE'S GROWLING BELLY HAD woken her a short time before, and now the sun was high in the sky. The trio had returned to the cave in the early hours, just before dawn. Before they had fallen into an exhausted sleep, Alice had taken a few minutes to scratch everything she could remember of the Mad Hatter's poem onto the cave wall with a charred stick.

Now they sat next to the small fire eating some animal Zander had hunted down. With its purple fur, Alice couldn't identify what it was. She was so hungry, though, she didn't care. As she took another bite, grease dripped down her chin, and she wiped at it with the back of her hand. She bit back a grin. Mother would be appalled if she could see Alice now.

We should go over this poem so we can figure out what it means. Chess sat back, licking a paw and washing his face.

Alice swallowed and wiped at her mouth again before she got to her feet. She trotted into the cave, Chess at her heels, and read what she had scrawled across the cave wall. Parts of phrases and single words stood in for the lines of poetry. She pointed to the second line that read "red and white flower."

"That can't be right. It doesn't rhyme with 'away' at the end of this line." She banged a fist against her thigh. "If only I'd written it all down. We'll never remember it."

Chess cocked his head. *And I thought I was the pessimist in this relationship, love.* He got up and mumbled as he paced. *Time, time ticks away. Something... something holds sway.*

Alice snapped her fingers. "I've got it. Time, time ticks away, flower red and white holds sway."

Chess rubbed against her leg and purred. *That's it, or close enough. Now let's figure out the rest.*

It took Chess and Alice over an hour to piece together the entire poem. Zander laid down in the cave entrance and watched them.

Alice put down her charred stick with a flourish and looked at Chess, a smile spreading across her face. "I think we've got it." She cleared her throat and recited the three stanzas.

Time, time ticks away
Flower red-and-white holds sway
Pluck at midnight
Blooms so bright
Breath of fire on the nectar
Melds the before and the after
Take them all to smear
Evidence of royalty will appear
None of Wonder the glass to take
Or the darkness will not break
Find the circle close at hand

Break it before falls the last sand

Now, we just need to figure out what it means.

Alice's smile dimmed. "Yeah, I guess this was the easy part." She turned to Zander. "You didn't hear the poem, but you could help us figure it out. You'd have more of an idea about what this means than I do."

The dragon cocked his head. *I'm not very good at this sort of thing. Chess is the clever one, not me.*

Nonsense. The cat's velvet voice was impatient. *It's not that you aren't clever. You just never enjoyed doing any of this type of work. You need to learn to like it, though. Once you get that crown, you'll need to do more than fight with a sword to deal with all those nitwits at court.*

Zander shook his head. *I am who I am, Chess. Putting a crown on my head won't change that.*

Afraid they were going to get off track, Alice jumped in again. "What kind of flower is red and white and blooms at midnight? There can't be very many of those."

The Jabberwock leaned forward, and his scaly eye-brows furrowed. *That has to be a dragon blood lily.*

"Well. That was easier than I expected."

Chess and Zander exchanged glances.

Alice narrowed her eyes. "What aren't you telling me?"

After a long beat of silence, Zander's voice scraped into her brain. *It's not so easy. The dragon blood lily is rare and hard to find.*

Chess twined around the Jabberwock's legs, a sly smile on his face. *I wouldn't say that, Zan.*

Chess. The Jabberwock's tone held a warning.

Chess wheezed out a laugh. *We both know where we can find a dragon blood lily. You just don't want to go there.*

Zander's nostrils flared, but he said nothing.

Alice looked between them. "Will one of you fill me in? I'm tired of being the only person who doesn't understand what's going on."

Zander avoided her gaze. Silence stretched in the cave until Alice's temper snapped. She jumped to her feet.

"This is ridiculous." She twirled a finger to encompass all of them. "All three of us have good reason to want this curse broken. You both need to stop acting like children, and tell me where we can find this lily." Chess and Zander both looked down at their feet. Alice rolled her eyes and wished she could just go home and leave these two witless wonders and all their problems behind.

It was Zander who answered. *It's the Pearl Queen. She grows them.*

"Who's the Pearl Queen?"

The dragon turned his head away. *She's part of the other royal family. Such as it is.*

Alice narrowed her eyes. "Why didn't you just say so in the first place?"

Zander didn't answer, but Chess hopped to his feet and twined around Alice's legs.

Let's just say the Queen and Zan have a history together, and like most of Wonderland, she doesn't realize he's still alive.

"A history? You mean you were her beau?"

Alice didn't think dragons could blush, but the mortified expression on his face said otherwise. *Our... relationship was over by the time Lyssandra cursed me. I'm grateful she wasn't dragged into this mess, too.*

Chess sat on his haunches and grinned. *Queen Citrine and Zander have been making eyes at each other since they were both in the schoolroom.*

We were not. The voice in her head was a whip, and Alice winced.

"Wouldn't she be willing to help you? Or what about her family? If she won't help, maybe one of them will."

At first, Alice didn't think Zander was going to answer. Finally his voice rasped in her head. *She has no family left. That's why I don't want her help. She'd become a target.*

"No family?" Alice's heart squeezed. She knew what that felt like.

Her parents are dead, and her brother went to the Mirror World. He never returned.

"That's terrible she's all alone."

Zander nodded.

"I'm surprised the Red Queen doesn't go after her kingdom, then."

The Pearl Kingdom doesn't exist anymore.

Alice blew out a breath. Getting the full story out of Zander felt a lot like getting caramel out from between her teeth. "And why is that?"

Zander let out a smoky sigh. *Her family lost power a long time ago. The estate is still in the Pearl Mountains, but it's worthless, as far as land goes. Besides a run-down palace, it's overrun with creatures. They're drawn there. It's part of the legacy.*

Alice wanted to ask about these creatures and the legacy, but there wasn't time to indulge her curiosity. "Then what would one lily hurt?"

It's better if we don't involve her.

Alice gritted her teeth and turned to Chess. "Is there anywhere else we can find this lily?"

In the northern bogs, but it would take at least two days, even if we flew. Chess cocked his head. *And the moon will be full tonight.*

Alice turned to Zander. "I don't think you have a choice. We need to go to the Pearl Queen."

Zander stood up, and the horned ruff around his head flared. Fire danced behind his clenched teeth. *I can't.*

Alice exchanged a look with Chess. "You're going to have to."

Flames shot out of the Jabberwock's mouth and scorched the rock in front of Alice's feet. She leapt back with a yelp. Chess arched his back and hissed.

Zander's eyes widened, and he snapped his mouth shut. The flames winked out.

I'm... I'm sorry. I'm so sorry. I don't know— He swung his head wildly from Chess to Alice before he backed away.

What is wrong with you? You almost burned Alice to a crisp! Chess's ears were flat against his head, his teeth bared.

Zander shook his head. His eyes dilated. *I don't know. I didn't mean to...*

Alice stiffened her knees and forced her feet to move until she stood right in front of the dragon. She hesitated, willing her hand to reach out so she could lay her palm on his snout. He jerked and tried to turn away from her. She put her hands on either side of his head and guided his face back so they were eye-to-eye.

"*This* is why we need to get the lily. Zander, you would never hurt me, but a Jabberwock might." She grimaced. "He's taking over, isn't he?"

Zander's eyes slid closed, and the steam from his nostrils warmed her face. His weary expression tugged at her heart. *If things go sideways, Citrine has nowhere to run.*

Alice leaned forward until her forehead touched the very end of his nose. "I know it's a risk, but I don't want you to lose yourself. I don't think Citrine would, either."

They stood that way for a long moment, and then Alice straightened and patted his nose. "Besides, I have a plan, one that will keep you both safe."

Chapter 35

THE WIND WHISTLED AROUND Alice. In her spot tucked behind the dragon's neck, it barely ruffled her dark hair as the prince winged his way towards the Pearl Queen's estate.

Alice kept repeating herself that it would be fine, that they'd get in and get out, but it didn't help the knot in her stomach.

"Are we almost there?" she asked.

Yes, the Pearl Mountains are just ahead. Remember, once we pass over the forest that surrounds the palace, the trees will awaken. They'll send the sentinels. You'll only have a very short window of time to get the lily.

Alice shivered. What was she getting herself into? Then she shook off her fears. This would work. She clenched her fists. It had to work.

She strained to see around Zander's muscled neck and gasped. A great shape loomed out of the darkness, glowing a pale, luminescent white in the moonlight. As they got closer, Alice realized it wasn't a reflection, but the actual rock was milky white.

They circled lower, and Zander coasted over the flank of the mountain, crowded with trees spearing into the night sky. Alice didn't have time to ask again how close they were because the forest of trees opened into a round clearing.

At its center was the Pearl Queen's palace. Alice hadn't been sure what to expect, but even from up here, it looked much more modest than the Red Queen's abode. In fact, it looked more like a sprawling manor house than a palace.

Zander coasted down downward, his big wings beating the air to slow his descent.

Alice scanned the clearing and the surrounding forest. "Where are these sentinels?"

They stay in the forest. There's a path, but nobody gets through without the trees waking them. That's why you need to hurry. I'm sure the trees have already done that.

"The trees?"

Do you really want to waste time on more explanations, love? Chess was in his usual spot, but with his black fur, he blended into the shadows of Zander's wings. Only his blue eyes were visible.

Zander banked sideways and glided to a stop just outside the forest line. Alice slid off his back. From the air, the clearing had seemed small. Now that she was standing in it, the pond seemed far away. She glanced towards the trees.

Go! Zander's voice in her head was urgent. *I can hear the creatures moving through the trees. You have little time.*

Alice gathered her skirts in one hand and took off at a sprint. The grass was short and the ground flat, but there was an imperceptible downward tilt from the tree line towards the house. The manor house lurked in the darkness, lights shining in only a few of the windows. Alice hoped nobody was looking out of them because the moonlight made her visible to anyone who might bother to glance outside.

She picked up speed, her feet hardly keeping up with the rest of her. The pond loomed in the distance. Through the sound of her own breathing and the thud of her footfalls, the faint brush of wings sounded at the edge of her hearing. A howl floated through the night air, making the hairs on the back of her neck stand up.

They're coming, Alice. I'll try to distract them.

A screech sounded far too close. She put on another burst of speed, almost losing her footing. The pond loomed up and, too late, Alice realized she was closer than she had thought. The downward slant of the ground worked against her as she tried to slow down. She stumbled towards the water. Throwing her weight back, she sat down, her tailbone jarring into the turf, but it had the desired effect. She slid, slowing at the very edge of the pond, one foot splashing the surface. Before she could yank it out of the water, she had lost one of her shoes. The water sloshed, and the lily closest to the edge floated out past her reach. Alice grunted and scrabbled to her feet. The howls of the guardians grew closer. Resolutely, she turned back to the pond.

The lilies floated closer to the shore, but when she reached for the flower, it was still too far away. Dropping to her belly, she was just able to snag the edge of a large leaf. As she pulled it towards her, something swooped over her and growled. Cold snaked up her spine, and she froze, the lily's leaves dripping water.

A series of yips made Alice jump.

She spotted movement off to her left at the edge of the pond. A wolf-like creature was crouched low. A responding grunt behind her made the creature on the other side of the pond slink forward. Her hand holding the lily shook as she scrabbled to her feet and turned towards the animal creeping up behind her. Terror clawed up her throat as she forced herself not to run.

The creature that stalked towards her was tall, its head almost to her shoulder. Its jet-black fur melded with the night, and its sharp wolf-like muzzle wrinkled to reveal long fangs. Its sleek leather wings flexed while its sharp-tipped tail whipped from side to side.

Zander roared, and the creature cranked its head towards the sound, growling low in its throat. In one part of her mind, she could hear the sounds of a fight in the air above them, but her gaze was focused on the threat in front of her.

Off to the side, a twig snapped, and her gaze swung back in that direction. She swallowed hard as her eyes darted between the two wolves closing in on her, She backed up, and a wave of water hit the back of her heels. She shivered as she tried to keep them both within sight.

The animals tensed to attack at the same moment, as if synchronized. Suddenly, they froze, eyes opening wide. Both whined low in their throats before they turned tail and flew away.

A large drop of water plopped onto Alice's head and ran down the back of her neck, making her body shudder. Heart already racing, she whirled, only to see a large gray-green neck. Her eyes followed it up and up and up.

A pair of large, fathomless eyes looked down at her from far above.

Chapter 36

ALICE SWAYED ON HER feet, and darkness closed in on the edges of her vision. She clutched the lily in her hands, unsure what to do. The flying wolves surrounded Zander. Half a dozen of the creatures darted in and out, trying to land a bite or a swipe of a claw. He couldn't help her, even if she could run fast enough to get away from the thing in front of her. It looked a lot like a dragon with its long serpentine neck. The rest of its body was hidden by the rippling water of the pond, but based on how long its neck was, it was huge.

It blinked at her, its expression mild and a little curious. Alice slid backwards a step and then another, easing away from the edge of the pond. A rusty voice in her head stopped her.

Are you the one who woke me, child?

"I... I.... Yes," Alice stuttered out through lips numb with fear. She slid another step backwards.

It's been a long time since I was awake. The creature twisted its head around and let out a sigh. *Where is everyone? It's so empty.*

"It is midnight. I suppose everyone's asleep," Alice said, continuing to creep backwards from the pond.

The animal narrowed its eyes and looked at her more closely. *What do you mean, you suppose? Don't you live here? You must, if you're taking a dragon blood lily.* The voice had taken on a cranky tone.

A yelp sounded on the night air, and a torrent of fire lit up the sky. Several of the sentinels tumbled to the ground like flaming stars.

The creature in front of her looked from the sky and then back down at Alice. It shook its majestic head, and more cold pond water sprayed Alice.

Why is there a Jabberwock in the sky? I demand you tell me what is going on.

Alice tried to gather her wits and come up with a plausible explanation. It seemed that the animal didn't realize she was stealing the lily. Of course, it had just said it hadn't been awake for a long time so it would have no idea who she was.

"You know, I'm not sure. I just came out for this." She pointed at the lily in her hand. "And there was all this kerfuffle. I, ah, better go let someone know."

Before she could take more than a step, the serpentine neck darted forward, and his head blocked her path. The animal's snout snuffled over her. Alice's lungs ceased to work.

You smell like a stranger, not from the house of Pearl.

Ice skated across Alice's spine, and it was all she could do not to run. She doubted she'd make it very far. She only hoped to fool him.

"That's because I'm not from the house of Pearl. I'm visiting."

The enormous eyes narrowed again. He drew his head back and tilted it, considering her. *You have the Creature Gift, but you aren't from the house of Pearl?*

"That's right," Alice said. She continued to ease away now that he wasn't blocking her anymore.

Who are you visiting, then?

"Queen Citrine, of course. She'll be so jealous that I got to meet you." Alice was now several yards from the pond's edge.

The water guardian paused. *Citrine? It was young Peridot the last time I was awake.*

"Well, that was a long time ago. It's Citrine now." Alice tried to sound confident.

But how long has it been? The creature shook its massive head, sending another shower of pond water onto Alice.

"Years and years," Alice improvised, and then held up the large red-and-white flower in her hand. "She's waiting for this, though, so I'd best get going."

Yes, yes. The creature sank back into the water.

Alice's whole body sagged, and she turned towards the house. Her plan was to go around the back, and Zander could pick her up there.

She barely had time to register the splash before a row of sharp teeth appeared in front of her.

Before I let you go, answer this: What is my name?

"Your name?" Alice's voice rose to a squeak.

Nobody from the house of Pearl would be so foolish as to send you to my pond without knowing my name. Only a thief and an imposter wouldn't know it. Tell me and I will allow you to go.

Alice grimaced, her mind a blank.

"Erm, Citrine didn't say anything."

The roar blasted hot breath over Alice, and she squeezed her eyes shut.

You are a thief and a liar! The rusty voice rose to a boom in her mind, and she clapped her hands over her ears, splattering wet plant on her face. *Leave the plant, and I may let you live.*

Alice clutched the lily to her chest and gave up her pretense. "I can't! Please, I just need the one. We have to break the curse."

The creature's wrinkled lips drew back from sword-length teeth. Alice's breath froze in her lungs. She willed her paralyzed legs to run, but nothing happened.

"Grenmar! Enough!"

The clear feminine voice rang out from the courtyard. Alice peeked in that direction. A tall young woman was hurrying towards them, her red hair streaming out behind her like a banner.

She stopped next to Alice and pushed a pair of spectacles up her nose. The creature gave a large inhalation and then bowed in the woman's direction. Even though he wasn't talking to her, Alice could still hear him.

Pearl Queen. Granddaughter of Queen Peridot. It is an honor to see you.

The woman dipped her own head in response. "It is an honor for me to see you as well."

Alice's legs remained rooted to the ground, even though she knew she should take advantage of the distraction.

This thief woke me and was trying to steal from you.

"It's all right, Grenmar. I am happy to give her the lily." She glanced behind her at the fight still taking place in the sky, and her mouth thinned into a flat line.

The water creature tilted his head, his eyes narrowed at Alice. *If you are sure you do not need me...*

A smile softened Citrine's sharp features. "I'm sure. Thank you, Grenmar, for your faithful service."

The guardian bowed his head again and sank back into the water. Alice heard him give a loud *harrumph* before his head disappeared from view. The young Pearl Queen stared at the flat water of the pond and then turned a hard gaze on Alice.

"I should take my leave," Alice said. "I'm sure I've outstayed my welcome." She gestured towards the forest.

Citrine ignored her. Instead, she closed her eyes, a low hum rising from her throat. It took Alice a moment before she realized the flying wolves were peeling away from Zander and heading back towards the forest. Zander didn't pursue them. Alice eased away from the Pearl Queen, but she hadn't gone more than a few steps when Citrine's eyes snapped open. The other woman pinned Alice with her gaze.

"Before you go, I think you'd better tell me why there's a Jabberwock setting fire to my wolves and why you're stealing my lily."

Chapter 37

CITRINE TURNED AND WALKED towards her front door without even waiting to see if Alice was following. Alice hesitated and glanced towards Zander. He was hovering in the sky, and even from here, she could read the indecision in his body language.

With a sigh, she followed Citrine up the steps to the front door. It swung open, and a large wiry-haired dog strained to greet them, his tail wagging. A tall man Alice assumed was the Pearl Queen's butler stood at attention, holding both the door and the dog.

He bowed his head and in a placid voice, asked, "Would Madam and her guest like some refreshment? Cook would be happy to prepare something."

"That would be heavenly, Bliss, but I told you, you didn't have to stay up on my account." Citrine framed the struggling dog's head with her hands and stared into its eyes. After a moment, she leaned over to press a kiss on its head, and the dog dropped to his haunches, tongue lolling in a doggy grin. She turned to the butler. "Cook was probably in her bed, wasn't she? I'm perfectly capable of fixing..." She turned to Alice and raised an eyebrow. "Oh dear, I'm afraid I haven't even learned your name."

"Alice, my name is Alice."

"I can fix Alice and me a snack in the kitchen."

Alice held out her hand to the dog, who gave it a big slurp with its huge tongue. His joy rolled over her as the word *friend* repeated like a chant in her head. She couldn't help but smile as she scratched the dog's ears.

The young queen smiled at Alice. "Seamus likes you, and he's an excellent judge of character, aren't you, boy?" The dog's large tail thwacked against the walls.

"If Madam wishes, I will serve her and her guest in the library."

The young queen sighed, but a smile tugged at her mouth. "I suppose you and Cook won't go to bed, even if I insist on fixing my own food."

The butler drew back his head, and his eyebrows climbed towards his hairline. "It won't be necessary for Madam to go to the kitchens." Alice bit back a smile at the look of disgust on the man's face. You'd think the Pearl Queen had suggested she go empty all the chamber pots.

"Bliss is right about one thing," the other woman said. "The library is much cozier." Citrine slid her arm through Alice's and led her towards the back of the house. Alice wasn't sure if the woman was being friendly or if she was trying to keep Alice from escaping, but at this point, she wasn't sure it mattered. As they wound their way through the sprawl of the first floor, Alice could see that at one time, the Queen's home had been quite lavish. Now, though, it looked shabby in the lamp-light.

"Things aren't as grand as they used to be when I was growing up," Citrine said. Alice flushed at being so obvious in her perusal of the place. The Pearl Queen didn't seem to mind, though. "Since Mama and Papa died, I've let a lot of the staff go. It seemed silly to have so many people just to wait on me. But it has made things more difficult to keep up."

Something whooshed over Alice's head, and she ducked as a brightly colored bird landed on Citrine's shoulder. The Queen's face lit into another brilliant smile, and she reached up to scratch the bird's scarlet chest feathers.

"This is Pierre. Isn't he divine?"

Alice nodded and then ducked as something else swooped over her head. Citrine chuckled and wagged a finger at the enormous raven that was perched on the wall lantern. "You can tell the rest of them we have a guest and her name is Alice, but I don't want anyone disturbing us."

The raven tilted his glossy black head, his beady eyes seeming to drill a hole in Pierre.

Citrine rolled her eyes. "You know Pierre's nest is in the library." She waved a hand. "Now leave us, please."

With a flutter of black wings, the raven sped off and disappeared around a corner.

Citrine smiled at Alice. "Ravens are always terribly nosy."

Alice felt tongue-tied, so she nodded.

When they reached the library, Citrine gestured for Alice to go in. A huge fireplace, in which a fire crackled, dominated one wall. Two plump chairs nestled close to the fireplace, their floral patterns faded. Stationed in front of one chair, a round footstool rested. The other three walls of the room had floor-to-ceiling shelves of books. It was only when a shadow moved that Alice realized that there were dozens of cats of all shapes and sizes lying amongst the shelves.

She looked around, wondering what other creatures would pop up. On one side of the room stood a sturdy oak table. Papers, pens, and inkpots were scattered across its surface.

Citrine gestured at the chair with the stool and took the other one for herself. "I'm sure you're all done in after your run-in with old Grenmar. Who knew he was so cranky?"

Feeling slightly hysterical, Alice swallowed down a bubble of laughter. She wasn't sure what to think of the Pearl Queen's sudden friendliness. She had seemed almost angry outside. Alice's brain felt tired trying to keep up.

"I believe he thought, at first, I was one of the family. It wasn't until he realized..." She trailed off and looked down at the lily she still clutched in her hand.

"You were stealing one of *my* lilies from *my* pond?" the other woman finished for her.

Alice's eyes flew to Citrine's, and her shoulders tensed. Zander said he thought she'd help, but what if she was still upset with the prince? Or what if she just didn't want to get involved? Citrine must have seen Alice's hesitation because she gave a half smile. She pointed to the flower that was dripping pond water on

Alice's dress. "I'm guessing you need that to help the infamous Jabberwock somehow?"

Alice didn't see any reason to deny it. "Yes."

Citrine wrinkled her nose and pushed her glasses up. "What I am wondering is, why?" She tilted her head. "You clearly aren't from here, and the rumors are flying about the girl from the Mirror World who is conspiring with the Jabberwock to bring down the Kingdom."

Alice clutched at the lily. "But... how...?"

Citrine lifted both eyebrows. "You'd be surprised how quickly things like that travel, even all the way out here. Birds are the biggest gossips."

Alice remained silent, her mind turning over what she should and shouldn't say to this woman. Chess had argued that they needed her help, but could they trust her?

Citrine waved a hand. "Of course, I dismissed it all as ridiculous. After all, whyever would someone from the Mirror World come here? And to conspire with the Jabberwock would mean the person would have to have the Creature Gift. It all seemed so illogical." She paused and tapped a long finger against her mouth. "And yet, here you are. With the Jabberwock and with the Creature Gift. I must admit, I am quite puzzled by it all."

The Pearl Queen leaned forward, her eyes sparking with an emotion Alice couldn't identify. "I need you to tell me why the Jabberwock is here, Alice. Why do you need that lily?"

Alice took a deep breath and decided. Zander wasn't here, and they needed this woman's help, even if he didn't agree. She needed to tell Citrine what was going on and hope that the other woman really was an ally.

Citrine sat back and let out a puff of air. "You don't trust me."

"No, it's just—"

Before Alice could get the words out, Citrine's hand snaked out and clamped onto Alice's wrist, twisting it so her palm was face up. Alarmed, Alice tried to pull away, but Citrine's grip was like iron. The firelight glinted off a small knife that had materialized in the Queen's other hand.

"I think I know how I can help you with that."

Chapter 38

BEFORE ALICE COULD REACT, Citrine drew the knife down her own palm. She squeezed her hand into a fist, and several drops of bright-red blood splashed onto Alice's own palm. She winced at the contact.

The Pearl Queen's gray eyes were large behind her glasses, her expression intense. "On my blood as a woman of the house of Pearl, I will tell the truth and deal honorably with you and any information you share with me."

She held Alice's gaze for a long moment before her face cleared and she leaned back. She snatched a napkin off the trolley and wrapped it around her palm. "There, now you understand you can trust me and speak freely."

She beamed at Alice, who drew her hand back and wiped off the blood. That seemed a bit... unnecessary, but any doubt she'd had evaporated. It was obvious the woman took honor seriously.

"The Jabberwock flew me here so we could get this dragon blood lily. He needs it." Alice cast about for a way to break it gently that the prince was still alive and flying around outside. But she didn't have to worry about that.

"That's not really a Jabberwock, is it?" The truth shimmered in Citrine's eyes.

The muscles in Alice's neck and shoulders relaxed. She may not have all the pieces, but the Pearl Queen knew... something.

Alice shook her head. "No, it's not. It's... the prince."

Citrine closed her eyes briefly as if absorbing a blow. Alice pressed on into the silence. "The Red Queen cursed him, and if we don't break the curse before midnight on his birthday, she'll become the permanent ruler."

Citrine's chest rose and fell as she took in the new information. Her mouth pressed into a tight line. "All this time, and he didn't come to me. When I could help him. Why would he do that?"

Alice shrugged helplessly. "He was trying to protect you."

Citrine's eyes flashed, and she clenched her fists. "Protect me?" She jumped from her chair and stalked back and forth. "Oh, I should have known. Of all the pigheaded, foolish..." She whirled back towards Alice. "And now he's wasted almost an entire year because of that blasted chivalry of his."

While Alice couldn't blame Citrine for her hurt and anger, she had some sympathy for Zander's feelings, too.

"To be fair, the Red Queen is rather... unpleasant."

Citrine flung herself back into the chair. "Unpleasant?" She gave a bark of laughter. "That's rather an understatement. She's a wretched witch, is what she is. I just didn't realize it was quite literal until now." She waved a hand and the scarlet bird now perched on the back of her chair flapped its wings and flew up to a nest tucked into the corner of a shelf. "Of course, everyone recognized she was marrying the Red King for power. The man was old enough to be her father." Citrine rolled her eyes. "Unfortunately, that kind of thing happens all the time." She gave a delicate shudder. "I'm so glad Papa and Mama didn't offer me up on the matrimonial altar to some old man—but I'm getting off track. Tell me, why do you need this lily? Is it part of breaking the curse?"

Alice nodded. "The Mad Hatter gave us this riddle, and it's clear we needed this lily. I don't know how we're supposed to use it, though."

Citrine leaned forward, her eyes bright. "A riddle? Tell me how it goes."

Alice recited the poem to the other woman. After having gone over it so many times with Chess, it came easily to her now.

Time, time ticks away
Flower red-and-white holds sway
Pluck at midnight
Blooms so bright
Breath of fire on the nectar
Melds the before and the after
Take them all to smear
Evidence of royalty will appear
None of Wonder the glass to take
Or the darkness will not break
Find the circle close at hand
Break it before falls the last sand

Citrine listened intently and then closed her eyes, humming under her breath. Alice waited. An awkward silence stretched out. Just as she was about to say something, the Pearl Queen's eye popped open, and she jumped up from her seat. Darting over to a bookcase on the far wall, she scrambled up the ladder that ran on a track around the room. Near the top shelf, she turned to look down at Alice.

"I think Zander must have been Creature Cursed, but I don't quite remember..." She ran her hand along the spines before pushing herself further down the shelf. Alice watched as Citrine used the ladder to zip around the room, stopping now and then to peruse the titles.

Finally, Citrine let out a loud huff and clambered back down. "There's a volume somewhere that talks about how to reverse that curse. I remember Mother consulting Father about it for some poor chap when I was a child." She frowned. "There's more to it, though. I just can't remember what it is."

Alice sank back into her chair. Disappointment and weariness washed over her. She had hoped Citrine would have a simple answer.

Citrine plopped back down into the chair. "Don't despair, dear. I think I know where to find that old book. In the meantime, the riddle doesn't seem that difficult to figure out, at least for the first part."

Alice gave a wan smile. "I hope you're right, but we don't have a lot of time."

"The first thing you need is right here." Citrine tapped the lily. "And honestly, the next part isn't too difficult. The nectar has to come from the lily, and the breath of fire must come from the Jabberwock himself. The last stanza is a little more tricky to decipher, though, but I'm sure—"

The door creaking open interrupted Citrine.

"I beg your pardon, Madam," the butler said, giving a grave bow with his head, "but there is someone to see you outside."

Citrine wrinkled her nose. "Outside? Why don't you show whoever it is in?"

"I'm afraid your guest won't fit." He nodded his head towards the tall library window. Citrine looked startled for a moment, and then her eyes narrowed.

Alice followed her gaze to find the Jabberwock staring through the glass.

Chapter 39

CHESS WATCHED CITRINE MARCH towards them. He didn't know if he should feel sorry for Zander or enjoy the show.

Citrine wrenched open the window, and even from his perch on Zander's back, Chess could see her gray eyes flashing. With her flushed cheeks and red hair curling wildly over her shoulders, Citrine probably didn't realize how pretty she looked. He understood her well enough to keep that tidbit to himself, though.

With a smirk, he hunkered down and waited for the show to start. He didn't wait long.

Citrine stuck a long, slender finger under Zander's nose and shook it. "You, Zander Phillipe Royce Alivaras, are a complete and utter idiot!"

Zander gave a loud snort, but Citrine waved that finger at him again. "Don't even try to excuse yourself. There is no excuse. It's been a year. A whole, entire year, and I thought you were dead." She paused, her mouth working. "I cried for you, Zander. Me! You know I hate crying above all else, and yet you let me believe you were dead! How could you?"

There was a long silence.

"Well? What do you have to say for yourself?"

I wasn't sure if you were done berating me, Trinny.

Citrine crossed her arms, her eyes narrowed. "Don't expect you'll soften me up with that old nickname, either." She tapped her foot. "I'm waiting for an explanation, Zander, and it had better be a good one."

The window was narrow, but Zander pushed his head closer and nudged Citrine's arm with the end of his nose. She batted it away and took a step back so she was out of reach.

Trinny... Citrine, if I had come to you for help, I'd have put you in terrible danger. I couldn't bear the prospect of anything happening to you.

Citrine opened her mouth, but Zander kept talking. That was a good move on his part, and Chess patted the scales underneath him as encouragement.

You know Lyssandra and what she's like. Before I even realized how poisonous she really is, you had already taken her measure. You might have helped me talk to the Mad Hatter, but you can't break the curse. Only someone from the Mirror World can do that. Chess has been telling me that from the beginning. Zander lifted a scaly shoulder. *Since it was the Queen that told him, I didn't believe him... but the riddle seems to back that up.*

"I could have at least interpreted this poem for you, instead of leaving it to the very last minute."

Yes, but, Trinny—the benefits of you knowing didn't come near to outweighing the risks for you. You're all alone up here.

"I have my creatures. I'm not helpless!" Citrine's body was still stiff, but some of the heat had gone out of her words.

I didn't say you were. But you're not invincible, either. Zander lowered his head again, pushing his snout through the open window.

Chess saw the anger drain out of Citrine. She took a step forward and laid a slender hand on the Jabberwock's snout. They stayed there for a long moment, staring into each other's eyes.

After what Chess deemed an appropriate amount of mooning, he pranced over Zander's head and leapt into the room. He sauntered over to Citrine and rubbed up against her leg.

It's good to see you again, Citrine.

She looked down at him and shook her finger at him next. "I notice you got caught up in this curse nonsense, too. Why am I not surprised?"

I wouldn't be a very good friend if I let Zander be banished all by his lonesome, now, would I?

Citrine scowled, but her eyes twinkled. She raised an eyebrow. "Don't assume you're off the hook, Chess. You should have talked him out of this foolishness."

Chess sat in front of her and grinned. *You underestimate my influence, and in this form, I certainly can't outmuscle him.*

Citrine laughed and scooped him up into her arms. He purred and shot a sideways glance at Zander. Steam rose from the Jabberwock's nostrils, but the prince didn't show any other sign of emotion. Still, no need to torture the man. Chess squirmed until Citrine set him on his feet. Then he scampered over to Alice and leapt up into her lap. He turned in a tight circle before he settled into her lap.

"Make yourself at home." Alice's tone was dry.

He grinned up at her and purred.

Now that you've all got that out of your system, can you help us with this blasted riddle, Citrine?

"I'd love to do that, Chess, but as I was telling Alice, the book I need isn't here."

There are more books somewhere else? Chess raised an eyebrow.

Citrine laughed. "Yes, believe it or not, Mama packed away her older books."

Chess stood and swished his tail. *I don't mean to be rude, but we're rather tight on time.*

"I've a good idea where it is, but it'll take me some time to sort through things. You all look like you need some rest."

Chess sighed. *I suppose you're right. We may as well sleep while we can.*

He hopped off Alice's lap and walked towards the library door.

Citrine stood and grabbed a nearby candle. "I suppose you'd like to get settled now. Let me show you to a guest room." She glanced over her shoulder and said, "I'm afraid, Zander, the only place big enough to accommodate you is the stables. You're welcome to try them."

Zander drew his head away from the window. *As much as I appreciate your hospitality, it would be best if I found somewhere else to stay. I doubt any of your horses would welcome my presence.*

"Well, we shall see you in the morning, then." Citrine walked towards the door of the library without another backwards glance, and Alice followed her. Chess was already waiting for them in the hall, weariness weighing on him.

Citrine led them down several hallways and up a set of stairs. By the plainness of the stairwell, Chess surmised this had previously been the servants' stairs.

Citrine reached the top of the staircase and pushed open a door. They walked down a hallway, the once beautiful carpet runner dusty and threadbare. "I'll just get you both settled into guest rooms. Goodness knows there are plenty to choose from."

She stopped in front of a door and turned to Alice. "This room should suit you well enough." She turned the handle and pushed open the door. The room beyond was simply furnished with a four-poster bed, a dresser, a plump green chair, and a plain dressing table over which hung a round mirror, its frame wrought iron. "There are nightclothes in the top dresser drawer, and Bliss will bring you up some hot water for a bath and some of my things to wear." Alice murmured her thanks and stepped into the room. Chess followed at her heels.

Alice frowned down at him. "What are you doing?"

Chess grinned. *Getting settled in a guest room?*

With her foot, Alice pushed him back into the hallway. "I don't think so. Don't forget, I know you're not really a cat. Go find your own room."

Just before she shut the door in his face, Chess caught the half smile on Alice's face. He let out a purr of satisfaction.

Citrine gave a hum of surprise. "Oh, I understand. That's how it is."

Chess stood and sauntered down the hall towards the next room. *I have no idea what you're talking about, Citrine.*

She chuckled. "Of course you don't."

Chapter 40

A SCREAM JERKED CHESS from sleep. He blinked and tried to orientate himself. A loud thump from the room next door shot adrenaline through him.

Alice!

He leapt from the bed and bounded out into the hall-way. When he pushed Alice's door open and peered into the dim room, he could make out her form on the bed, twisting and thrashing. Another scream made his fur bristle.

He scurried across the floor and jumped up next to her on the bed. An arm came out of nowhere and knocked him back to the floor. He landed with a thump, and his bruised spine protested.

When he looked up, Alice was peering over the edge. Her face was white and her eyes shadowed.

"Are... are you all right?" He could hear the tremor in her voice.

He grinned up at her in the dark. *Don't worry about me. Cats always land on their feet.* He shook himself and leapt back up next to her. *The bigger question is, are you all right?*

She scooted towards the headboard to make more room, and he settled next to her hip. "I'm fine." She stroked a hand down his back, but her body trembled. He pressed into her leg and upped his purr to a loud rumble. She sniffled, and Chess tensed. Tears always made him feel so helpless.

That must have been some doozy of a nightmare, love. Remind me to duck next time.

As he intended, she gave a soft laugh, the sound watery. Then her fingers dug deeper into his fur and a shudder rippled through her. "It was horrible." Her voice was quiet.

Chess rubbed his head against her leg. *It was just a dream. You're safe now.*

"It wasn't me. It was you and Zander... you both died. And it was my fault." Her voice broke on the last word.

Chess sat up. *Whatever happens, love, it won't be your fault. There's many people at fault here, but none of them is you.*

"But I'm the one who's supposed to break this curse. What if... what if I can't?" Her fingers plucked at the blanket, and she wouldn't meet his eyes. "What if Zander loses himself? It'll be my fault."

Chess climbed into her lap and put his paws on her shoulder. Never had he longed so much for his human form. There were limitations to what you could do as a feline. *Look at me, love. If you want to blame anyone here, blame me. This whole thing is my fault, not yours.*

Alice's eyes widened and her mouth dropped open to form a little *o*. "Did you just admit you were wrong?"

Chess smirked. *Don't get used to it.* Then he sighed. *I knew what the Queen was before Zander did, and I didn't move fast enough to protect him.* He dropped his paws and sat back on her lap. He stared into her face, willing her to believe him. *And I dragged you here and put you in danger. We needed your help, but...* He looked down at his paws. *You deserved to have a choice.*

Alice blinked and wiped at her eyes. "I... thank you." She flushed and bit her lip. "And I'm rather glad you came along when you did. I mean, I'm not glad the Red Queen cursed you and Zander or that she wants to kill all of us. But I'm not sure how things with Hadley would have ended if you hadn't come along."

Chess's lip lifted into a snarl. *You mean that puffed-up idiot that was mauling you in the barn?*

Alice wrinkled her nose. "He is an idiot, but he's smart enough to have backed me into a corner—if he's telling the truth, that is. It's why I need to get back home, to see if what he said about Papa James is true." She sighed. "Not that any of that is your problem."

Chess figured getting Alice to talk about her life in the Mirror World would get her mind off of her nightmares. Besides, he was finding he had an urge to protect her. *You'd be surprised what I care about. What's the lout done?*

Alice bit at her thumb and peeked at him out of the corner of her eye. "He wants me to marry him."

The idea of someone like that claiming Alice as his bride made Chess's fur bristle. *You'll tell him no, right?*

"It's not that simple. Hadley's father is the head of one of the major banking houses in London. He said Papa

James took out a loan, and if I don't marry him—well, he insinuated..." Her voice trailed off.

He'll have his father call in the loan. Is that it? A growl rumbled up in his chest, but Chess swallowed it down. Instead, he rolled his eyes. *Are all the men in the Mirror World so asinine?*

Alice shook her head. "Oh no! Finn—that's my sister's fiancé —he's marvelous. He was a hero in the Great War, and if he ever found out what Hadley did, he'd pummel him right into the ground."

Chess felt something twist unpleasantly in his chest at Alice's glowing admiration of her soon to be brother-in-law. He sat up a little straighter. *Your problem is easy to fix. All you need is money.*

"It's only easy if you actually have money."

Chess grinned at her. *But I do, and Zander has even more. And he'll owe you if we break this curse. For that matter, so will I. Plus, there is the bonus I could break his nose a second time.*

Alice giggle and the sound spread warmth through Chess. She reached out and scratched him under the chin. "I couldn't let you do that, but thank you."

You don't want me to break Hadley's nose?

Alice smirked. "Oh, that part I'd be fine with." Then her smile fell away and her shoulders drooped. "All of that won't matter at all if I can't break this curse. If I don't, we'll all be doomed. You and Zander will lose your humanity, and I'll never get home."

Chess stood on his hind legs and pressed his head under Alice's chin. *Stop worrying. I didn't make a mistake when I picked you. I have an instinct about these things, and I think we've already established I am rarely wrong.*

Besides, you have Zander and Citrine and me to help you.

Alice's arms came around him and she pulled him closer, burying her face in his fur. After a minute, she set him back in her lap and wiped at her eyes with the backs of her hands.

Her mouth tipped up into a half smile. "Why are you being so nice to me all of a sudden?"

He stood and swished his tail. *I'm always nice to you, love.*

Alice rolled her eyes. "What a lot of tosh. I didn't even think you liked me."

Chess stared into her face. *That's never been the problem, love, trust me.*

She tilted her head. "I think I'm starting to."

The moment stretched, and Chess wished he could be human again, even for a little while. He shook off the feeling and stood up.

I should leave so you can get some sleep. Who knows what the next few days will hold?

Alice slid down until her head was once again on her pillow. She lowered her eyes. "I... I'm afraid to go to sleep."

I don't mind staying.

After a brief hesitation, she nodded her head, her cheeks turning pink.

Chess turned in a circle and settled himself on top of the blankets next to her. Her hand moved to rest on his back, her fingers clinging to his fur.

He didn't want to examine the warmth that glowed through him too closely, but as Alice's eyes slid shut and her breath evened into sleep, he realized what it was: happiness.

Chapter 41

A SCRATCHING SOUNDED AT the door of Alice's bedroom. She fumbled with the boot in her hand.

"Just a minute!"

They sent me up to retrieve you. Citrine is waiting along with our breakfast.

The sound of Chess's voice made her cheeks turn hot. When she had awoken this morning, he had been gone. She might have dreamt he'd been there at all, but a round indention in the covers said otherwise.

She didn't know if she could attribute her peaceful sleep to his presence or not, but she was thankful for it. At the same time, the idea that he had spent the night in her room sent waves of embarrassment over her.

Hopping on one foot, she pulled the boot on. Bliss had left them for her with a pair of trousers, a soft cotton shirt, and some underthings when he had the hot water toted to her room last night. She checked to make sure her shirt was tucked in all the way and then walked towards the door.

She grabbed the doorknob but then stopped. Turning, she took a last look around the room. Her eye caught on a pile of pale purple. She wrinkled her nose as she went over to pick it up. She held the dress at arm's length. It was beautiful. Her throat tightened. An image of an ax glinting in the sun flashed through her mind. She shivered, pushing the thought away. As far as she was concerned, they could burn the dress, but she didn't want to just leave it on the floor. She gave it a brisk snap, and something tumbled to the floor.

She squatted down. Four cubes, two pink and two blue, lay on the carpet, along with a pile of crumbly dust. She frowned. Oh yes, the Mad Hatter—! Alice picked up the cubes and turned them over. They looked like...

What's taking you so long? She jumped and almost dropped them.

"I'm coming!" Alice shoved the cubes into her pocket. She'd worry about them later.

When she opened the door, Chess paused in mid-pace. *It's about time! I'm starving, and Cook's outdone herself.*

She quirked an eyebrow. Thank goodness! Chess wasn't acting any differently. She gestured towards the hall. "I'd hate for you to starve to death. Lead on."

It surprised Alice when he led her, not to a breakfast or dining room, but back to the library. In daylight, she could truly appreciate the room with its tall shelves of books and tall windows that let in the morning light.

Citrine was sitting at the big square table. Bowls of food steamed all around her, but her plate was empty. She had pushed the jumble of papers, pens, and ink bottles off to one side, and she had a large leather book pulled in front of her and was skimming the lines with the finger of one hand. Her nose was almost touching the page, and her glasses had slid down to the end of her nose. She held a pen poised over a notebook with her other hand. She hadn't even heard them come in.

Alice and Chess had barely entered the room before Bliss slid in behind them, pushing a cart laden with bowls of fresh fruit. He clasped his hands behind his back. "Would Madame like me to serve?"

Citrine jumped, and a blob of ink landed on the notebook. "Oh, I didn't even realize you'd both arrived." She pushed her glassed back up her nose and left a smudge of ink on one cheek. "I hope you haven't been waiting long."

"Oh no, we just got here," said Alice. She walked over and took a seat at the table while Chess jumped up and sat next to a plate. He stared at the bowls and licked his lips.

Bliss removed the tops of the various bowls and served eggs and fried potatoes onto their plates. He placed a bowl of fruit in front of Alice and Citrine. He hesitated in front of Chess.

"Would sir care for fresh fruit?" the butler asked.

Chess shook his head, and Bliss poured everyone a cup of tea before trundling back out of the room.

Alice opened her mouth to tell Citrine *good morning*, but the other woman held up her hand. "I've almost got it."

Alice waited in silence as Citrine scribbled on the notepad. She checked the book several times, added a few words, and then shut the book with a bang and flung herself backwards in her chair.

Her smile was triumphant. "There! I found the book, but it was harder to find the curse. It wasn't the one I was remembering at all. In fact..." Her smile melted away and she frowned at Chess. "Tell me what happened when she cursed you. Were you in your human form or this form?"

Alice's eyes widened at the question.

Chess didn't answer at once. When he did, his voice was cautious. *I was a man, but when I came back to myself, I was in this form.* His eyes darted to Alice and then back to Citrine. *I couldn't shift back.*

Citrine's face paled and her mouth tightened. "Did... did the same thing happen to Zander?"

Chess gave her a level stare. "You'll have to ask him that."

Citrine held his stare, and her knuckles whitened as her grip on the arms of her chair tightened. Alice chewed a mouthful of egg. A buzz of tension filled the room, and she looked between Chess and Citrine. Shifting forms? What was going on here?

A loud bang at the window made all of them jump. Zander had arrived.

Citrine closed her eyes and gripped the edge of the table. After a moment, she pushed herself to her feet and stalked over to the window. She flung it open.

Zander lowered his head and pushed his snout towards her. *Good morning...*

Citrine shoved a shaking finger at Zander. "Do you have the Drifter Gene?"

Zander pulled back and eyed her warily. *Why would you ask me that?*

Alice noticed he hadn't denied it, whatever this Drifter Gene was.

"Just answer the question, Zander."

His gaze slid away from hers. *If you'll let me explain—*

"Just tell me—yes or no?"

After a long moment, Zander nodded his head once.

Citrine spun from the window and paced back and forth. As she spoke, she punctuated each word with a wild gesture. "All this time, and you never told me. You said you loved me. We talked about marriage—marriage, Zander!—and you never told me you have the Drifter Gene?" She flung a hand in Chess's direction. "Why didn't you trust me with this? I learned about Chess, and I kept his secret."

It's different for him.

"It's not different. In fact, it's probably worse. He's half fae. You know everyone watches him for that wild streak they're so afraid of. Yet, he shared that part of himself with me. Because he's my friend and he trusts me. Unlike you!"

He's not the prince.

"And you thought, what, I would betray you?"

Of course not, but I couldn't just tell you something like that.

"Actions speak louder than words, Zander. It's quite obvious you don't trust me. Not when it counts."

That's not true!

"It is true, and it's why you didn't come here when this happened, isn't it?"

Zander shook his head. *No, I told you I feared for—*

"Oh, you were afraid all right, but not for my safety." Citrine gave a bitter laugh. "The only person's safety you were worried about was your own. You were afraid I'd figure out your secret. You're a coward, hiding behind noble excuses!"

Zander's eyebrows lowered, and steam rose from his nostrils. His voice scraped like ice in Alice's brain. *Believe what you want, Citrine. I've only ever wanted what was best for you. If we had decided to marry, I would have told you. You were the one who broke things off. Or don't you remember?*

Citrine narrowed her eyes. "And you agreed it was for the best, for both of us."

Zander drew himself up and stared down his nose at her. *No, Trinny, it was best for you. Not me.* Without another word, Zander launched himself in the air and was gone.

Citrine gripped the windowsill with both hands and bowed her head, the anger leaking out of her body. Alice looked at Chess, unsure what to do.

Chess hopped down off the table and made his way over to Citrine. He twined around her legs. *He'll be back.*

Citrine spoke in a choked voice. "I don't know, Chess. How could he not tell me? Did he really believe I wouldn't..." Her voice broke and she wrapped her arms around her middle.

He should have told you, and you have every right to be angry. But you and I both realize if anyone found out, it could cost the royal family the crown. You understand how people are about the Drifter Gene. It doesn't mean he didn't—doesn't—trust you. Fear makes us do stupid things.

Alice bit back the questions that wanted to burst out of her mouth.

Citrine wiped at her eyes. Then she sniffed and straightened. She blew out a big breath and turned around. "We don't have time for all this nonsense. Finish your breakfasts. I'll be right back. I think I've figured out how to break the curse."

Chapter 42

ALICE PUSHED THE FOOD around on her plate. All the questions running rampant in her brain had chased away her appetite.

Chess looked up from his plate. *Are you going to eat that?*

Alice pushed it towards him. "Help yourself."

He didn't need a second invitation. He spoke between bites. *Go ahead and ask, love. I can see it's killing you not to.*

Alice felt her cheeks heat, but her curiosity won. "What did she mean, you are half fae?"

Chess gave the plate a last lick and sat back. *My mother was one of the flower maidens from the Queen's court.*

Alice's eyebrows lifted. "Really?"

I wouldn't lie about something like that.

She crumpled her napkin and then smoothed it out again. "But if they are part of the Queen's court, then why... I mean, Citrine seemed to imply that being fae is a problem."

Chess stood and stretched. *It's rather a long story, but the bottom line is, people fear the fae, even half-flits like me.*

"But why?"

Chess strolled across the table and sat down in front of her. *They think of them as wild and unpredictable. Add in the fact that they have multiple magical abilities, and...* He winked. *Let's say I don't advertise everything I inherited from my mother.*

Alice pushed some crumbs on the table into a little pile. Her mind flashed back to her conversation with Buttercup, the other girl's shorn wings. She wondered if Chess had wings, and she blushed. "If everyone is so afraid of them, why are they in the palace with the Queen? That doesn't make much sense."

Chess licked a paw and ran it over one of his ears. *The fae are beautiful and exotic. People like the idea of being around a creature they consider dangerous, especially if there's no real danger. The flower maidens are mild-mannered and one of the less... wild of the fae races.*

Alice wrinkled her nose. "Yes, Buttercup told me they had to have their wings clipped." She shuddered. "That sounds so... so uncivilized, I guess. I mean, you're people, not some kind of exotic pet."

That's the problem, though. People in Wonderland don't consider fae of any kind truly people. And that's why, besides my father and a few close friends, the only things people thought I inherited from my mother were my devastating good looks and undeniable charm.

Alice remembered her conversation with Buttercup and how the girl had seemed so surprised and grateful that Alice had even noticed her enough to ask nosey questions.

Chess butted his head against her arm. *I can see you have another question you're dying to ask. Go ahead. Unlike Zander, I won't go off in a huff of smoke.*

"All right, if you're sure." When Chess stared at her, she continued. "When you say *abilities*, what do you mean? Well, besides the cat thing, of course."

Chess grinned at her, and her eyes widened as he started to disappear, first his tail and then his back half until only a smile floated in front of her. And then that winked out, too. She hesitated and reached out her hand. She felt soft fur. A deep, rumbling purr sounded out of nothing, and he popped back into view, and she yanked her hand back.

"That... that's amazing."

It comes in handy.

Alice opened her mouth to ask more, but Citrine bustled back into the room. "Oh good, you're done." She came to stand next to Alice and pushed all the plates and utensils out of the way. Then she laid a small green book on the table. She tapped it with her finger. "This is one of my mother's journals." She rolled her eyes. "You don't know how many of those she had. I found this book on curses right away, but it took me practically all night to find the journal from the correct time period."

Alice ran her hand over the cloth cover. "You said last night you thought Chess and Zander were Creature Cursed." She hesitated, not wanting to bring up a sore subject. "Erm, you seem to have changed your mind."

"The Creature Curse didn't fit with what I found in the *Encyclopedia of Curses*. For one thing, Chess and

Zander should have been in the same animal form, and they clearly aren't."

Alice raised her eyebrows. "You have an encyclopedia of curses?"

Citrine scrunched up her nose. "Yes, of course. How else would you find out about a particular curse? Not that anybody is supposed to read up on curses. They're illegal to perform." She frowned at the book. "If people knew I had this, I might get in trouble." Her face cleared, and she waved a hand. "It shouldn't be a problem, even if someone found out, because I don't have the Alchemist Gift. I couldn't use any of them even if I wanted to. Which I don't." Citrine stopped and took a big breath. "Oh dear, I'm getting off track."

Chess chuckled and stretched out on the table. *Don't get her talking about her books, Alice. She'll never shut up.*

Citrine narrowed her eyes at him. "You should be thankful for that. How else would you find answers?"

Alice tried to bring them back on track. "So if it isn't this Creature Curse, what kind is it? I mean, as interesting as all this is, the important thing is breaking this curse."

Citrine pulled the large leather volume towards her and flipped through the pages to the one she had bookmarked. "The Red Queen used the Jabberwock Curse."

Chess whistled. *She wasn't playing around, was she?*

Alice leaned forward so she could get a better view of the book. It surprised her to see handwritten words scrawled in a small, crabbed script that had probably been hard to read even before the words had faded so much. "What's the Jabberwock Curse?"

Citrine pressed her lips together. "It prevents those with the Drifter Gene from changing back into their human form. Worse, the longer the curse lasts, the more the person loses their humanity and reverts to the creature whose form they've taken. This curse has caused a lot of problems, especially for those with that particular Gift."

Alice rubbed her temples. "I am completely confused right now."

Citrine plopped into a chair, her face brightening. Chess rolled his eyes. *Oh no, now you've done it.*

Citrine ignored him and leaned towards Alice. "All the people of Wonderland are born with a Gift, almost without exception. Some are born with more than one. My parents both had twin Gifts, and I do too. Those things run in families, as well as types of Gifts. One of those Gifts is the ability to change yourself from a human being to an animal. It used to be called the Drifter Gift. Now that it's banned, they no longer call it a Gift."

"How can they ban something you're born with? I mean, you can't help it, can you?"

Citrine grimaced. "If a parent learns their child has this ability, they hide it. Our Gifts are like muscles in many ways. If you don't use them, the ability gets weaker, and in people whose Gift wasn't that strong to begin with, they can lose the ability altogether."

Alice stared at the yellowed pages of the book. "So, someone could only use the Jabberwock Curse against someone with this Drifter Gene. Wouldn't it be simpler to stop people from using the curse?"

Citrine scowled. "It's stupid, isn't it?" She sighed. "But a century ago or so ago, one of the Red King's sons,

Gervais, was cursed. Nobody could break it because, at the time, only the fae could get to the Mirror World, and they weren't interested in helping us. The prince was stuck in his animal form for so long that he ended up losing his humanity. His Drifter form was also a Jabberwock, and as you saw, they are large and dangerous creatures. Gervais ended up going on a rampage in the south of the kingdom. He killed many people and burned down an entire village. The King had to stop him, but of course, he was reluctant to kill his own son. Phineas Sacklepenny was the one who came up with the answer. He had created the Looking Glass which allowed people to travel by simply stepping through it. It took a lot of tinkering, but he eventually discovered how to use it to get to the Mirror World. Sacklepenny was finally able to break the curse, but it was too late."

Alice leaned forward. "Too late? Why?"

Citrine's voice dropped to a whisper. "Because even though his body returned to his human form, the prince never regained his human mind."

Alice put a hand over her mouth. "That's awful. What happened to him?"

Citrine nodded. "They had to lock him away. Anyway, the King and Queen were so horrified by what had happened—not only to their son, of course, but also to the Kingdom—they banned the Drifter Gift." She bit her lip. "Zander is right to be afraid of people finding out. It's too close to what happened before. He really could lose his crown. I don't know if the people of Wonderland would tolerate someone with the Drifter Gene ruling them, especially since he's been cursed. It's their worst fears realized."

Chess yawned. *Which is why we need to hurry and break this curse before anyone finds out what really happened.*

Alice and Chess both looked at Citrine. Citrine smiled. "Tell me again what the Mad Hatter told you?"

Alice recited the poem again, finishing with, "Find the circle close at hand, break it before falls the last sand."

Citrine nodded. "Now that last stanza makes sense."

"Well, what about the circle? That could be anything!"

Citrine flipped open her notebook. "According to the book, the curse has to be contained in something clear, like glass or crystal. In order to break the curse, we need whatever glass ball or sphere that's holding it. We have the dragon blood lily. We'll need to heat it to extract the nectar and then smear that on the glass object. Mama wrote in her journal that the last step is to smash it, and that should release you both from your animal forms."

Chess stretched out and put a paw on the book. *That's fine, but how do we know where or what this container is? Something round and glass doesn't narrow it down much.*

Citrine offered an apologetic smile. "I'm still figuring that out."

Alice jumped up and paced around the room. Several of the cats on the shelves sat up and watched her. "The palace is enormous. It could be anywhere."

Chess sat up. *But could it? It has to be something the Queen keeps close at hand. So, we don't have to search through the entire palace. We just have to look at what the Queen keeps close by.*

Citrine jumped up and pointed at Chess. "That's brilliant!"

Chess smirked. *Charm, beauty, and brains.*

Alice rolled her eyes. "That's all well and good, but do you have any idea what it could be?"

Both Citrine and Chess deflated. Chess jumped off the table and wandered over to the windowsill. *If she keeps it close by, it has to be somewhere she frequents the most.*

Alice walked over and rested her forehead against the cool windowpane. "You would know more than I. Besides the dungeon, I only saw my bedroom and the Queen's garden room."

Chess stopped pacing and stared up at her. *I'm not the brilliant one. You are! I know what it is—it's that garden globe. She brought it with her from her home, and she always has it with her in her garden room. It's glass. It's round, and it's always close at hand.*

Citrine clapped her hands together. "It fits." Then she frowned. "But who's going to go get it?"

Chapter 43

ALICE CROUCHED NEXT TO Chess in a row of hedges at the rear of the palace. It was late, the full moon high over-head, but Chess wanted to make sure all the servants were asleep before they went inside.

The leaves behind them rustled, and Alice looked over her shoulder. She could make out the outline of Freddie, the night pegasus Citrine had asked to fly them to the palace. Its midnight-blue-and-black coat made it blend into the darkness.

Alice shifted, and the tools in her pocket clanked to-gether. "Can't we go in now? Nobody's been around for ages."

Just a little longer. Trust me, love, we want to be sure.

Alice shifted again and stretched out her left leg. It prickled as blood flowed back into it.

Would you be still?

"I'm not a cat—I can only crouch here so long."

Chess peered around one more time and then crept out into the open. He waved a paw at her, and Alice followed. They scurried across the courtyard, and Alice drew in a ragged breath when they reached the wooden door flanked on both sides by large, bushy pots of herbs.

Hurry up, but be quiet about it.

Alice rolled her eyes and fished out the two long hairpins she had brought. She knelt in front of the lock and inserted both pins. She could feel the tumbler, but the top pin kept slipping.

Hurry!

"I'm trying!"

I thought you said you were good at this.

She stopped and wiped her hands on her trouser legs. "Unless you want to have a go at it, can you just be quiet? I can't concentrate."

She pressed her lips together and jabbed the pins back into the lock, her face inches from the door. The back of her neck prickled, but she resisted the urge to turn around.

Instead, she bent closer still. The pin caught. Carefully, she pushed on the other pin, and something clicked. She sat back on her heels and grinned. "We're in."

She grasped the doorknob, but Chess stopped her. *Wait, we don't want any surprises.* He pressed a furry ear to the door. Alice stared into the empty courtyard, her eyes flicking to the hedges and various outbuildings. She hoped nobody needed to relieve their bladder or had decided to meet a sweetheart. She studied the shadows by the stables. It was too far away to see clearly, but nothing moved.

Something brushed her hand and she bit back a yelp. It was Chess.

Come on! I thought you were the one in a hurry.

Alice bit back a retort. The sooner they could get in and get out, the better. She didn't have good memories of the palace, and the sooner she was away from the place, the better.

She pushed the door open. The hinges creaked, and she cringed. Chess ignored it and stepped inside. She followed on his heels.

The kitchens were dark and empty, but the large table in the middle of the room was mounded with food. Chess leapt up next to a tray of custard tarts.

"What are you doing? We don't have time for a snack!"

Chess ignored her and continued to nose around. After a few minutes, he jumped back down.

I can't believe it!

"Can't believe what?" Alice asked as they skirted the large table and slipped into the butler's pantry.

Chess paced back and forth, shaking his head. *She's having a ball. The Red Queen has the gall to hold a coronation ball for herself.* He paused to point Alice towards a desk in the corner. *There should be a candle here somewhere.*

Alice found one in the top drawer. She had to rummage longer to find the matches and sandpaper. "Don't most royalty hold some kind of celebration when they're crowned?"

Well, yes, but you'd think she'd want the deadline to quietly pass without a lot of notice.

Alice shrugged. "She doesn't seem the type to let anything pass without a lot of notice."

Chess chuckled. *You're right about that.* Then he noticed her fumbling with the matches. *Don't light it yet. Wait until we get into the servant's hallway.*

She slid them into her pocket and followed him to-wards a shadow. As they got closer, it morphed into a doorway. He slid through, and Alice shuffled after him. It was inky black in the narrow hallway, and she groped for the wall.

"Wait, let me light this candle."

Not yet. Someone might see it if they come into the kitchen.

Alice's palms dampened, and she gripped the candle tightly. With her other hand, she felt along the wall. She could no longer see Chess. Blackness yawned in front of and behind her. She scuttled forward, her nerves jumping at every creak of the palace.

Time ticked out one tentative step at a time. Finally, Chess's disembodied voice floated out of the darkness.

I think it's safe now.

She pulled the match and sandpaper out of her pocket and fumbled to get the candle lit. The small flame illu-minated a plain hallway. Alice's chest loosened.

Chess trotted down the passage and made several turns before he stopped. Alice had to do a quick sidestep so she didn't step on his tail.

This will take us to the garden room. We'll search there first.

Alice held up her candle. She frowned. It was a large panel, not a door. It took a moment before she saw the recessed handle. The door slid open without a sound, and they were in the Queen's garden room.

Moonlight filtered through a large glass window set in the ceiling onto the trees and plants, casting the cav-ernous room in shadows. The splash of the waterfall was the only sound in the room.

Chess stepped out of the passageway, but Alice hesitated. An uneasiness settled in her stomach. She pinched out the flame before she followed him into the room.

"Where should we look first?" Alice whispered.

Chess shrugged a shoulder. *It could be anywhere, but if I were a betting man, I'd lay odds it's near the waterfall. She and her maidens spend a lot of time there.*

That made sense. It was where she had met the Queen. They walked down the pathways made by the pots of trees, flowers, and plants.

A branch crackled, and Alice stopped. "Did you hear that?"

There are birds and other little creatures in here. It's fine.

Alice's eyes darted around. Did that shadow move?

"Chess, I don't know..."

Come on. The waterfall is just around here.

Alice followed, and they stepped out of the path into the little clearing by the waterfall. There it was. The globe rested on a wrought iron pedestal next to the moss-covered seat where Alice had first met the Queen.

Alice moved towards it, but Chess stopped her. *Let me check it out. The Queen isn't stupid. She might have put some kind of protection on it.*

He circled the pedestal, his tongue flicking in and out and his tail lashing. Eventually he nodded at her. *Grab it and let's go. I don't know if your paranoia is making me nervous, or what. The sooner we're out of here, the better.*

Alice plucked the globe from the stand. It wasn't large, about the size of a cantaloupe. The back of her neck prickled, and Alice stopped. She looked around. Except for her and Chess, the room seemed empty.

Off to the left of the path, leaves rustled. Alice swung towards the sound, the globe clutched in her hands. Two eyes glowed from the shadows.

Chapter 44

"Chess, I think we have a problem."

Stop making me nerv— He broke off as he turned and caught sight of the eyes. He swore as a shriek shattered the silence. A large griffon bounded out of the shadows.

Grab my tail and whatever you do, don't make a sound.

"Shouldn't I try to, I don't know, talk to it?" The Commander's griffon had been somewhat friendly, so maybe—

No! Chess glared at her and waved his tail at Alice. She latched onto the furry length as it was disappearing from view. She bit back a cry when her arm and then the rest of her faded into nothing.

Chess bounded up the pathway in the opposite direction from the griffon. Alice struggled to keep up and not drop the globe. It was surprisingly disorientating to run when you couldn't see your feet. Chess raced back into the room's jungle of plants.

Behind them, trees toppled over as the griffon pursued them. Chess led Alice around the edges of the room until the griffon was in front of them. Alice saw the tops of the potted trees moving, pinpointing its progress.

"Can't we just hide somewhere until it, I don't know, forgets about us?" Alice's voice was barely a whisper.

The question was no sooner out of her mouth than the trees in front of them stopped moving. Her stomach clenched. The creature reversed directions and headed their way.

I told you to be quiet. Griffons have excellent hearing.

They scuttled up one path and crossed through the clearing by the waterfall again. Once again Chess had maneuvered them so the griffon was in front of them.

To answer your question, no, we can't hide. It'll be able to track our scent and hunt us down.

Ice skated up Alice's spine. What were they going to do? She didn't dare speak the question out loud.

Chess moved them down another path, but it didn't take long for the griffon to adjust course and move towards them again.

Chess was right. Even if they managed to do this all night, with the start of a new day, they'd get caught. If only she could send her thoughts into Chess's head like he did into hers.

They backtracked in a large circle. Alice's grip on the globe was slipping, and she hiked it higher.

Chess's velvet voice scraped in her mind. *I'm going to maneuver you towards the servants' entrance. You can hide in that cluster of potted willows over there. I'll create a distraction on the other side of the room. You should have enough time to get out of here before the griffon realizes where you went.*

Alice sucked back the protest on her lips and squeezed his tail instead. No way! She was not leaving him here. What would happen to him?

I'll be fine. I know another way out of here.

He moved forward, but Alice planted her feet. She couldn't even glare at him because they were both invisible.

We don't have a choice, love. If we both get caught, that's the end of it—for all of us.

He crept in a twisting route towards the panel in the wall, and she reluctantly followed him. He was right, even though the idea of leaving him behind made her chest ache.

It took another quarter of an hour before they made their way to the servant's entrance.

Alice let go of Chess's tail, her hand cramped from clutching it so long. She popped back into view. Chess butted his head against her leg, and she slipped into the midst of the cluster of potted trees and crouched down, the globe hugged to her chest.

I'll meet you in the forest, love. If I take too long, leave without me. I'll find my way back.

Alice shook her head and gripped the globe harder.

Don't worry about me. I've got at least half of my nine lives left. He winked at her and was gone.

It didn't take long. A loud crash sounded on the opposite side of the room. An answering shriek pierced the quiet.

Alice shot to her feet. Her hand was slick as she fumbled for the hidden handle. She thanked whoever had oiled the door as it slid open without a sound and she slipped into the passage. With a shaking hand, she closed it behind her. Blackness enveloped her.

Blast it! She had no idea where the candle had gone, and she couldn't see a thing in here. She put her hand on the wall and shuffled back the way they had come. At least she hoped it was the right way.

Something hit against the wall, and it shuddered under her hand. She swallowed a yelp.

With everything in her, she wanted to run back into the garden room, but that wouldn't help Chess. He was right. If she didn't get this globe back to Citrine's, they'd all be doomed.

She bit her lip and plodded onward. It wasn't until the first turn that she lit a match. Relief flooded her when she saw there was only one choice.

On and on she walked, only lighting matches when she came to a turn. She was grateful she only had to choose right or left a handful of times.

The third time, she chose incorrectly and had to back-track. The tension in her shoulders eased when she recognized the doorway into the kitchens.

Hesitating out of view, she listened for a moment before stepping out of the hallway. She hurried to the back door.

It opened with a creak, and she poked her head out. She half expected the area to be crawling with soldiers, but it was empty and quiet. Keeping close to the wall, she scurried towards the hedge. Behind her, lights were shining from windows that had been dark an hour ago.

The hedge was only a few yards away.

A voice rang out. "Halt! Who goes there?"

Alice ignored it and ran.

The thud of hooves came from ahead of her, and she swerved. Perspiration broke out on her body, and her eyes darted wildly around the courtyard. Where to go?

Then the pegasus burst into the courtyard. He stopped long enough for her to swing herself up on his back before he spread his wings and launched himself into the air.

Chapter 45

THE WINGED HORSE CIRCLED high in the sky, and Alice clung to his back. It was too bad she hadn't thought to bring some kind of bag to carry this stupid globe. It wasn't the easiest thing to hang onto, and if she dropped it, this would all have been for nothing. She hugged it tighter to her body.

The pegasus whinnied. *Leave now?* The words sounded deep and melodious in her mind.

She shook her head. "We can't leave Chess. Let's take another look around for him."

The animal snorted, and Alice thought she heard the word "dolt," but Freddie flew in a large circle. She scanned the ground. With his black fur, Chess would be hard to see. She squinted, not wanting to miss him.

On the ground, the courtyard was no longer quiet and empty. Groups of soldiers gathered in clumps. One of them pointed to her, and she guided the pegasus closer to the palace, out of reach of the soldier's arrows. At least she hoped that was the case.

More windows throughout the place lit up. They wouldn't be able to wait much longer. They circled around again. Alice strained her eyes, hoping for a glimpse of Chess.

Something whistled through the air, and her horse reared backwards to avoid an arrow. Alice's grip on the globe slipped. Her stomach dropped as she fumbled with the slick glass, snagging it back at the last minute. Her body tightened and her nerves stretched.

She knew they should leave. Instead, she instructed the pegasus to circle around the palace one more time. He tossed his head, but he did as she asked. Several more arrows flew in their direction, but none were close enough to hit them.

They flew low over the roof of the palace. A black blur caught Alice's eye. "There! I see him!"

But he wasn't alone. A soldier was scrambling across the shingles after him. There was no way they could land without all of them risking capture. Alice bit her lip, not sure what to do.

Chess's body lengthened out to a full run. He was racing towards the edge of the roof, the soldier keeping up with him. Alice urged the pegasus towards the far edge of the roof. Freddie banked steeply, his wings spread wide.

Chess reached the end of the roof and launched himself through the air. Alice squeezed her eyes shut and gripped the globe to her chest with one arm, clinging to the pegasus with the other.

Chess thumped onto the back of the flying horse, and the animal bucked and whinnied. Alice twisted. Chess crouched on the animal's rump like a burr, his nails sunk into flesh. No wonder Freddie was unhappy.

After a frantic moment, the pegasus evened out. Chess scrambled closer to Alice. With several sweeping beats of his wings, the pegasus headed away from the Red Palace.

Chapter 46

THE PEARL PALACE LOOMED up in the dim predawn light.
Alice clutched the globe, thankful she could hand it off
to someone else soon.

Freddie glided towards the front lawn. Citrine sat on
the front steps, her chin in her hands. She stood as they
touched down on the lawn.

Chess leapt down before the pegasus' hooves touched
the ground. Alice took longer to swing herself down
since the globe made it awkward. Her knees almost
buckled, and she gripped the silky mane. Freddie stood
still until she got her balance. She laid a hand on his
neck.

"Thank you!"

The creature tossed his dark head and snorted. Then
he bunched his hindquarters and leapt into the air. Alice
watched him go before she turned back. Only then did
a shadow separate itself from the wall. She clutched the
globe and looked for somewhere to run.

Zander's rumbling voice stopped her. *Alice, I'm so
relieved you both made it back in one piece.*

Alice nearly dropped the globe in her surprise. Citrine was at her elbow in an instant. "Zander, you didn't need to scare the life out of her." She glared at the Jabberwock, and he ducked his head.

Citrine led Alice over to the steps. She took the globe and set it on the grass before she helped Alice to sit. "Are you all right, dear?"

Alice nodded. "It's just been a long few days. I'll be glad when this is all over." She looked up when a large snout came into her field of view. She smiled up at the dragon. "I'm glad you're back."

He exchanged a long look with Citrine. *I am too.*

Alice noted the way Citrine and Zander leaned towards each other, their body language loose. It was like the fight from this morning—or was it yesterday morning?—had never happened. Questions bubbled up in her mind, but Alice pushed them down. It was none of her business, and they had more important things to attend to right now.

As if he had read her thoughts, Chess inserted himself in their midst. *You'll excuse me for being impatient, but the sooner we break this curse, the better.*

Citrine inclined her head in Alice's direction. "Are you up for this or do you need a bit of a rest?"

Alice shook her head. Chess was right. The sooner they got this over with, the better. She rubbed her hands on her trouser legs and pushed herself up. "I'm ready when you are."

Citrine stood too. "I'll be right back." She strode into the house.

A few minutes later, she came out carrying two lilies and some kind of contraption. She gestured to them from the gravel path that led up to the palace.

"Bring the globe, won't you?" Citrine said.

Alice scooped up the globe, glad she would be rid of the thing soon. They all formed a loose circle and watched as Citrine set up an iron tripod with a ring at the top. She set a small cast-iron bowl with a funnel in the middle into the ring. Next, she hooked a small glass bottle underneath the bowl.

Alice frowned. "What's that?"

"We have to extract the nectar from the dragon blood lily." Citrine held up the two flowers.

"When did you get the second one?"

"After you all went to bed last night, I decided it wouldn't hurt to get a second flower, as a precaution." She handed one flower to Alice. "I'm not sure how much you have to do to break the curse. Most likely it refers to the actual breaking of the globe." She shrugged. "It's better to err on the side of caution, though. Go ahead and put this in the bowl."

Alice did as Citrine instructed and then waited to see what would happen next.

Zander lumbered closer. *Everyone, please back away. I don't want to burn anyone.*

The three of them took several large steps backwards. It made sense now why Citrine didn't want this contraption on the grass.

Flames flickered behind Zander's teeth, and he opened his mouth. A thin stream of fire lit the bowl, the flower disappearing in the white-hot flames. When Zander stopped, a clear red liquid was dripping out of the bottom of the bowl into the bottle. Steam rose from the mouth of it.

After the first bottle cooled down, they repeated the process. Citrine slipped the second bottle into her pocket.

She handed the other one to Alice. "You need to pour it on the globe and smear it around. At least, I think that's how it should work."

Alice took the bottle and hesitated before she poured the contents over the glass. The red liquid slid down the sides and dripped on the ground like the object was bleeding. Using her fingers, she smeared the liquid, so it covered the top half of the globe. She looked at Citrine. "Do you think that's enough?"

Citrine frowned. "It should be. Now, you just need to smash it."

Alice hesitated. A bird sang from a nearby tree. The sun's rays were just peeking over the horizon. Everyone's eyes were trained on her. She trembled, and she drew in a shuddery breath. It was now or never.

"Do I need to say anything, do you think?"

"No, just break it."

Alice lifted the globe over her head. She shut her eyes and slammed the globe towards the ground.

Silence fell over the early morning, broken only by Citrine's inhalation.

Alice cracked open her eyes. And gaped. The globe had rolled harmlessly off to the side, bits of gravel stuck to the red, sticky nectar of the flower.

The sun's rays touched on Zander's olive scales, turning them an oily bronze, and Chess flicked his tail.

She had failed.

Alice's arms dropped to her sides. "What did I do wrong?"

Citrine put a hand on her shoulder. "Nothing." She bent and picked up the globe. The early rays of the sun bounced off its surface, turning it opaque. It was almost like the globe was mocking them. Alice shook the image away. How silly of her. It was just a garden globe—a very ordinary one, after all.

Alice clenched her hands. "But it should have worked."

Citrine shook her head. "Not if it's the wrong circle of glass."

So, we're back to square one? Chess's tail flicked back and forth.

"It would seem so." Citrine's gaze landed on each of them. "Do any of you have any ideas? It has to be circular and made of glass or crystal."

They stared at each other blankly.

Zander stood. *This is hopeless. My birthday is tomorrow. There isn't even a full day to find whatever holds the curse. It could be anything.*

Citrine grimaced. "There's still time. We can't give up yet." She pressed a fist against her forehead. "We just need to think. There are only so many things that are the right shape and material. It's a process of elimination."

Yes, of the entire contents of the palace. Zander shook his head. *It's too late. You and Alice need to figure out what you're going to do next. Neither of you will be safe once Lyssandra's got the crown for good.*

You may be willing to give up, but I'm not, not yet. Chess stalked back and forth. *There are other decorative globes she has around the palace. It's possible any of them is the right one.*

Zander snorted. *And what are you going to do? Steal them all? Be sensible, Chess. We need to get the girls to safety while we still have time... and our wits.*

They were all silent for a moment as the gravity of his words sank in. This wasn't just about the crown. The specter of the last prince who'd been Jabberwock-cursed loomed over them. The idea of Zander hurting anyone would have been laughable to Alice if she hadn't seen him lose control. She hadn't known him very long, but she understood even the thought of doing so would bring him great pain.

Citrine lifted her chin. "I'm not going anywhere. This estate is my responsibility."

Lyssandra knows that. She'll use it against you.

Citrine bared her teeth in a fierce smile. "She can try."

Chess stepped between the two. *Look, I agree, the ladies' safety is important, but it's not midnight yet. We still have today.*

Fine, we have today—not that it will do us much good. But plans must be made, and soon. I'm not sure how long I'll be... myself. Zander's head drooped. *I can't allow myself to hurt my people.*

Zander's expression was haunted. Alice's eyes prickled, and she turned away.

Citrine moved to Zander's side. She reached up and wrapped her arms around his snout. "I won't let it come to that, Zander. You have my word."

He pushed into her and closed his eyes. They stood together, a conversation without words flowing between them.

Alice wandered several yards away. She felt like she was intruding on something intimate and private. Chess followed her. She sank down onto a boulder and put her head in her hands. "He means for Citrine to..." The words stuck in her throat.

Chess leaned against her knee. *You can't blame him, Alice. Jabberwocks are dangerous creatures.*

"Why can't he, I don't know, fly off somewhere far away from people?"

I'm hoping it won't come to that, love. I've been speculating, if we can't find the object we need, I can go to my mother's people. Fae magic is powerful, and they know things humans don't.

Alice lifted her head. "Do you really believe they could help?"

Oh, they definitely could. It's more a question of, would they?

"Couldn't your mother go with you, since they're her people?"

Chess blinked up at her. *Go with me?*

Alice wondered if his relationship with his mother was strained, too. She hated to poke into a sensitive area, but this was important. "Yes, couldn't she travel with you to wherever the fae live and persuade them to help you?"

The confusion on Chess's face cleared, and he shook his head. *My mother already lives with the fae. She left when I was about fourteen.*

Alice tried to stroke his fur, but he moved away from her. *It's not important.*

"But that had to be—"

She's been gone a long time, Alice, and most of her kind would have most likely left much sooner.

Alice lapsed into silence, not sure what to say. She could hardly keep up with all the information she'd been presented with over the past few days. Pressing her fingers against her temples, she tried to squeeze her thoughts into order.

They might be willing to take you home, too.

"But how? Zander said it was impossible to go back through the Rabbit Hole."

Chess lifted his eyebrows. *Not for a full-blooded fae. Unlike a half-flit like me, they can move between the worlds easily. I could get you here, but taking you back would be beyond my abilities.*

Under other circumstances, Alice would have so many questions about how that worked, but the clock in her imagination was ticking too loudly. "There has to be a way to save Zander, to save you both. I can't bear to think that..." The lump in her throat blocked the rest of her words. She reached for her necklace and slid the pearl back and forth.

Chess butted his head against her thigh, and she stroked his back. Something niggled at the back of her mind.

The rush of wind almost pushed Alice off her perch. Citrine had backed away as Zander flapped his wings and launched into the sky. If he wanted to be alone, Alice couldn't blame him.

Citrine came to stand by her, and Alice pushed to her feet. Her new friend's eyes looked red behind her spectacles, but her chin was up and her shoulders were squared.

"Zander will be back. He just needs some time." Her throat worked, and she ran the back of her hand over her eyes. After a minute, Citrine continued. "We should go in the house. Cook will have breakfast ready. Maybe after a good meal, we'll come up with something."

Alice's appetite was gone, but she nodded anyway. It would give them something to do. Together, with Chess following, they strolled towards the front door.

"Whatever is holding the curse has to be close to the Queen," Citrine mused aloud as she clasped her hands behind her back. "What did the poem say again?"

They were now at the front steps. Alice paused, her foot on the bottom one. She closed her eyes and clasped her necklace. She ran through the poem in her mind. "Find the circle close at hand."

The niggle at the back of her mind took shape: a delicate crystal ball hanging from a chain, a drop like blood swirling in its center.

Her eyes popped open. "I know what it is! It's the Red Queen's necklace!"

Citrine's face lit it up, hope warring with desperation. "You might be right."

What are we waiting for, then? Chess grinned up at them. *Call Zander. We need to crash a party.*

Citrine's forehead wrinkled. "What party?"

Chapter 47

NIGHTTIME CAME ALL TOO soon for Alice. Once Citrine had called Zander back—unlike Alice, she could use her Creature Gift over distances—they had spent the morning planning and the afternoon resting, or trying to, anyway. When they met together for an early teatime, nobody had eaten very much.

Now, it was time. Alice's stomach clenched as she climbed onto Zander's back. Citrine clambered on behind her, and Chess leapt up to his usual spot. Alice patted her shirt pocket where the last bottle of dragon blood lily nectar rested.

Butterflies churned in Alice's stomach at what lay ahead, but at least the wait was over.

Zander's voice rumbled through her. *Are we all ready?*

Alice shrugged. "I don't know that it matters. Let's just go."

His powerful muscles bunched beneath her, and he leapt into the air. The air whistled by Alice's head, and she wondered if this would be the last time she'd ride on a dragon. She tried to stay in the moment, but her mind kept skipping ahead. All the ways this could go sideways flipped through her mind like a newsreel.

Before she was ready, the palace loomed in front of them, ablaze with lights. The sounds of music and people spilled through the French doors onto the back lawn. Twinkling lanterns hung around the expanse of lawn, and large pots of flowers and shaped shrubberies created an exotic garden. A few couples seemed to be taking advantage of the shadows.

They circled overhead, but the scudding clouds and the noise of the party covered their arrival. Zander flew away from the palace and then banked back around.

Up ahead, the stained glass window yawned in front of them. Each beat of Zander's wings brought them closer. In a dim part of her mind, Alice heard someone's exclamation, but her focus was on the window.

Duck down. Zander's voice boomed across her mind and Alice flattened herself against his warm scales. She felt Citrine press against her as he struck the window. Glass shattered and rained across Alice's back and hair. The sound of a thousand tinkles of glass hitting the floor added an oddly harmonious note to the music. Zander skidded into the ballroom, and his roar shook the chandelier, making the hundreds of candles shiver in their holders.

A sudden, absolute silence fell over the ballroom. Several hundred pairs of eyes turned in their direction. A woman towards the edge of the dance floor slid bonelessly to the floor in a dead faint. Her companion didn't even seem to notice. Alice's eyes darted around the ballroom, looking for only one thing...

She spotted the Red Queen.

She had been dancing, but both she and her companion, a tall, sandy-haired man, paused. A mocking smile played over the Queen's mouth as her dark eyes met Alice's. She tipped her head in Alice's direction before she turned and barked out in a loud voice, "Commander Felinas, get your men and take care of this beast, once and for all."

Her voice broke whatever spell had held the ballroom in stillness. All the sound and noise rushed back in as people shouted and scrambled towards exits, pushing chairs, tables, and other people out of their way in a mad stampede away from the Jabberwock in their midst. As the attendees tried to get out, the doors flung inward and armed soldiers poured in. One burly man herded the guests into a quivering huddle, breaking the bottleneck that had developed at the entrances to the ballroom.

Alice's eyes bounced over the jostling bodies, trying to find the Queen again. Her gaze snagged on movement. She squinted. It was the Mad Hatter. He smiled and waved wildly. A smile tugged at her mouth before she turned back to scan the crowd.

There, over in the far corner. A group of soldiers had surrounded the Queen. Alice felt anger pool in her stomach. Next to the woman was a pedestal that held the crown that didn't belong to her.

"She's over there!"

Zander slid towards the tight knot of soldiers, his fire licking the floor at their feet. Several of the men scrambled out of the way. Alice didn't hesitate. She slid from Zander's back and darted through the gap of bodies towards the Queen. Citrine had already melted into the crowd.

Instead of running or hiding, the Red Queen stepped into her path. Her childlike face was alight with delight, and her dark eyes sparkled.

"Darling, I have to say, I underestimated you," she said, her voice sincere.

Alice eyed the crystal pendant swinging over the Queen's white skin. "It's over, Lyssandra. You won't win."

The soldiers' ranks were thinning as they attempted to keep Zander at bay. The Queen *tsk*ed and flicked her wrist. A glittering blade slipped into her hand. "I do so admire your spunk, my dear." She sighed. "I wish you'd at least try to see things from my perspective. You'd make an excellent ally. You don't have to die. The only one I want dead is him." She waved her blade in the prince's direction.

Alice's lip curled. "No thanks—I'll take my chances with the prince."

The Queen shook her head. "I was so afraid you'd say that." Her hand snaked out and curled around Alice's wrist. The Queen yanked her closer, the blade poised to strike. Alice tried to pull away, but the woman was stronger than she looked. Desperate, Alice folded her fingers into a fist. She drew back her arm. Her punch landed squarely on the Red Queen's nose. The other woman staggered back, dropping her knife to cover her face. The blade clattered to the floor, blood gushing between her fingers. Alice scooped up the knife and darted forward, her hand closing over the rose-gold chain.

A searing pain lanced through her scalp as the Queen jerked her hair. Alice pulled at the chain, and after some brief resistance, it snapped.

"No!" the Queen shrieked. She let go of Alice's hair and backhanded her across the face. Alice's head snapped to the side, and the Queen shoved her, hard. Alice landed painfully on her hip. The Queen's mouth contorted into a manic grin, her teeth smeared with blood.

"I think you have something that belongs to me." She extended her hand. "Give it to me and I'll kill you quickly."

Alice scrabbled to her feet and jabbed at the Queen with the knife. The woman smacked her arm, and the knife clattered to the floor. She grabbed Alice's fist that held the necklace. Her mouth twisted into a snarl, and she ground the bones of Alice's fingers together. Alice gasped as the Queen forced her hand open, and she lashed out with her foot. It connected solidly with the Queen's knee. The other woman's leg buckled and she jerked sideways. The necklace flew out of Alice's hand and landed somewhere among the dozens of feet that trampled over the ballroom floor.

"You stupid girl." The Queen's voice held a hiss, and she tilted her head, the movement strangely reptilian. The Queen twisted her head in a strange circle and rolled her shoulders. Dread pooled in Alice's stomach, and she slid backwards a step. Her eyes darted to the side. Where was it?

"I gave you your chance."

Alice snapped her gaze back to the Queen. Behind them, Alice could hear the twang of arrows, and Zander's roars shook the room, but all she could see was the Queen's dark eyes. They glowed in the candlelit room. The woman's small face stretched, and she threw back her head, her laugh high-pitched. Her hands curled into claws, talons ripping through her fingertips. Alice kept backing up as the Red Queen's body stretched and elongated. There was a loud ripping sound as her petal-pink dress shredded to reveal scales. A long tail slid across the black-and-white checked floor.

Icy cold spread across Alice's body as her eyes met the Queen's chocolate-brown gaze, now set in a snub-nosed dragon's face. Her body was covered in vivid scarlet-red scales. Alice backed up another step and bumped into the table. The leathery lips drew back in a smile and a long tongue flicked out. The creature opened her mouth, and Alice could see the red glow at the back of her throat. She squeezed her eyes shut, unwilling to watch her own death come at her.

Chapter 48

A SHRILL CRY BROKE the air, and Alice's eyes popped open. Instead of a stream of fire, a flurry of feathers blocked her view. Hesperus was diving, aiming at the Queen's eyes. The red dragon screeched.

A hand locked on Alice's wrist and jerked her to the side, just as a flash of bronze scales crashed into the crimson dragon, and the two creatures rolled into the table where Alice had just been standing, smashing it flat.

"I have to get the necklace."

"And you have to remain alive to do it," said Citrine, her mouth tight. Behind her stood the Commander.

"Get her out of here," he said, his voice clipped.

The two Jabberwocks clawed and snapped at each other. The guests who were standing in a quivering huddle where the guards had herded them earlier threw themselves out of the way of the two fighting dragons.

More soldiers surged into the room. Citrine pulled Alice down into a crouch, and they scuttled to the other side of the room. Alice twisted back in time to see the necklace skid across the floor. It landed near the far wall.

"I have to get to the necklace," she repeated to Citrine.

"I know that. But if you go over there, you'll get crushed."

"We don't have time to wait. I don't know how long Zander can hold out." Alice winced as another series of arrows thudded into Zander's side. The Red Queen took advantage of the distraction and raked claws across his face, dangerously close to his eye. Alice rose from her crouch, trying to see where the necklace was now. A long tail almost hit her head. She dropped back down next to Citrine.

"What am I going to do?"

Citrine's face was grim. "Maybe Hesperus can get to it." Her eyelids drooped again, and she hummed, but a blast of fire set the table next to them ablaze. Both women scrambled away in the opposite direction of where the necklace lay.

Suddenly, a face appeared, topped with a hat bedecked with feathers and gems. "Pink to shrink, blue and you grew."

Alice blinked up at the Mad Hatter. "Erm, hello?"

He smiled and pushed up his round spectacles. "Sugar, one lump or two. It's all up to you."

What in the world—? Then it clicked. The *sugar cubes* the Mad Hatter had given her. She had shoved them into her pocket a million hours ago. She scrabbled for them now, and her fingers touched the cubes. Some of them had crumbled, but there were still two left, one pink and one blue. She looked up to ask him to repeat his rhyme, but he had disappeared.

A loud crash shook the floor, and she looked up to see Zander lying on his side, his body riddled with arrows. He was trying to stand, but the Queen blasted him with fire. He roared, the sound weak.

Alice took a chance and popped the pink sugar cube into her mouth. There was a rushing around her, and tall wooden poles surrounded her. It took her a moment to realize they were table legs. She felt a moment of relief as she realized her clothes and the vial had made the size change with her.

Chess appeared next to her. *I'll take you to the necklace.*

She clambered onto his back, using his fur to haul herself up. Chess ran, dodging under tables and around broken china and furniture. He leapt over a crushed cello, almost skidding out on the slick floor. A tail landed with a crash in front of them. He swerved, and Alice clung to his back.

The candlelight glimmered off the crystal pendant. It was just ahead. Chess leapt over a broken chair and continued running. Alice shut her eyes and hung on. They slid up to the necklace as a large taloned foot stomped down, just missing them.

Jump. I'll distract her.

Alice didn't have time to argue. She threw herself one way and Chess leapt the other as a blast of fire almost singed them both. Chess darted under the red dragon while Alice scrambled for the necklace. A loud snap rustled her hair, and Chess leapt onto the Queen's tail and bit down, hard. A roar shook her bones, and Alice heard Chess yowl. She hoped he was all right, but there wasn't time to check.

Alice shoved a blue cube into her mouth as she ran. The crunchy sweetness melted over her tongue. There was a rushing, and then her head was brushing the ceiling.

The Red Queen looked no bigger than a medium-sized dog. Alice's gaze took in Zander lying on his side, surrounded by soldiers. Chess was a small black lump by the far wall. A slice of pain on her ankle made Alice gasp. The red dragon reared back, opening her mouth, and Alice kicked the creature. The dragon screeched as it skidded across the floor. It hit the wall with a thump that knocked several candles from the chandelier.

Alice grabbed the necklace, which had grown with her. She fumbled with the bottle's tiny lid and lost her hold on the glass bottle. She grabbed at it—but it slid through her fingers.

The bottle bounced once, then twice on the floor before cracking. The nectar seeped out. Frantic, Alice dropped to her knees, shaking the entire ballroom.

In the distance, a clock bonged. She fumbled with the crystal pendant and rolled it in the nectar. As the last chime sounded, she squinted at the necklace. Was the crystal fogging? The soldiers and the few guests who hadn't been able to escape stood frozen, staring up at her. As Alice watched, the red dragon twisted and shrank until the Red Queen lay on the floor. She wobbled to her feet.

"You're too late," she screamed. "It's already midnight."

Already Alice was getting smaller. "I can still save the prince."

The woman cackled. "Not if you want to go home."

Alice hesitated and looked down at the necklace in her hand. Even as she glanced at it, a face appeared inside the pendant.

The Queen's smile spread across her face. "If you break the curse, you'll be tied to Zander forever."

Alice was now almost normal sized, and her gaze found Citrine's. The other woman shook her head and lifted her shoulders.

Alice looked at the crystal pendant in her hand and then at Zander. He lifted his head, and his green eyes met hers.

Time slowed. The surrounding faces blurred.

Alice's grip on the necklace tightened. "You're lying."

"Try it and see."

Alice's hand trembled, and the faces of her family flashed through her mind.

"You can go home. I'll make sure of it." The Queen reached out a hand still tipped with claws. "Just give it to me."

Time resumed. "I don't think so." Alice bared her teeth. "You can't fool a street rat."

Holding the Queen's stare, she smashed the pendant down to the ground. It bounced once and then cracked down the middle.

A red vapor rose from the broken shards of glass and enveloped the Jabberwock. When it cleared, a young man lay on the ground in tattered clothes. There was a gasp as he stood, blood streaming from numerous wounds. He swayed on his feet. Alice recognized the shaggy bronze-brown hair and moss-green eyes. It was the same face she remembered from the portrait, striking rather than handsome, with a nose that was a bit too large.

Murmurs rose from the soldiers, and a few of the guests gasped. The words "the Red Prince" spread around the room. The prince looked at the Red Queen. Her doll-like face was twisted in rage. The Commander stood back while two of his soldiers strode across the room. They reached to take her arms, but Zander held up his hands. "Wait."

The Queen smiled and wagged a finger in the prince's direction. "You always were a smart boy. It's after midnight. The crown is mine."

Zander stepped over and picked up the crown. "Not if I challenge you for it."

"Do you think the good people of Wonderland will still want you for their king once they know your little secret?"

The muscle in Zander's jaw ticked, but his voice was even. "I think they'll agree that it's better than the alternative."

The Queen laughed. "Even if they accept you, do you think they'll be happy with a Mirror Worlder?"

Zander's eyes widened.

The Queen turned to Alice, a sneer on her face. "I told you not to do it, but you didn't listen. I do hope you're as fond of the prince as you seem to be."

Zander scowled. "Enough with your riddles. What do you mean?"

The Queen laughed. "Your fates are bound now." When it was obvious nobody understood her meaning, she rolled her eyes. "Look at your wrists."

Alice glanced down and frowned. An intricate filigree of twisting vines encircled her wrist like a sepia-colored tattoo.

Zander had a matching one on his wrist.

"Speak plainly. What does this mean?" He held out his arm.

"I told you, your fates are bound together." She gestured towards Alice with a flourish of her hand. "Meet your love."

Alice's stomach flipped, and the room telescoped inward. It couldn't be true. A hand steadied her as Citrine materialized by her elbow.

Alice turned to her. "Is that true?"

Citrine's face was bone white, and she shook her head. "Not as the original curse stands, no, but..."

"But what?" Zander's face was stiff.

Citrine shrugged helplessly. "She could have put a trap in the curse." Her eyes narrowed at the Red Queen. "But only very skilled Alchemists can do that. It seems you've been holding out on the royal family about more than one thing, Lyssandra." She squeezed Alice's arm. "Don't worry. We'll figure something out and get you home."

"I wouldn't try sending her back. The bond will tear her in half," the Queen said. Then her mouth twisted into a nasty smile. "Of course, death breaks the bond, so at least one of them will be free."

Alice rubbed at the pattern on her wrist and then took a step towards the Queen. "Whether or not I stay, it won't change the fact that they'll execute you for treason." She narrowed her eyes and gave a nasty smile of her own. "I hope the executioner has good aim."

The Queen's eyes lit up. "I wish things were different, Alice. In another life, we could have been friends." She wiped at her face with the back of her arm, smearing blood across her cheek. She winked. "I'll be in touch." Then she whirled and ran. With a last cackle, she shifted back into her dragon form and flew out of the broken window.

Chapter 49

THE SILENCE THAT HAD fallen over the room during this last exchange erupted as the Commander barked orders at his men, and everyone started talking and shouting at once. Alice stood frozen as people and soldiers swarmed around the prince, who had sagged once the Queen was gone.

The mark around her wrist burned. Chess. She wanted to talk to Chess. She twisted around, but he was nowhere. Her chest squeezed. He'd been hit.

She ran to where she'd last seen him, but instead of a cat, she found a young man, lying as if asleep. His skin was a deep brown, and close-cropped silky black curls covered his head. She knelt beside him and felt his throat. A faint, thready pulse beat under her fingertips.

At her touch, his eyes fluttered open. Long lashes framed blue eyes, blurred in confusion. Alice's breath hitched as he finally focused on her face. He moved his hand in front of his eyes with difficulty and then wiggled his fingers.

"You... did it. You broke... the... curse." He struggled to speak and a bit of blood trickled from the side of his mouth. Her heart hammered, and her throat was thick with tears, but she forced a trembling smile.

"Only because of you."

His eyes narrowed. "Am... I... dying?"

Alice blinked back tears and shook her head. "No, of course not. Why would you say that?"

"You're... being... too... nice." A smile ghosted across his face. "Or maybe you... just... like what... you see."

She gripped his hand in her own and gave a shaky laugh. "Now I know you'll be okay."

He smiled. A cough shook him and he grimaced. Alice frowned. "We need to get you a doctor."

One side of his mouth tipped up. "I'll live. I think." His eyes settled on her wrist and his brow furrowed. With effort, he lifted his other hand and traced a finger over a sepia-brown vine. "What's this?"

Alice bit her lip. "I..."

A hand touched her shoulder. Citrine stood behind her, a tall man clutching a leather satchel next to her. "This is one of the royal physicians. He'll take care of him." Chess's hand tightened on hers, and she didn't want to let go.

Citrine's smile was gentle. "I think he's broken some ribs, and hurt his lung." Seeing Alice's expression, she shook her head. "No, dear, don't panic. He'll be just fine, but we have to let the doctor help him."

Alice turned back to Chess, but his eyes had slid closed again, his breathing raspy. She let his hand slip from hers as Citrine drew her to her feet. "Come along, dear. We'll let the others take care of things in here. You look like you could use a good, hot cup of tea."

Chapter 50

ALICE SAT IN THE cozy library of the Pearl Palace and shifted restlessly under the blanket Citrine had insisted she keep over her knees. It had been three days since *the Great Ballroom Battle*, as it was now called. Besides the news that both the prince and Chess were healing nicely, she had heard nothing from either of them.

Until today.

She folded and unfolded the paper that held the message from Prince Zander.

"If you twist that paper anymore, it's going to disintegrate." Citrine sat across from her, a large orange tabby on her lap.

Alice smoothed out the paper.

"It says he's coming here." Alice looked up.

Citrine shrugged her slim shoulders. "That's not surprising, under the circumstances."

"But he's bringing the Council and someone called Sir Lapin Blanc with him." Alice wrinkled her nose at the name. It meant *white rabbit* in French.

Citrine nodded. "That was wise of the Council to consult with Sir Blanc. He's an old and powerful Alchemist. He lives in seclusion most of the time, which explains why we haven't heard from anyone until now."

"What can he do?"

Citrine nodded. "I just told you, he has a powerful Alchemist Gift. If anyone can figure out how to undo this trap Lyssandra attached to the original curse, he can."

"So she was telling the truth about this?" Alice held up her wrist.

Citrine's expression darkened. "Yes, I'm afraid she was." Her forehead wrinkled. "Although how she did it, I still don't know. That's complicated magic."

Alice turned to stare at the fire. She could hardly look at Citrine. All she'd wanted to do was help, and look at what happened? Would this council make her marry Zander? He was nice, of course, but...

A black-and-white cat leapt into her lap. His purr rumbled like an engine. A smile tugged at her lips, and she ran her fingers through the soft fur. It reminded her of Chess. Her chest tightened, but she pushed the thought away.

"It's not your fault, Alice."

Alice blinked at Citrine. "How did you—"

Citrine waved a hand. "You have guilt written all over that pretty face of yours." Her mouth lifted in a half smile. "You realize that Zander and I aren't, can't, be together, right? My duties as the Pearl Queen, and now that he's the King..."

Alice shrugged. "I still feel horrible."

Citrine leaned forward and put a hand on Alice's arm. "I appreciate your sympathy about this difficult situation, but you saved him."

Alice looked up and met Citrine's intense gaze. "Yes, but—"

"But nothing. If you hadn't broken the curse, I would have been forced to..." Her voice faltered, and she cleared her throat. "Trust me, this is an outcome I can live with much more easily."

The clock bonged the noon hour just as Bliss appeared at the door. "Madam has guests. Would she like to greet them in the parlor?"

Citrine straightened in her chair. "No, bring them in here, if you would."

"Very good, Madam. Would you care for tea? Cook has some lemon scones."

Citrine shook her head. "This isn't that kind of meeting, Bliss, but tell Cook thank you. Alice and I will have some after everyone leaves. It'll be something to look forward to."

Citrine stood. Alice placed the black-and-white cat back on the floor and stood, too.

A few minutes later, Bliss opened the door. Zander came in, followed by an elderly man and two women, one short and round and the other tall with fiery hair.

Alice couldn't help searching for a dark, curly head. The knot in her stomach got bigger when she realized Chess wasn't with them. She didn't want to think too much about how disappointed she felt.

Unsure what to say, Alice lowered her head and dipped into a curtsey. When she straightened, she almost fell over.

Behind the prince was a white rabbit. And not just any white rabbit. This one was over six feet tall and walked on his back legs. He was also wearing a linen suit with a waistcoat. A fancy watch chain sparkled in the light coming through the window.

Alice's mouth hung open before she remembered herself and snapped it shut. "Someone could have mentioned he was an actual rabbit," she muttered under her breath.

Citrine must have heard because she smothered a laugh, coughing into her hand before making the introductions.

She pointed to the older man. "This is Lord Beecher, and these lovely ladies are Lady Perma and the Duchess. Lord Whistlewaith is indisposed, and Lord Dordo couldn't be with us today."

The Duchess rolled her green eyes. "Thank goodness for small favors," she muttered.

Alice bit back a smile and nodded her head at both in turn. Citrine crossed the room and took the tall rabbit's arm in hers. "And this is Sir Lapin Blanc."

The rabbit patted Citrine's hand with a furry paw. "It's so nice to see you again, my dear. It's been too long."

"Yes, it has. I must apologize. I should've invited you out here ages ago."

The rest of the group hovered in the doorway. Zander shifted from foot to foot. He offered a tentative smile to Alice, and she returned it. It still felt strange to see a person and not a Jabberwock.

Citrine's voice interrupted her thoughts. "I thought we'd all be more comfortable in here." She gestured to the square table. "Shall we sit?"

Alice, thankful Citrine took charge, sat along with everyone else. An awkward silence descended. Alice shifted in her seat. It felt as if everyone was staring at her. She glanced down at the pattern twining around her wrist and rubbed at it.

"Well, at least she's pretty." The sharp voice belonged to the Duchess.

"Leticia, what a thing to say!" The other woman shook her head. She smiled at Alice. "I'm sure you're a lovely girl."

Zander cleared his throat. "We're here to talk about our options. Sir Blanc, can you share what you've learned?"

The large rabbit pulled out a pair of spectacles. He patted at his jacket pockets. "Ah, here it is." He pulled out a sheaf of papers with a flourish. "Now then." Before placing the papers on the table, he scanned them. Leaning forward, he folded his paws on the table.

He peered at Alice over the top of his glasses. She resisted the urge to squirm in her seat. Instead, she sat up straighter and placed her own hands on the table. His nod looked approving.

"Now then," he started again. "I'm afraid we can't erase the extra condition that the Red Queen attached to the curse."

Alice's mouth was dry, and she wished she had a glass of water. She swallowed and nodded.

"However, because of the language of this added magic, there are several interpretations we can conclude."

"Does that mean she doesn't have to marry the prince?" Lady Perma bounced in her seat, her bosom jiggling.

The Duchess frowned at her. "Do be quiet, Henrietta. Lapin is trying to tell us what's going on, but if you keep interrupting, we'll never be done."

The other woman subsided with an audible *harrumph* and a glare at the other woman.

The rabbit cleared his throat. "Ahem, as I was saying, this magic ties you to the prince and his fate. However, that does not mean you have to marry him or stay in Wonderland forever. You simply have to affect his fate. Once you do that, this part of the curse should dissolve, and you'll be free to leave."

"How do I do that?"

The rabbit pushed up the spectacles that had slid down his nose. "The most obvious answer is to become the prince's champion."

Alice knotted her hands together. She had no idea what it meant to be anyone's champion.

Zander shot to his feet. "There has to be another option for her. That would be much too risky."

The Duchess tilted her head, her sharp gaze darted between Zander and Citrine. She reminded Alice of a bird of prey. She decided it was probably wise to stay on the woman's good side.

Lapin shook his head, his large ears flopping. "Young man, I've looked closely at this curse, and I assure you, while we can interpret the language several ways, the curse will know if you are trying to pull a fast one."

"But I can't ask Alice to risk her life again for me." The prince raked a hand through his bronze hair.

The rabbit sniffed. "Then I suggest you ask her to marry you instead." He held up his paw when Zander opened his mouth to argue. "I'm sure there would be other opportunities for this young woman to affect your fate, but who's to say how long before one of those opportunities presents itself?"

Zander crossed his arms. "I can't take over her life like this. It isn't fair to her."

The rabbit nodded. "I agree with you, but we are dealing with a curse. They aren't often fair, son. There really are just the two options. If you choose to wait, you can't marry until another opportunity for her to affect your fate presents itself. You could both be waiting until you're as old as I am, and I don't know if there would be any nasty side effects of waiting too long, either." He shook his head again. "No, it's quite clear. She can marry you or be your champion."

"You dear boy," said Lady Perma. "This is such a shame, but I think we have to agree with Sir Blanc. Either marry the poor girl or let her be your champion. There has been so much upheaval, we can't risk the curse causing some other catastrophe if you wait around." She wrung her plump hands.

Zander bowed his head against his clasped hands, his expression shuttered. "I'm so sorry, Alice. I hate that I've put you in this impossible situation."

The Duchess snorted. "I don't want to be contrary, Your Highness, but as pretty as she is, the girl is a no-body from the Mirror World. Marrying you is only an improvement, I'm sure. Who complains about marrying a prince?"

Alice bit back the hot words she wanted to say, and instead forced her lips into a smile. "It's not your fault, Za—I mean, Prince Zander. You're in just as bad of a position as I am."

After a long moment of silence, Lord Beecher banged his cane on the floor. "She can't be your champion. She's female. So, ask the girl to marry you already, and get it over with. Then we can all go home. I, for one, am old. I don't have time to wait around all day for you to act." He fished out a dingy handkerchief and blew his nose. Then he glared at the prince. "I certainly hope this isn't a preview of your kingly abilities, young man."

Alice looked over at Citrine. The whiteness of her face was the only sign that the discussion bothered her at all.

Zander ran a finger around the collar of his shirt and pushed to his feet. Before he could move, Alice shot to her feet. She looked around the table and swallowed.

"I didn't ask to come here, but when I did arrive, the first person I met was the prince. He's proved over and over that he's a good man. He deserves—no, he needs—to rule the Kingdom of Wonderland." She met Zander's eyes across the table. "I know you don't want to marry me"—she gave an apologetic smile—"any more than I want to marry you. I miss home and my family, and they need me." She looked around the table. "Since it's my life, I think it should be my choice what I do." She drew in a deep breath. "And I choose to be Prince Zander's champion."

CONTINUE THE STORY IN *JABBERWOCK'S CHAMPION*, BOOK 2 IN THE *LOOKING GLASS CHRONICLES*, *available June 27, 2023.*

Wondering how Prince Zander ended up cursed? Find out in Jabberwock Prince, your free gift for signing up to my newsletter. Just scan the code below.

One secret may cost him everything.

Prince Zander thought he had years before he would ascend the Kingdom of Wonderland's throne.

But then he is summoned back to the palace and finds his father dead. Before he even has time to mourn, he's informed that the Queen will be the interim ruler until his 21st birthday. Which is news to him.

Suddenly, he is thrust into a cat and mouse game with his stepmother. And she knows more than she's saying.

If he doesn't thwart the Red Queen's schemes, he won't survive long enough to blow out his candles or claim his crown.

About the Author

R.V. Bowman spends her days teaching high school students in an effort to instill a love of reading and writing. By night, she hits her keyboard to write fantastical tales full of magic and heart. She is also the author of the middle grade fantasy trilogy, *The Pirate Princess Chronicles—Hook's Daughter, Pan's Secret,* and *Neverland's Key*.

She currently lives in Northwest Ohio with her husband, The Coach, two sons, and a nosey dog named Sherlock. You can find out more about her and her books at www.rvbowman.com or follow her on Instagram under the handle @r.v.bowmanfantasyauthor.

Acknowledgments

Writing can be a solitary endeavor, but once you move into the publishing part of things, that's not something you do by yourself, not by a long shot. There was a small, but mighty team that helped me get this book out into the world. First, I'd like to thank my beta readers who were the first eyes to see this story. Emily Bontrager, Amanda Sutton, Julian Jamar, Ticia Messing, and Steph Hesseling gave me invaluable feedback. Thanks, ladies – without you, this story would not exist in its current form.

Another invaluable set of eyes was my editor Jody Skinner, of Skinner Book Services. She did a stellar job. Not only was she easy to work with, but her eagle eye caught a lot of important things I would have completely missed, including historically appropriate language. Finally, what's a book without its cover? Elona Bezooshko from Psycat Studio created my gorgeous cover. I also want to thank JacQueline Vaughn Roe, who was a huge encouragement during this entire process. It's always wonderful to have writing friends to make the journey more enjoyable.

Of course, I also want to thank my family. My husband and kids had to deal with leftovers too many nights to count and my absentmindedness as I was mulling over plot points, and then later, as I was in the final stages of the publishing process. Writing the first draft is the easy part, but the revising, editing, and getting the entire thing ready for my readers takes a lot of time and attention, and the people who allowed me that time and focus was my family. I also want to thank my mom, Mary Ann McColm, who had to listen to me nattering on about various plot points and characters when I'm sure she would have rather talked about other things. Thanks, Mom! You're the best!

Finally, I want to thank you, my reader. Without you, there would be no point in writing because a story is just words on a page until readers brings it to life. I'll never get over the sheer magic of how my ideas and your imagination meld so that characters, worlds, and events spark into existence. So, thanks for joining me in making that magic happen!

R.V. Bowman

Made in United States
Orlando, FL
11 February 2024

43574062R00202